"Lady Diana Westover, allow me to present Lord Adderley."

The viscount reached out and took her hand. "Delighted, Lady Diana," he murmured, his deep voice perfectly suited to his coloring, making her think of secrets whispered in the dark. Then he pressed his shapely mouth to the back of her gloved hand.

No mere brush of the lips from him! The pressure of his mouth was firm, and lingered. Pleasure seemed to spread out from the place he touched her, seeping through her body until it was like being enveloped in a velvet blanket.

Oh, *this* was what she had imagined—except that the man eliciting such a response was a scoundrel.

Other AVON ROMANCES

MARGARET MOORE

Kiss Me Quick

AVON BOOKS

An Imprint of HarperCollinsPublishers

This is a work of fiction. Names, characters, places, and incidents are products of the author's imagination or are used fictitiously and are not to be construed as real. Any resemblance to actual events, locales, organizations, or persons, living or dead, is entirely coincidental.

AVON BOOKS
An Imprint of HarperCollins*Publishers*
10 East 53rd Street
New York, New York 10022-5299

Copyright © 2003 by Margaret Wilkins
ISBN: 0-06-052620-3
www.avonromance.com

First Avon Books paperback printing: May 2003

Avon Trademark Reg. U.S. Pat. Off. and in Other Countries, Marca Registrada, Hecho en U.S.A.
HarperCollins® is a registered trademark of HarperCollins Publishers Inc.

Printed in the U.S.A.

10 9 8 7 6 5 4 3 2 1

With thanks to my two great kids and wonderful husband, for their support, patience, and especially the laughs.

Chapter 1

The mysterious stranger filled Evangeline with both excitement and a nameless dread.

He bowed, then kissed her hand. "Permit me to introduce myself," he said. "I am the Count Korlovsky."

From the first draft of
The Castle of Count Korlovsky,
The Westover Papers

Bath, England
1817

Her plan was all very well in theory, Lady Diana Westover decided as she marched toward the Pump Room alongside her aunts. Unfortunately, the execution was going to be rather more difficult than she had assumed. Her hands were definitely clammy in her gloves, and her heart beat with a wild rhythm she hadn't experienced since her horse had bolted on her when she was ten years old.

To be sure, Bath was no longer the epicenter of fashionable life it had once been, but that didn't lessen Diana's uncomfortable sensation that she was too countrified and woefully unprepared. Maybe she should claim a headache and return to her aunts' townhouse—or all the way back to Lincolnshire.

Except that she had a plan that she couldn't abandon now, and that meant being around fashionable people.

Well, men. She needed to meet men.

And to do that, she needed her aunts who lived in Bath, a spa town famous for the hot spring that had been used since Roman times. Aunt Calliope and Aunt Euphenia were only too delighted to take her under their wing, as Diana knew they would be. Indeed, they'd been anxious to do that for years.

So now here she was on this fine day in May, trooping toward the large building where the supposedly restorative spring water was dispensed, dressed in a lilac pelisse, a bonnet she thought had been overly decorated with a riot of flowers, thin kid gloves and carrying a reticule that contained smelling salts and little else. Aunt Calliope had insisted that no proper young lady left the house without smelling salts, even though Diana had assured her that she had never needed them before, even when her horse had bolted.

That had been shocking enough for Aunt Calliope, but the poor woman had had to lie down when Diana also admitted she often walked for miles in the country, and without a chaperon.

As they neared the Pump Room, Diana again glanced surreptitiously at her aunts, one on either side of her like a guard of honor. Lady Calliope FitzBurton was dressed very stylishly, although her bonnet adorned with false fruit and ribbons looked more suited to a buffet table than a middle-aged woman's head. She was, however, as sharp and bright-eyed as a woman half her age, which could be something of a problem when one was trying to keep a secret.

Lady Euphenia Harbage, older, wiser and calmer, was dressed in a more muted fashion. She had much less money to spend on her clothes, thanks to a spendthrift, gambling husband now mercifully deceased. Like Diana, she was a guest in her widowed sister's home, albeit a permanent one.

Aunt Euphenia patted Diana's arm gently. "Since this is all very new for you, we won't stay long in the Pump Room," she assured her. "We'll see if any acquaintances are there, make a few engagements if we can, and then we shall leave."

Diana relaxed a bit. But really, what was she so worried about? It wasn't as if she had only this one chance to find what she sought, or that these fashionable, sophisticated people held any power over her.

She would just imagine that she was going into battle, like Hector at Troy. Achilles. The Spartans at Thermopolae.

Well, not the Spartans. They had all died.

"We must spend *some* time in the Pump Room,"

Aunt Calliope exclaimed, the force of her remark causing her bonnet to tilt dangerously. "Dear Diana must be noticed."

"I don't want to make a sensation," Diana said, meaning it. She was there to observe, not participate, or at least no more than necessary to gain some acquaintance of men who had not spent most of their lives in Lincolnshire.

"Of course not. That wouldn't be modest or proper, and you are a very modest and proper young lady," Aunt Euphenia replied. "You do look lovely, though, my dear, and I daresay some of the young men will think so, too."

Diana refrained from pointing out to her kindhearted aunt that while she looked as pleasing to the male eye as it was possible for her to be, her appearance was hardly likely to elicit rapturous approval from the young men of Bath.

"Has Madame Rotellini not outdone herself with that bonnet?" Aunt Calliope asked, addressing Aunt Euphenia.

"I absolutely agree and you were right about that color for Diana's ensemble. Lilac suits her perfectly and brings out the blue in her eyes. Mrs. Jenkins has fit the gown to perfection, too."

"I'm sure you won't be long in the marriage mart, my dear," Aunt Calliope said, speaking to Diana again. "Although I wouldn't talk quite so much about books. In fact, I wouldn't talk very much at all. Let the young men do that."

"Yes, Aunt," Diana obediently replied, but

with a gleam of mischief in her eyes. "I'll be on my very best behavior because who knows? Perhaps, if I am lucky and the ancient Roman gods of Aqua Sulis are with me, I may even meet my future husband this very day. Naturally I wouldn't want him to think I talk too much."

Aunt Calliope came to a dead halt. "For heaven's sake, Diana, don't talk about ancient gods being with you when we are in the Pump Room! People will think you're a heathen."

Diana nodded solemnly, although if her aunt had been a little more perceptive, she would have noted the gleam in her niece's bright blue eyes. "Very well, I'll refrain from discussing the Roman gods and their various activities. I agree that given the loose morals they evinced, it wouldn't be wise to mention them in polite company."

"Certainly not!" Aunt Calliope said as she began marching toward the Pump Room once again. "And *don't* mention future spouses, either."

"But isn't that what all the unmarried men and women here hope to do, meet somebody to marry?" Diana asked innocently. "Why else would they parade about like horses for sale at a county fair, whether in the Pump Room or on the street or in the gardens and promenades? I was thinking I should wear a sign noting that I am currently unmarried, my late father was the fifth duke of Dilby, and the exact amount of my dowry. It would save a lot of time and unnecessary conversation."

"Diana!"

Aunt Euphenia laughed. "Calm yourself, Calliope. Can't you see she doesn't mean it?" She frowned at Diana with mock annoyance and shook her head. "You had best take care, young lady, or I fear you'll send your poor aunt into a fit."

"I knew she was only jesting," Aunt Calliope said with a sniff. "But remember, Diana, if you must speak, confine yourself to suitable subjects."

"Yes, Aunt." Diana recited the list of forbidden subjects. "No politics, no religion, no mention of the Prince Regent's latest escapade or the king's illness. Nothing controversial or shocking in any way." *Or interesting.* "Fortunately, I was only planning to observe today."

Instead of alleviating her aunt's dread, her last remark made Aunt Calliope frown even more. "Whatever you do, don't stare. You have the most disconcerting habit of staring at people, Diana, and that simply will not do."

"I'll do my best, Aunt, but I daresay it will be uphill work. There are sure to be lots of interesting people to look at."

"But you mustn't *stare*, Diana!"

Diana didn't answer, because they reached the outer doors of the Pump Room.

Hesitating on the threshold, her throat constricted. If poor dear Papa could see her now, wearing this fussy gown beneath her velvet-trimmed pelisse instead of a simple muslin frock, her hair curled and dressed within an inch of its life, willing to be censorious of her speech despite his encouragement to always speak her mind, he would think a changeling had taken her place.

But her father was dead and soon enough, she would have to do the expected thing and marry. Before that, though, she had a dream to fulfill, and if that meant parading about the Pump Room of Bath in fashionable attire, trying not to notice anything unusual or talk about anything interesting, so be it.

Aunt Calliope led the way inside, then paused at the entrance of the large room, surveying the inner sanctum like an admiral on the bridge of his man-of-war. Sunlight shone in through the tall windows, lighting the pale walls. A three-piece ensemble played a Bach concerto on a little stage at the far end of the hall. Above it was a small gallery with a balustrade overlooking those gathered below.

People stood in clusters, or languidly strolled around the room. Snatches of conversation about balls and card parties and clothes drifted to her, the voices sounding as bored as the speakers looked. It was as if conversing was just too, too much trouble.

Diana wondered what would happen if she suddenly shouted, "Fire!" Would these oh-so-elegant people run, or would they slowly saunter out of the room, risking death rather than perspiration?

Even stranger, everyone's gazes drifted to the people nearby or even across the room, as if they were seeking someone more important or influential or interesting to talk to. Surprisingly, nobody seemed offended by this rudeness—but then, they were all doing the same thing.

Diana thought of the lively discussions she'd had at home. If *this* was what passed for polite conversation in Bath, she'd be glad to leave it.

A group of three young women nearby, fashionably attired in muslin gowns so thin and diaphanous Diana foresaw an early death from consumption, kept glancing at the small stage. The music was well enough, but hardly superb, so Diana couldn't make out who or what was so fascinating—until the crowd parted and her gaze lit upon a man standing nearest the cellist.

Like a bolt of lightning, happiness and excitement shot through her. Good God, she had found him already!

He was perfect. Absolutely perfect. Raven black hair. Lean and excellent features. Superb cheekbones. Firm jaw. Broad shoulders. Slim hips. An excellent leg for a riding boot.

A shiver of delight ran down her spine as she watched him lean toward the lovely young woman in front of him in an intimate manner. Unlike so many in this room, it was clear he was really attending to his companion.

Impressed, Diana cocked her head, studying the casual grace and elegance of the man's stance while wondering what they were talking about. Surely they couldn't be mere acquaintances. What must that young woman be thinking, and feeling, to have such a man speak to her? What would it be like to have him interested in you?

She'd probably never know. After all, the young lady was the very epitome of beauty—shining dark hair, swanlike neck, pale complexion, heart-shaped face. Her clothing bespoke wealth as well as style.

Although her own ensemble might be just as fine, Diana knew that in everything else, she could not compare. Her eyes were too large, her features not nearly so delicate.

Normally, she didn't give more than a moment's thought to her looks, and then only if she happened to catch her reflection in a mirror. Even when enduring her maid's dressing of her hair that morning, she'd spent more time reading than contemplating her face.

Why would she? Staring at her face wouldn't change it. She'd known she was no beauty since she was ten years old and overheard a neighbor's daughter say, with sweet malice, that it was a pity rank didn't also ensure a pretty face.

Diana turned her attention back to the couple. What if he was making an assignation with the lady? Would she agree?

Who was that elderly woman standing nearby, the one who seemed to be listening while looking the other way? Was she a relative of the beauty, or only a gossip shamelessly eavesdropping?

The astonishingly handsome man slowly straightened, a slightly puzzled look on his face.

What had the beauty said?

Then he swiveled on his heel and turned in Diana's direction, his dark brows rising in silent query.

Feeling as guilty as if she'd been caught spying on a stranger in his bedroom, Diana quickly turned toward her aunt.

Before she could think of something to say, Aunt Calliope grabbed her arm. "How dare he!"

Shocked, embarrassed, worried about making her aunts upset, Diana did the first thing that came to her mind.

She feigned ignorance. "How dare who?"

Heaven help her, she sounded like an owl.

"That . . . that *odious* man! How dare he look at me in such an insolent fashion!"

She had never heard Aunt Calliope so annoyed in her life. "Do you mean the man standing by the cello? Who is he? Why is he odious?"

"Never mind who he is," Aunt Calliope snapped.

Diana supposed she didn't have to know his name. It was enough that she'd seen him. But she was still dying to learn why her aunt was so upset by the sight of him.

"Whatever is the matter, Calliope?" Aunt Euphenia asked.

"Lord Adderley had the unmitigated gall to look at me. Impudent cur!"

"Impudent cur he may be," Aunt Euphenia said with her usual calm, "but he *is* a viscount, so please don't speak so loudly."

The title explained the courtly and elegant manner.

Aunt Calliope's small nose wrinkled with the same disgust rotten food elicited. "Lord Adderley is a complete cad," she said to Diana, obeying her sister's admonition and whispering as quietly as she could. "A lothario and a gambler, too. No military service for him, either, thank you very much. Not that he would have been much help, I'm sure, unless Wellington wanted to fight the war at the gaming tables."

No wonder Aunt Calliope, widow of General Lord Walter FitzBurton, spoke so harshly of him.

"Not every man is cut out for military service, Calliope," Aunt Euphenia noted. "I can't help thinking it would be better if some of these young officers decided not to purchase their commissions. I swear all some of them care about is how dashing they look in their uniforms."

Aunt Calliope leaned forward and spoke in a confidential whisper. "A thorough reprobate, that's what he is. There is talk of gambling and cock fighting and mistresses by the score. It's only his good looks and family name that enable Adderley to venture into polite society at all. Even so, I don't know what the world is coming to when he is not given the cut direct in the Pump Room."

"The man *is* charming," Aunt Euphenia said,

"as such men are, and pleasing to the eye. However, it's not as if anybody's proposing that Diana marry Lord Adderley. Nor would she accept him, for there may be some truth to the tales about—"

"*Some* truth?" Aunt Calliope cried. "I have it on the best authority!"

Which meant that her friends had told her about the viscount's nefarious activities in great salacious detail, Diana supposed.

"Then you have even less cause for concern, for if there is a grain of truth to the rumors, Diana has too much sense to encourage the attentions of a fellow like that. Don't you, Diana?"

Before Diana could answer in the affirmative, Aunt Calliope said, "I should hope so." She tapped Diana's hand to emphasize her point. "If he did pursue you, he would only be after your money, Diana. Remember that."

"Oh, I don't think you need fear," Diana replied good-naturedly, and sincerely. "Such men are attractive in fiction, but I'm certain they leave much to be desired in real life. Fortunately, I doubt my dowry would be enough to tempt him. I'm sure he wouldn't sell himself for anything less than fifteen thousand a year."

"Diana, please!" Aunt Calliope exclaimed. "Do not talk of anybody selling themselves! It sounds so . . . so *mercenary*!"

"I'll try," Diana answered gravely. "Yet I must point out that not everyone seems to share your poor opinion of the viscount. The expensively attired young lady talking to him, for instance. Who is she?"

"She's *not* a lady," Aunt Calliope retorted. "Adelina Foxborough is the daughter of a rum distiller. Her dowry, they say, will be twenty thousand a year and an estate in the West Indies, which no doubt explains the viscount's interest in her."

"The viscount is in debt?"

Aunt Calliope colored. "Well, no, that's the one bad thing I haven't heard about him—which doesn't mean he's not, of course."

Her aunt's logic was definitely faulty. Considering what else was being said about him, if the man was in debt, that rumor would be making the rounds of drawing and assembly rooms, too.

"If Adelina Foxborough lacks in birth, she's been well educated," Aunt Euphenia observed. "She'll likely make the viscount a better wife than he deserves, despite her lack of title."

"Well educated she may be, in terms of history and Latin and other dead things, but she's not been well brought up if she'll attach herself to Lord Adderley," Aunt Calliope said firmly. "And that woman who's supposed to be her chaperon is absolutely hen-witted, if you ask me, too busy gossiping to pay attention to her charge."

"Never mind them," Aunt Euphenia said. She nodded toward the counter where the restorative water was dispensed. "The marchioness of Ellis and her son, Lord Fallston, the earl of Dartonby, are here."

Aunt Calliope smiled happily. Apparently the odious, impudent Lord Adderley was no longer important.

"Excellent!" she cried. "He would be perfect for you, Diana, simply perfect! And he so deserves a fine young lady after that jilt ran off the day before their wedding."

"He was engaged before?" Diana asked.

"Yes, unfortunately, to some romantic chit of a girl who ran off to the border with a former friend."

"The viscount?"

"No, another man," Aunt Euphenia answered.

"It seems Bath is full of reprobates and cads," Diana noted. "Perhaps I should have stayed in Lincolnshire."

Aunt Euphenia smiled. "But that would have deprived us of the pleasure of your company, Diana, and while I don't wish to speak ill of my brother, you *are* a duke's daughter, and it's past time you took your place in society, as you deserve. Now come along, my dear."

Resisting the urge to look at the viscount again and feeling like a puppy on a leash, Diana followed her aunts toward the counter and the two people standing beside it.

Unlike her stylish aunts, the marchioness was plainly and simply dressed, and her son likewise. He didn't have high points on his collar or a jacket cut so tight his valet would have to wrestle him into it, or a waistcoat of brilliant colors in astonishing combinations. Indeed, he might be the most modestly dressed young man in Bath.

When he realized they were coming toward them, he gave Diana a tentative smile and brushed back a lock of chestnut hair that had fallen over his forehead. Although he was taller than Diana and certainly not a youth, that self-conscious action, and his smattering of freckles, made him seem like a shy little boy.

After her aunts had exchanged salutations and introductions with Lady Ellis and her son in their characteristic manner—meaning that Aunt Calliope was all delight and joy, Aunt Euphenia genial and calm—Lord Fallston stepped forward to take Diana's hand.

She stood absolutely still and held her breath. The only other men who'd ever kissed her hand had been of long acquaintance and old enough to be her father.

Lord Fallston's lips barely brushed her glove.

Was that *it*? Lips against a glove would hardly ever be the last word in excitement, she supposed, but she was disappointed nonetheless.

"I'm delighted to make your acquaintance, Lady Diana," he said as he straightened.

She gave Lord Fallston a smile. He could hardly be blamed for failing to live up to her no doubt exaggerated expectations.

"Would you care to take a turn around the room with me?" he asked.

She glanced at her aunts. Aunt Calliope looked enraptured, while Aunt Euphenia gave an approving nod.

Lord Fallston held out his arm, and Diana experienced another first as she slipped hers through that of a young man she'd only just met.

"You've not been long in Bath, I think," Lord Fallston noted as they set off around the room. "I haven't seen you in the Pump Room or the theater, or at the assembly balls. I'm quite sure I would have remembered you if I had."

Maybe her aunts were right about clothes and a hairstyle making a lot of difference. Maybe she did look better than she thought. "I had to purchase some new clothes in Milsom Street before I could venture into society. I've been in black gloves for the past year."

Lord Fallston looked suitably concerned. "I'm sorry. I didn't mean to arouse unhappy memories."

She gave him a little smile of forgiveness. "Before coming here, I lived very quietly in Lincolnshire with my late father. I rarely had cause or the opportunity to purchase stylish clothes. When I arrived in Bath, Aunt Calliope was appalled by my lack of fashionable attire and insisted I wait until I had new clothes before venturing out in society. *I* insisted on going to the circulating library, unfashionable clothes or not, so we compromised. We went to the shops one day, and the library the next, until I had an abundance of new clothes and books to read."

They strolled past a knot of elderly men hotly complaining about the country going to the dogs. Apparently it had been going to the dogs since 1749.

"You enjoy reading?" Lord Fallston inquired.

"Oh, very much! I have no skill or patience for embroidery, and even less for painting. I am a very unaccomplished young woman."

The moment the words were out of her mouth, she mentally cringed. Aunt Calliope would probably have apoplexy if she heard her say that!

Fortunately, Lord Fallston's expression didn't betray either shock or horror or disgust. "A well-read young woman is a rarity in Bath. I suppose you prefer poetry?"

"No," she admitted. "Unless it's the *Iliad* or the *Odyssey*, and some of Milton."

She did not tell Lord Fallston she liked Homer's battle scenes the best, and found Satan in *Paradise Lost* a fascinatingly evil character.

Lord Fallston smiled with relief. "I must confess, all that stuff by Byron and his ilk does not appeal to me, either. I tried to memorize some poems once, hoping to impress a young lady, but I just couldn't stomach most of it."

They passed three elderly ladies engaged in a

discussion of their various ailments and treatments, each one seemingly determined to outdo the other with the severity of the symptoms and the number of times the doctor had been summoned to her deathbed.

Diana also noticed that the impudent viscount had disappeared and the beauty was now standing beside her chaperon. The beauty looked rather peeved. Perhaps the viscount's disappearance had something to do with that.

"I prefer novels," Diana said, returning to the conversation, "and the more they make my spine tingle, the better I like them. *The Mysteries of Udolpho* is one of my favorite books."

Lord Fallston started. "You were allowed to read novels?"

"My father didn't censure my reading, except some parts of Ovid. But novels aren't so very bad, are they? They're just stories, after all."

"Yet they are hardly the sort of edifying tales a young lady should read."

Diana's first instinct was to inquire if he thought all reading had to be edifying, and if so, what edifying works had he read lately? However, her aunt's strictures were uppermost in her mind, so she restrained herself, although she couldn't be completely mute on the subject. "Surely you don't believe a novel can corrupt a woman?"

"They are a waste of time that could be spent doing better things."

"I think it is better to read than gossip, which seems to be how many young ladies spend their time."

"I don't disagree," Lord Fallston replied. "It is what they read that I question."

"What do you think they should read? *Pilgrim's Progress*?"

His steps slowed. "I didn't mean to offend you, Lady Diana."

She mentally cringed again. "I assure you, you haven't. I hope *I* haven't offended *you*, my lord."

To her relief, Lord Fallston smiled. "Let us agree to disagree. I'm glad you were honest with me. I'm tired of young ladies who just smile and simper and flatter and flirt. You're a very welcome change."

"I'm glad you think so and I believe I can give you my word that I won't simper."

From behind them, a deep masculine voice intruded. "Hello, Fallston. Won't you introduce me to this charming young lady who promises not to simper?"

Diana turned toward the speaker who had interrupted their conversation.

And found herself staring into the amused, chestnut-brown eyes of Lord Adderley.

Diana's heart missed a beat. Maybe two, because up close, the viscount was even more breathtaking. Not only was he handsome, masculine vitality fairly emanated from him, making everyone else in the Pump Room seem half dead by comparison.

Even Lord Fallston might have been an effigy, so rigidly was he standing. His verbal response was just as stiff, too. "Lady Diana Westover, allow me to present Lord Adderley."

The viscount reached out and took her hand. "Delighted, Lady Diana," he murmured, his deep voice perfectly suited to his coloring, making her think of secrets whispered in the dark. Then he pressed his shapely mouth to the back of her gloved hand.

No mere brush of the lips from him! The pressure of his mouth was firm, and lingered. Pleasure seemed to spread out from the place he touched her, seeping through her body until it was like being enveloped in a velvet blanket.

Oh, *this* was what she had imagined—except that the man eliciting such a response was a scoundrel.

The viscount let go and stepped back, smiling the most compelling little half smile Diana had ever seen while his dark-eyed gaze burned into her. He made her feel happy and wary and warm all at the same time.

"I don't like women who simper, either," he said, his deep voice as fascinating as his eyes.

"Why not?" she asked, her curiosity overcoming her aunt's admonitions.

His smile grew, and his approval suddenly seemed like the greatest compliment any man could bestow. "Because it shows a lack of assurance. I prefer a woman who has opinions and isn't afraid to voice them."

Her father had always said that an intelligent, confident man would welcome discussion and never seek to censure anyone, male or female, who cared to participate.

"I didn't think there was a woman you didn't like, one way or the other," Lord Fallston said, still stiff as a soldier on parade.

Diana couldn't quite believe what she had heard. The implications were so clear and so vulgar, she could hardly reconcile the sentiment with the amiable man beside her.

The viscount assumed a shocked expression that was patently fraudulent. "Really, Fallston, is that any way to speak in front of a lady?"

Diana didn't disagree, yet as Lord Fallston flushed with embarrassment, she recalled all that her aunts had said about the viscount. If he was a gambler and a rogue, it wasn't *his* place to correct Lord Fallston.

"It's very kind of you to be concerned for my sensibilities, Lord Adderley," she said, assuming an affable mien that was as false as his indignation, "but while I may have grown up in the country, I assure you that I am well aware of how some young men choose to spend their time, and with whom. It's a most unfortunate choice, given they have all the advantages and opportunities the world has to offer, but thus it is. What can one do but shake one's head over the waste, and regret that women do not have the advantages and opportunities instead?"

The viscount's brows lowered. "You think women would be less likely to engage in frivolous pursuits?"

"*Frivolous pursuits* are not what I would choose to call such activities. However, I am not so ignorant as to assume women are more virtuous than men, in general. That said, I do believe they couldn't do much worse." She gave him a very bright smile. "Now if you will excuse us, we should rejoin my aunts and Lady Ellis."

Her arm still in the stunned Lord Fallston's, she turned and headed back toward her aunts and Lady Ellis, who were watching with their mouths agape. The crowd made way for them, and whispers followed their progress like the sound of dry leaves blowing in a breeze.

Blushing, she bit her lip. She hadn't wanted to make a sensation, but apparently she had, and not a good one. Perhaps she shouldn't have said anything. . . .

"I say," Lord Fallston murmured before they reached their relatives. "That was marvelous! I've never seen Adderley so shocked." His cheeks colored. "I apologize for what I said to him at the first—"

"It's really quite all right," she replied, relieved that he wasn't upset.

Her relief lasted until she reached her aunts. Aunt Calliope looked about to choke, Lady Ellis regarded her as if she were a freak of nature and even Aunt Euphenia seemed rather worried.

Aunt Calliope immediately drew her aside. "I thought I would have an attack of nerves right here in the Pump Room when I saw you talking to that wastrel, Diana," she whispered. "Whatever possessed you?"

"Lord Adderley spoke to me. It would have been rude to remain mute, wouldn't it?"

"You could have and you should have!"

"Don't be angry with her," Lord Fallston said, coming to her aid. "She gave Adderley a marvelous set-down. You should have heard what she said."

Much to Diana's chagrin, he then began a long and exaggerated account of what had happened, making it sound as if she'd delivered a notable oration in parliament instead of bantering in the Pump Room.

By the time he was finished, however, she had to be grateful for his version of their conversation. Lady Ellis seemed a little less frosty, Aunt Euphenia was obviously relieved, and Aunt Calliope was delighted.

"Good for you, my dear!" she exclaimed. "It's about time somebody put that man in his place."

"Indeed, yes," Lord Fallston said eagerly. "She was wonderful."

Aunt Euphenia gave Diana an approving look. "I'm not surprised she could hold her own against such a fellow. She's very clever."

That quality didn't seem to impress Lady Ellis overmuch. "If you'll excuse us, I think I've spent enough time in the Pump Room for one day," she declared in a tone of command that would brook no dissent.

Lord Fallston wasn't completely under his mother's thumb, apparently, for he ignored her. "We're going to Sydney Gardens tonight for the gala," he said to Diana. "Will you be there?"

"Of course we shall!" Aunt Calliope cried, sparing Diana the necessity of answering. "We wouldn't miss it for the world. Dear Diana has never seen fireworks before, have you, Diana?"

As she shook her head, she realized that Lady Ellis didn't look pleased. Clearly, she hadn't made the best of impressions on the woman. Well, she was used to being considered somewhat odd, given her country upbringing and penchant for reading. And Lady Ellis hadn't made a particularly good impression on her, either.

Lord Fallston grasped Diana's hand and again raised it to his lips. This time, he kissed with more pressure, but it still didn't give her the thrill the viscount's kiss had.

Why was that, she wondered. She liked Lord Fallston. He was a comely, modest young man. She should prefer his attention to that of a rake and a scoundrel.

Except that she found it hard to believe Lord Fallston was capable of any real passion, whereas the viscount. . . .

She realized Lord Fallston was smiling at her. "I look forward to seeing you later," he said fervently, like a little boy eager for a present.

"Come along, Crispin!" his mother commanded.

Diana gave him an encouraging smile as Lady Ellis turned and marched off, her son dutifully at her side.

"I'm so pleased we were able to meet Lord Fallston today!" Aunt Calliope exclaimed when they were out of earshot. "He's a very fine young man. Well educated, mannerly, modest."

"He seems quite nice," Diana agreed.

"And more importantly, he is obviously very taken with you. I can't remember him ever walking about the Pump Room with any other young lady." Aunt Calliope fairly beamed.

"He's a fine young gentleman of spotless reputation," Aunt Euphenia confirmed.

"Not like that nasty Adderley," Aunt Calliope said. "And now you have even more reason to avoid that reprobate in the future, Diana. Lord Fallston hates him."

Diana found it difficult to believe the genial Lord Fallston was capable of any strong emotion. "Why?"

"Some sort of prank at Harrow that went wrong. Poor Lord Fallston nearly drowned,"

Aunt Calliope explained. "Adderley promised to be his friend if he'd take the headmaster's punt out onto the river in the dead of night, but the boat had a leak. Lord Fallston is convinced it was scuttled on *purpose*."

"A villainous viscount, indeed," Diana murmured.

"So you *must* avoid him in future. And you must be sure not to say too many shocking things to Lord Fallston tonight, Diana, or he might cease to be impressed and think you're odd."

Diana didn't want to upset her aunts anymore, so she nodded. "I promise to do my very best to be ladylike and demure in Sydney Gardens." She caught Aunt Euphenia's cautioning eye. "And everywhere else in Bath, too, of course. May we leave now?"

"Of course," Aunt Euphenia replied. "I think we should rest if we are to go out again this evening."

Aunt Calliope appeared reluctant to go, until a swift glance around the Pump Room confirmed that they were still the object of some curious speculation. "Yes, that might be best."

Diana happily accompanied them from the room, although she had no intention of resting. She wanted to commit her thoughts about the viscount to paper while their encounter was still fresh in her mind.

His looks, his manner, his deep, seductive voice, the incredible power of his dark brown eyes, the sparks of anger that came to them when she bested him in their verbal duel. . . .

Yes, he *was* perfect—the perfect model for Count Korlovsky, the villain of her novel and the nemesis of the fair Evangeline.

Chapter 2

Evangeline opened her eyes, then looked around. The contents of her baggage had been looted and strewn about the road. There was no sign at all of her traveling companions.

A man came around the side of the overturned vehicle, saw her and rushed toward her. "My dear young woman, what has happened?"

She recognized the familiar face of Count Korlovsky, who knelt beside her and took her hand. "Are you injured? Ah, wait! You are the young and beautiful lady I met at the party, the one engaged to the Farinelli boy."

"Yes," she said as he helped her to her feet. "I was on my way to meet Rodolpho when the coach was attacked. What happened to my companions?"

"I do not know," the count replied. "I have just arrived here." His voice lowered to a gentle plea. "You must allow me to offer you my assistance. My home is not far off. You must come there until you are recovered."

"But Rodolpho—"

"When you are rested, you may have my carriage to continue on your way." The count looked and sounded as if his heart would be bro-

*ken if she refused his request. "You cannot stay
here. The outlaws may return."*

*Evangeline barely knew the nobleman, but
what else could she do? She was alone, in a desolate, dangerous countryside, and weak with thirst
and hunger. The count seemed so kind and concerned. She would accept his generous offer.*

The Castle of Count Korlovsky

Later that morning, Edmond Terrington, Viscount Adderley, strode into the library of
the Honorable Brixton Smythe-Medway's house
in Queen Square. The odor of cheroots lingered
in the stuffy atmosphere of the well-appointed
room paneled in age-darkened oak, along with
the scent of furniture wax and leather bindings
unopened for a quarter century. Several portraits
of stern relatives in amazing wigs looked down
from the walls, as if wondering how their noble
lineage had produced the slender, sandy-haired
Brixton.

At present, Brix himself stood in front of a
small table bearing three decanters and several
glasses, his untied cravat dangling about his neck,
and the dark circles under his green eyes telling
Edmond he hadn't slept all night.

"A bit early for the brandy bottle, isn't it?" Edmond asked as he threw himself into an over-
stuffed wing chair.

Brix stopped in mid-pour. "It's the first I've had

all night." He glanced at the sunlight streaming in through the tall windows. "Or morning, either."

"What was it this time? Cards? A woman?"

"If you must know, I got lost in the labyrinth in Sydney Gardens. I swear they've rearranged it."

"What, without telling a single soul in Bath?"

Brix grinned, looking exactly like the boy Edmond had first encountered at Harrow who had a penchant for proposing the most astonishing pranks the ancient school had ever witnessed.

"Oh, very well," Brix said with a laugh, "I just plain got lost trying to avoid Fanny Epping. Honestly, one kiss fourteen years ago and apparently I'm hers for life. I swear I spent half the night in there stumbling around in the dark."

Edmond shook his head more with dismay than manly sympathy. He'd never understood why Brix just didn't confront the young woman and tell her he didn't reciprocate her feelings. Every time he tried to suggest that, Brix made a joke and changed the subject.

However, he wasn't here to talk about Brix and Fanny Epping.

His more serious purpose must have shown on his face, because Brix ran a measuring gaze over him and said, "You look like you could stand a stiff drink yourself. What the devil are you doing here this early? Not something amiss with the delightful Miss Foxborough, I hope?"

Edmond leaned his head back, closed his eyes

and groaned. "Miss Foxborough? Oh, God. I forgot all about her."

Brix spilled the brandy. "You *forgot* a beautiful woman worth twenty thousand pounds a year?"

Edmond rubbed his eyes. This day was fast turning into a disaster. "You would have, too, if you'd been in my place."

Brix poured two brandies. He handed one to Edmond, then sat on the faded sofa opposite him. "You'd better explain these extraordinary circumstances, and in words of one syllable, if you please. I'm exhausted."

Edmond downed his brandy before answering, enjoying the familiar warmth as the drink slipped down his throat while he contemplated what exactly he would say. "I was talking to Miss Foxborough in the Pump Room. She was rattling on about last night's concert when I had the oddest sensation, as if I was being spied on. I turned and discovered a young woman watching me from across the room. I swear, Brix, the way she stared at me made the hairs on the back of my neck stand on end."

Brix looked puzzled. "People stare at you all the time. You should be used to it by now."

He'd never get used to it, Edmond thought as he twisted his empty glass in his hand. He'd been stared at from childhood, and it had been years before he'd known it was because he was good-looking. In their righteous zeal to stamp out any vanity he might possess, his parents had always spoken of his appearance as an unfortunate cross he'd have to bear, and they'd never allowed a mirror in their home. He had been convinced he must be horribly ugly or disfigured, until the day he'd overheard the new scullery maid telling the cook what a handsome boy he was and wasn't it a pity he was such a solitary little fellow? He'd immediately run as fast as his eight-year-old legs could take him to look at his reflection in the mill pond and discovered he wasn't so terribly ugly after all.

"This was different and definitely odd," he said, trying to explain why Lady Diana's scrutiny bothered him more than most. "At first, I thought there must be something wrong with my cravat, or that the seam in my jacket was ripped, but I've checked and it wasn't that."

Brix's grin widened and he relaxed against the cushions. "Well, it was a woman, wasn't it? She was probably overcome with admiration."

"No, you don't understand," Edmond replied, searching for a comparison. "It was like Buggy watching the spiders he used to keep in a jar in our room at school."

Grimacing, Brix shivered. "Gad! I kept expecting him to go blind. Or start eating them."

"Well, that's exactly how this young woman was looking at me. Like she was Buggy and I was a spider."

Or as if he'd encountered an agent of the Spanish

Inquisition trying to discover his deepest, darkest secrets.

The ridiculousness of that comparison struck him, and the worst of his tension eased. After all, it wasn't as if he'd actually done half, or even a quarter, of the shameful things people said about him.

"Then the woman realized I'd noticed her," he continued. "She looked away quickly enough, and had the grace to blush."

As he remembered the pink flush that had spread across her cheeks, it reminded him of a pale pink rose opening in bloom.

He put away such fanciful thoughts to go on with his story. "I decided to find out who she was. Since she was with Fallston, I made him introduce me."

Brix's mouth fell open again. "Fallston? That disgusting little rodent?"

Edmond shrugged his broad shoulders. "What else could I do? I didn't want to wander around the Pump Room asking a lot of questions. People might assume I was interested in the chit and I'm not, beyond wondering who she was and why she stared at me like I was some sort of creature."

"She's not pretty, then?"

Edmond frowned as he set down his glass on the scarred side table. There was a certain vivaciousness to her features, particularly the intelligent sparkle in her cornflower-blue eyes, but he doubted Brix, or most other young men in Bath, would appreciate that intriguing quality. They would compare her to the conventionally beautiful, like Adelina Foxborough, and find her lacking. "That wouldn't have made a bit of difference anyway."

"Yet you were so determined to find out the identity of this odd woman that you went and talked to Fallston." Brix shook his head. "He probably wanted to strangle you on the spot. He's never forgiven us for that dunking at Harrow."

"He should be over it by now. Still, he was quite civil, for him."

This suddenly struck Edmond as rather odd. It was as if Fallston was on his very best behavior—to impress his bright-eyed companion, no doubt.

"So, who was she, then?" Brix asked.

"Lady Diana Westover."

Brix's eyes widened.

"You've heard of her?"

"Haven't you?"

"If I had, I would hardly come rushing over here to ask you, would I?" Edmond pointed out.

"I suppose not."

"So, is she touched in the head or otherwise deranged?"

"As far as I know, she's not, but her father was definitely eccentric. Worse for you, Lady Calliope FitzBurton is her paternal aunt."

Edmond stared into his empty glass. Now the young woman's cutting remarks made perfect sense—but they still rankled, perhaps more so because of the way she'd smiled when she said them.

"So I don't think you need have the slightest fear you're losing your appeal to the fairer sex. I don't doubt Lady Calliope has painted you the worst sort of lascivious cad. Fallston has probably told the young lady you're evil incarnate."

"Yes, I'm sure between the two of them, Lady Diana must think me the worst villain in England." He stifled a weary sigh.

"Why don't you refute the lies Fallston tells about you?"

"As I've told you before, Brix, it's not worth the trouble. And a gentleman should be above such pettiness."

"I don't call it petty to stop him from implying that you have mistresses spread hither and yon across the country, that you gamble for days at a time, that you—"

"That's enough!"

When he saw his friend's expression, Edmond regretted his harsh retort. "I'm sorry, but those stories are damned annoying."

"Which is why you ought to nip them in the bud."

"Brix, I don't want to discuss it," he said, his tone a cross between an order and a plea.

"I know, I know." Brix grinned, the merry comrade once more. "I suppose being the subject of gossip and rumor and speculation is the onerous price one must pay for being so handsome. Thank God I'm spared. I dye my hair this color on purpose, you know, just to make myself less attractive."

Edmond laughed. Brix could always jolly him out of a foul mood. He was able to see the funny side of any situation—quite a contrast to Edmond's humorless, undemonstrative parents, which was one reason Edmond liked him so much. "It doesn't quite work. You're not unattractive, Brix, if you'd care to comb that mop of hair once in a while."

Brix looked offended. "And risk being stared at by strange women in the Pump Room? No, thank you!"

"So, how exactly was Lady Diana's father eccentric?" Edmond asked, returning to the original subject of the conversation.

Brix got up and poured them both another drink. "After the death of his wife, the fifth duke of Dilby took himself off to the most remote estate he owned in Lincolnshire and—"

"Her father was a *duke*?"

Brix nodded. "After he got to Lincolnshire, he never set foot out of doors again, or so they say. He kept his daughter with him, in a manor that, according to Mama, was a perfect ruin. Like something out of one of those gothic novels you're always reading. *The Mysteries of Otranto* and that sort of thing."

Edmond had often thought that his parents

would turn over in their tomb if they knew that the gruesome stories they had provided that were intended to terrify him into good behavior had only whet his appetite for more lurid tales, whether they gave him nightmares or not. "It's *The Mysteries of Udolpho* and *The Castle of Otranto.*"

"Whatever," Brix replied, waving his glass in airy dismissal. "I don't think Lady Diana even went to school, but I could ask Mama. She'll know."

Edmond wondered what Lady Diana's father had been like. Was he simply a shy, retiring sort of man who preferred the quiet country life, or had there been a darker, more selfish element in his self-imposed banishment?

If the latter were so, he would expect Lady Diana to be a quiet little mouse of a thing, scarcely willing to open her rather shapely lips, which she most certainly was not.

Likely, then, the former was true—her father had merely preferred the quiet country life. Deep in his heart and despite what she had said to him, Edmond was glad to think so. He wouldn't wish the sort of loveless upbringing he'd had on anybody, even bold, impertinent young women who stared.

Brix refilled Edmond's brandy. "So if Fallston was genial and she only stared at you, why were you so angry?"

Edmond wished he hadn't been. "The lady

said . . . something," he explained, the answer sounding weak even to himself.

Brix settled himself back on the sofa, drink in hand. "What did she do, curse you on the spot?"

"It wasn't what she said so much as the way she said it," he reflected. "It was as disconcerting as her staring." He took another sip of brandy. "Ah, well, Fallston is welcome to her," he said, meaning it. His tranquility had been disrupted enough.

"So you'll continue pursuing the beautiful Miss Foxborough?"

"I'm not interested in Miss Foxborough solely because of her looks."

Brix raised his glass in another wry salute. "Of course not. She's the most wealthy heiress in Bath."

Edmond decided he should give up trying to convince Brix that while he admired a pretty woman as much as the next man, a lovely face and large fortune were not the first things he would consider when it came to choosing a wife.

Brix sighed dramatically. "Alas, how can I, the lowly youngest son of an earl, compete for the hand of the fair Miss Foxborough and her twenty thousand pounds when Lord Adderley has his eyes—and quite possibly more—on her?"

"I've been a model of decorum, Brix."

"Have you really? Well, well."

"Brix, answer me honestly. Do you want to court Adelina Foxborough?"

Brix's first response was a genuine, friendly

smile before he shook his head. "No, although I confess it's tempting to see just how upset my family could get. A distiller's daughter—they'd probably fall into fits. But I don't intend to wed until I'm past my prime and merely in need of an heir to carry on the family name. Do *you* want to marry the rum heiress?"

Edmond honestly wasn't sure how to answer that question. "I haven't decided. But I don't want her angry at me, although she'd be perfectly justified after the way I left her this morning."

"I'm sure she'll forgive you if you ask nicely enough, which no doubt you will," Brix said genially. "She's not likely to let you—and your title—slip through her lovely fingers."

Edmond sighed. "You make me sound like a stallion being brought to stud."

Brix laughed. "It's what we all are, one way or another. All I ask is a placid mare and a foal to carry on the family name at some far distant day."

"You're incorrigible, Brix."

"Which is why we are the best of friends, my lord. Peas in a pod, and all that."

They weren't exactly similar, but Edmond knew what he meant. They'd been partners in pranks and fast friends ever since the first day they'd met.

"Speaking of which," Edmond said, "before I deserted Miss Foxborough in the Pump Room, we had planned to meet in Sydney Gardens tonight to view the fireworks. Care to join us?"

"What are the chances Fanny Epping will be there two nights in a row and I'll have to hide again?" Brix mused aloud. "Then again, I don't suppose you'd want me sticking with you like a burr the entire evening. It sounds like the perfect opportunity to make your apologies to Miss Foxborough."

"I'd thought of that." Edmond gave his friend a saintly smile. "And I promise to be on my very best behavior."

Brix gave him a wry grin. "Somehow, I don't think that's quite what Miss Foxborough expects. You wouldn't want to disappoint her, would you?"

Edmond didn't answer before he took another drink.

Diana put down her pen. She was supposed to be napping, resting for this evening's festivities in Sydney Gardens, but she was much too excited to nap or even lie still. She'd simply had to make the changes to the meeting between Evangeline and the mysterious count based on her confrontation with Lord Adderley this morning.

She looked at the page in front of her and reread the section she had just revised.

The handsome stranger filled Evangeline with both excitement and a nameless dread.

He bowed, then took her hand in his, bringing it to his remarkable lips for a kiss. Although his action

*was merely courteous, an unfamiliar warmth
flooded through her as he pressed his mouth to her
flesh, a warmth that increased when he raised his
dark, piercing eyes to regard her steadily.*

*"Permit me to introduce myself," he said, the
low, deep timbre of his voice making her tremble.
"I am the Count Korlovsky."*

"Much better," Diana muttered, sighing with
satisfaction.

She put the pages away in the writing desk that
she had brought from home, locked it, then
tucked the key in the pocket of her petticoat. It
wasn't that she didn't trust her aunts or the servants; it was simply that she dreaded their reaction if they discovered her work in progress.

Aunt Calliope would be baffled at first, then
horrified when Diana revealed that she was writing a novel. She would exclaim that no relative of
hers should sink so low, voicing an opinion many
of the *ton* would share.

Aunt Euphenia might not disapprove of her
niece's wish to be a writer, but she'd probably be
dismayed by Diana's choice of story. She wouldn't
understand why tales of mysterious men, ruined
castles and life-threatening danger thrilled her so,
and Diana wasn't sure she could explain. She supposed one either shared that enjoyment, or one
didn't.

Lord Fallston most certainly did not, and it was
easy to guess what he would think of a woman

who wanted to write such a book. That was rather too bad, because he did seem like a nice young man. She hadn't expected to encounter such a matrimonial prospect so quickly.

Indeed, she'd rather hoped she wouldn't, so that she would have more time to pursue her dream of becoming a published writer before settling down to married life. The vast majority of men of her class would surely share Lord Fallston's opinion of a woman who wanted to write novels and have the public read them.

Of course, many things could happen to prevent an engagement, not the least of which was learning more about each other. There was no need to feel that she was already losing what freedom she possessed, or that her time to accomplish her goal was growing short. Besides, his mother didn't seem to like her, which was a very comforting thought.

She stopped short in her progress to the bell pull. She shouldn't feel that way. She should want the mother of such an eminently suitable young man to approve of her. She should try to ensure that she overcame whatever bad impression she'd made, no matter how troublesome that seemed. After all, she did want to be married. Some day. To a good man, not some darkly dangerous rogue.

Was Lord Adderley's mother still alive? she mused as she continued toward the bell pull. What was she like? No doubt she would disapprove of a writer in the family, too. Would he?

Diana shook her head at her own folly as she rang for Sally, her maid, to help her dress for dinner. She shouldn't be thinking about Lord Adderley, let alone his mother.

Nevertheless, she couldn't help wondering if he would be in Sydney Gardens tonight—but only because a little further study of the viscount would be beneficial for her book.

Or so she told herself as she tried to disregard the excited little thrill that surged through her body at that thought and ignored the realization Lord Fallston inspired nothing like it.

Chapter 3

The castle sat on a cliff overlooking the sea. Gulls wheeled and cried about its ruined roofs, and a large part of the outer wall had crumbled and fallen down onto the rocks below. The sea, whipped by the wind, churned and frothed as if angry to be disturbed by the noise of the black coach and four that rumbled through what was left of the barbican, beneath the murder hole that now yawned open to the darkening sky. In days gone by, Evangeline knew, the castle's defenders would have lurked there, ready to rain down stones or boiling oil on invaders passing below.

Seated beside her, the count smiled and his dark eyes gleamed like polished obsidian. "Do not be afraid, dear lady. My castle is old and in need of repair, but inside you will find every comfort a woman's heart desires."

Evangeline shivered.

The Castle of Count Korlovsky

The beautiful Adelina Foxborough's gray-green eyes were distinctly cool as she regarded a penitent Edmond. As her costly perfume warred with the dew-damp foliage of the many trees and plants, Edmond realized he preferred the foliage.

A short distance away from them, Mrs. Jesser, her companion, stood listening to the orchestra on the back balcony of the tavern at the end of Sydney Gardens, and only occasionally looked back over her shoulder at her charge. Other people, there to enjoy the music, the fireworks and the gossip, meandered along the graveled walk. Nearby were several boxes, rather like covered stalls, for private parties and refreshments; further inside the gardens were arbors and faux grottos for even more private activities. Lamps provided illumination in the rest of the park, and lovely ironwork bridges led over the Kennet and Avon canals.

"I'm really very upset with you, you bad man," Adelina said with an exaggerated pout, tapping Edmond on the shoulder with her fan as she leaned toward him and spoke just loudly enough to be heard above the music by him, but not the hard-of-hearing Mrs. Jesser. "It was very rude of you to abandon me in the Pump Room."

"I know," he began sincerely, "and I'm—"

She hit him again, a little harder. "It's too noisy here! I'm sure you're going to apologize charmingly, and I don't want to miss a word. Is there not somewhere more private we could go? One of those picturesque little grottos, perhaps?"

Edmond wondered if it was possible Adelina was ignorant of the activities that sometimes took place in those grottos. They were hardly suitable places for purely innocent rendezvous.

Yet they were private, and not very far away. He could apologize quickly and without interruption, and they could be back before their absence was noted. Since he was finding that he didn't particularly want to spend much time with the beautiful Adelina tonight, that suggestion had undeniable appeal. "Very well. To a grotto it will be."

"Since you insist," Adelina whispered, looking around furtively and apparently forgetting that had been her suggestion. "But only for a few moments. I wouldn't want my reputation to be compromised."

She might as well be wearing a large sign reading *We are about to sneak off together,* Edmond thought, not impressed by her lack of subtlety.

Indeed, she seemed so excited, he began to doubt it was simply the possibility of being alone with him that brought that hungry gleam to her eyes.

A little warning bell went off in his mind. There might be more to this than Adelina wanting to hear him clearly, or even share some clandestine kisses. Maybe she had other plans, ones with serious consequences. Maybe he should reconsider.

He didn't get the chance. The moment the next firework exploded in a shower of golden sparks, Adelina grabbed his hand and headed toward the grottos.

He thought of ordering her to stop, but he suspected she might make a scene if he did, which was something he most certainly did not want.

He decided to make the best of it—apologize quickly and get her back to her duenna as fast as he could.

As they hurried past the labyrinth, he thought of poor Brix wandering around looking in vain for the exit. He should have suggested that the next time Brix ventured inside, he use some string to find his way back out, like Theseus.

They reached a grotto even more secluded than most by virtue of a huge willow near the entrance, and Adelina pulled him into the cool, dark confines as if they were fleeing an invading army.

He shrugged off his qualms and told himself they were the result of too many lectures about the wages of sin in his childhood. Adelina likely sought nothing more than a titillating tale to tell over the teacups with her friends.

With that in mind, he immediately assumed a melodramatically mournful expression. "I am very sorry that I left so abruptly this morning, Miss Foxborough. I should have taken proper leave of you. Can you forgive me?"

Adelina picked at the edge of her fan and spoke without looking at him. "I was very upset, my lord."

She was obviously going to drag this out as long as possible.

Stifling a sigh, Edmond decided that if she wanted titillation, he'd give it to her, and get this over with. Hopefully one kiss would suffice.

He put his knuckle under her chin, lifting her head so that she was looking at him. "Is there nothing I can do to make up for my lack of consideration?" he whispered, leaning closer and smiling his most devastating smile.

She twisted her head away before he could kiss her. "I thought perhaps you found that other young woman more interesting. You certainly looked interested when you spoke to her."

He put his hands lightly on Adelina's shoulders. "A morbid fascination, my dear, and nothing more."

She continued to pout. "And just what was so morbidly fascinating?"

He hated a grown woman pouting nearly as much as simpering, but given that he was supposed to be apologizing, he tried not to show his distaste. "Why, the fact that she was with Fallston and engaged in a lively conversation with him. But she's too insolent for my taste, I assure you."

"You don't like bold women, my lord?" Adelina inquired as she slowly dragged her fan across her chest just above her cleavage.

Edmond had met some very experienced courtesans who were experts at that sort of practiced gesture designed to draw a man's attention to a physical feature. This time, however, his suspicions were the only thing aroused, despite their seclusion and Adelina's physical attributes.

Gad, he was tired of this, the coy looks, the sly banter, the teasing, the game of love, the perpetual sizing up of partners with no thought of lasting happiness, only gain or physical pleasure. He was bored of Bath and its society. The only time he hadn't been bored lately had been when he was reading—or skirmishing with Lady Diana.

Determined to speed things along, he drew Adelina close, shifting slightly so that the long white feather in her bonnet didn't poke him in the eye. He put his arms around her shapely body and kissed her with slow deliberation and a complete absence of passion.

Much to his chagrin, Adelina didn't draw back, or protest. She relaxed against him and her response increased in passionate fervor.

Obviously, his strategy was having the opposite effect to the one he intended.

He broke the kiss and stepped back. "Am I forgiven then?"

Adelina wrapped her arms around him and insinuated her body against his. "Of course you are, my lord," she whispered before standing on her toes to kiss him again.

If he really wanted to, he could probably seduce her right here and now. However, he wasn't the lascivious cad certain young ladies with bright blue eyes and studious miens thought him to be. "Adelina, we shouldn't—"

A sudden rustle of leaves audible above the distant explosions of the fireworks made him fall silent. There was no breeze tonight.

"What is it? Is somebody there?" Adelina demanded as he turned to look over his shoulder toward the wide entrance of the grotto.

He glanced sharply back at her. She sounded curious, not worried or upset. "I don't know," he said brusquely, wondering if she had planned this all along, thinking that if they were discovered together in a compromising position, he would have to marry her.

If that was what she hoped, she was going to be disappointed, he thought as he strode outside. Adelina was a pleasant young woman in her way, but he wasn't about to get trapped into a marriage, not even for twenty thousand pounds a year.

Feet planted, arms akimbo, he slowly surveyed the area.

He spotted the skirt of a blue dress behind the curtain of willow leaves.

He waited, tapping his toe and glaring at the bit of blue, silently daring the woman to come out and denounce him for trying to seduce the virtuous Adelina.

The bit of blue didn't move.

Perhaps Adelina's confederate, if she was one, was wisely reconsidering.

"Were we seen?" Adelina asked anxiously behind him.

He faced her. "You had best go back to Mrs. Jesser, just in case, and we must take special care not to be seen together again tonight."

For the first time, Adelina looked frightened, but whether that was because her plan had gone awry or because he was not doing the best job of hiding his annoyance, he couldn't say.

Taking her hand, he began to hurry back the way they had come. He slowed his steps a little when he realized she was panting, but not by much. He wanted to get back to that willow tree as quickly as he could, to discover who had seen them kissing and if Adelina had sent her to spy on them.

He halted when they neared the crowd still listening to the orchestra. "Mrs. Jesser is right where we left her. She hasn't even realized you've been gone. You'd best hurry and join her."

Thankfully—and wisely—Adelina obediently hurried off without a protest, while he turned on his heel and headed the other way. He looked around for any woman wearing a blue gown, and saw none.

Had the spy been too afraid to leave the shelter of the willow?

Then he spotted her. Her back to him, her skirt lifted a bit to aid her speedy progress, bonnet-covered head lowered, she was hurrying away from the grotto toward the labyrinth. She must have waited until she was sure they were gone before leaving her hiding place.

His lips turned up in a smile. She wasn't going to get away from him that easily.

The woman stopped at the entrance to the labyrinth, fished in the little reticule she carried, and paid the entry fee. The man taking the money looked askance, as well he might. What sort of woman ventured alone into that place at night?

Trotting up to the entrance, Edmond tossed a coin at the startled man and went inside. He paused and looked around, then spotted a flash of blue hem disappearing around a corner.

His heartbeat quickened. This was like some of the nights at Harrow, when he and Brix and his friends had gone about their prankish business. Putting the Latin master's desk on the roof. Stealing all the eggs and putting them in the headmaster's bed.

There! The blue skirt disappeared around another corner. He broke into a run. She was fast, whoever she was, he'd give her that. He wouldn't wager a shilling on any woman of his acquaintance being so fleet of foot.

The labyrinth was deserted tonight—thank God. It made his job easier. Must be the fireworks. But where the devil had she gone?

His chest heaving, he skittered to a halt as he came to a fork. He had no idea which way to go. He held his breath a moment, listening, to see if he could hear her.

Nothing. Not a sound nor sign of her. It was as if she'd completely disappeared.

Looking around, he ran his hand over his sweaty face. The woman had wisely chosen the best place in Sydney Gardens to hide, just like poor befuddled Brix.

And then Edmond realized he, too, was lost.

He'd been so intent on finding the spy, he'd paid no attention to where he was going, except that he was following her.

He considered a moment, then decided the best thing to do would be to forget the woman and go back the way he'd come—but before he could move, somebody came rushing round the corner behind him and ran smack into him.

He reached out to steady his inadvertent assailant and realized it was a woman. A rather shapely woman. Wearing a blue gown. A very familiar blue.

"Now I've got you!" he cried triumphantly, his hands gripping her arms.

The brim of her blue bonnet tilted, revealing a ruched lining of silver, and the face of Lady Diana Westover.

As he bit back a curse and let go of her, she made a surprisingly graceful little curtsy and damn if she didn't look completely at ease and barely out of breath.

"I beg your pardon, Lord Adderley," she said in her melodious voice. "I didn't expect to find you here."

Edmond forced himself to ignore her subtle perfume, which was like the sweet, cool breeze in the summer, full of the scent of wildflowers.

"Obviously, I didn't expect to run into you, either, Lady Diana," he said, bowing stiffly. "Or to have you run into me. What are you doing here?"

"I got separated from my aunts. I believe they're in here somewhere." She cocked her head as she regarded him with that discomfiting intensity. "Did you get lost in here, too?"

The answer to that was none of her business. "Were you spying on me?"

"Where? Here? Of course not," she said, her voice having the same genial friendliness that Brix's usually did. "I accidentally bumped into you."

"I didn't mean here in the labyrinth. I meant in the grotto."

Her expression was innocence itself. "Why ever would I do that?"

"I'm sure you were. I recognize your gown."

She glanced down at her dress, which reminded him of bluebells. "Suppose that were true, my lord—and I'm not saying it is—why do you think I would spy on you?"

He struggled to keep a lid on the exasperation that threatened to boil into anger. "How the devil should I know what your motives are?"

"Really, my lord, such language is hardly becoming to a gentleman addressing a lady."

"Don't try to change the subject. You *were* spying on us."

Her delicately arched brows rose quizzically. "Us?"

He bit back another curse and changed tactics. "Perhaps it was envy that compelled you."

She smiled again with that same affability, as if they were two old friends conversing casually in the Pump Room or her aunts' drawing room. "I don't envy anyone except Mrs. Radcliffe."

Another unexpected—and fascinating—answer. "The writer?"

Her brows shot up even more. "You know of her?"

He crossed his arms over his chest. "Unlike the false reports spread about me by certain parties, I am not a complete ignoramus. I am well aware of her work."

Lady Diana smiled again and he realized what a charming smile it was—open and honest and pleasant. "Since you know Mrs. Radcliffe's works, I will admit that I do find you a very interesting man."

He'd received many compliments since leaving his parents' house, but nothing had ever made him feel quite as this one did, as if he really was interesting, and for more than his looks.

His anger drifted away as he began to wonder why she didn't desire him. Then he told himself it didn't matter how she felt about him.

"However you came to be here, you shouldn't be wandering about the labyrinth or the gardens without an escort," he warned. "It can be dangerous."

"I didn't mean to be. I told you, I got lost and perhaps if young men wouldn't stand stock-still blocking the path just around a corner, it wouldn't be so dangerous."

A little annoyed by her pert answer, he took a step toward her and gave her a wolfish grin. "That's not the sort of danger I meant."

Lady Diana tilted her head again, reminding him of an inquisitive squirrel. "Oh, do you mean there are other lascivious men prowling about, and that as a momentarily unescorted female, I may fall prey to their unconstrained lust?"

Other . . . ? Edmond's anger flared. "If anyone was prowling about, it wasn't *me*."

She didn't seem at all nonplussed by either his anger or his answer. "However misplaced your concern, I assure you I can defend myself if I must."

He barked a laugh. "Your waspish tongue may not be enough."

"No?" she inquired, still annoyingly calm.

Before he could say anything more, her gloved fingers suddenly shot out straight into the base of his throat above his collarbone and below his cravat.

"Damn!" he gasped, his breathing labored from the sharp blow as he stumbled backward.

She smiled that charmingly friendly smile again.

"You see, my lord, a young woman raised in the country is not necessarily a babe in the woods. I am well prepared against men who wish to do me harm."

"I don't wish to do you harm," he panted as he regained his balance. His curiosity got the better of his wounded pride. "Where did you learn to do that?"

"My father's groom spent time with the guerrillas in Spain fighting the French. He had many interesting skills."

"I'll wager he did. And he showed you all of them, did he?" he asked with an exaggerated leer.

He still couldn't get a rise out of her.

"I daresay it is difficult for you to appreciate that a man and a woman can have any sort of relationship other than a carnal one," she said calmly. "But Benton was fifty years old, my lord, and married, so all he taught me was how to defend myself."

"I can and I do have relationships with women that aren't carnal," he retorted.

"Really? I must confess I'm surprised. However, I believe you should follow your own advice and leave the labyrinth."

"I'll go when *I* decide."

"Have it your own way, my lord. But I recall our conversation before, when we spoke of whether or not women would be more virtuous than men if given the same opportunities. You may remember I have my doubts that women would be. Therefore, you may not want to risk being discovered in your present weakened condition by some other young woman who may be overwhelmed with admiration for your broad shoulders and handsome face. You might not be able to fend her off should she decide to have her lascivious way with you."

The idea of Lady Diana having her lascivious way with him was a surprisingly appealing notion.

He ran his gaze over her body. She was long of limb, slender of hip. Her small, round breasts would probably fit perfectly in his cupped palm.

She'd responded to his words with no false coyness, no fraudulent maidenly modesty. She'd been bold, frank, even brazen. He could well imagine she would be the same in bed, making love with eager joy and unabashed delight.

A vibrant image burst into his head, of this bright-eyed young woman naked beneath him, her eyes shining not with curiosity but with desire, her body undulating as he pressed his lips to hers.

Her long legs would wrap about him, pulling him closer as he thrust inside her. He could almost hear her whispers, soft moans and cries of delight as he pleasured her. And by God, how he would!

He eased toward her, closing the space between them. As she stared at him, her lips parted and her breathing grew rapid. Her expression changed, to something that was not calm composure.

Nor was it fear.

It was something he was sure he recognized, for he was feeling it himself.

"Perhaps I wouldn't fend *you* off, Lady Diana," he whispered, his voice hoarse with suppressed desire, the force of it overwhelming his urge to intimidate her. "Would you care to try?"

She laughed. She actually laughed in his face.

"I amuse you, do I?" he asked, a hint of real warning in his voice as he moved closer yet, trapping her body against the labyrinth.

"Because I know you can't be serious, my lord," she answered, apparently unaware of how truly tempting she was. "I'm no beauty, and have little to recommend me to your sex. As I said, I find you interesting, but my interest is purely platonic, as I'm sure yours is for me if you are at all sincere."

Platonic? He'd show her platonic.

He slid his hands up her slender arms. "You're wrong, Lady Diana. I find you very attractive."

Lady Diana met his gaze with that brazen, yet strangely innocent, boldness he was coming to expect. "Do you plan to kiss me, my lord?"

His fingertips skimmed her soft cheek. "I was certainly contemplating it."

She closed her eyes and stood perfectly still, her whole body rigid.

"What are you doing?"

She opened one eye. "Why, I am waiting to be kissed. It's sure to be a novel experience."

She sounded so very matter-of-fact, his passionate desire instantly dissipated.

She truly was odd, and if he were wise, he would have nothing more to do with her, images of her in his arms notwithstanding.

Both of her eyes opened. "I gather from this delay that you have changed your mind about kissing me, my lord."

She didn't have to look so relieved. "I have reconsidered, yes."

She reached out and patted him on the chest. "That's quite all right, my lord. I really didn't think you would."

"Which doesn't mean it's safe for a young woman to be wandering about Sydney Gardens at night, whether you think you can defend yourself from physical harm or not," he retorted, telling himself she must be the most frustratingly naive young woman in Bath. "You're putting your reputation at risk, at the very least."

She laid her hand over her heart and drew back as if shocked. "Why, how kind of you, my lord, to counsel me on propriety and the guarding of one's reputation. You, of course, are a model on both counts. So now, ever mindful as I must be that a woman's reputation is so much more delicate than a man's, I must beg your leave to be excused—"

She turned to go but he reached out to make her stay, resisting the sudden urge to pull her into his arms and see if her kisses would be as exciting as he expected. "*Were you spying on me?*"

She looked down at his hand with an expression of revulsion. "Unhand me, my lord, or I may be forced to hurt you."

Like flame to tallow, her challenge heated his blood. "I would like to see you try."

"I doubt that. Benton was a very excellent teacher. It might be embarrassing for you to explain to your valet how you came to be so bruised. Now will you unhand me, or are you the cad my Aunt Calliope believes you to be?"

He released her immediately. "No doubt your Aunt Calliope has described me as quite the blackguard."

"As a matter of fact, she has. It's really very shocking, some of the things she says of you."

"They're lies."

She got a little studious wrinkle between her brow as she gave serious consideration to his words. "Are you accusing my aunt of lying?"

He wanted to press his lips upon that little wrinkle and make it go away. "Not deliberately," he said, his anger lessening. "She's merely repeating lies other people have told her."

"Then you deny that you've got a score of mistresses all over England?"

"I don't even have one."

"At present?"

Damn, he was actually blushing like a schoolboy. What could she possibly know of *his* world, to stand there so cool and composed and make him feel like he ought to be ashamed? He'd had enough of that in his youth.

Before he could reply, two female voices rose nearby. "Diana! Oh, Diana dear, where are you? Lord Fallston is waiting!"

She smiled. "My aunts are at hand, my lord. I suggest you flee. You're very attractive in your own way, but I wouldn't want to feel compelled to marry you for the sake of my ruined honor should we be discovered together, and I don't think you'd want to marry me under those circumstances, either."

Was there ever a more frustrating, aggravating female? "I wouldn't marry you under any circumstances, not even if they found us naked together," he growled.

She laughed again, a low, intimate chuckle of glee. "Then run, my lord, as quickly as you can."

He didn't run, but he walked very fast.

When he was gone, Diana let out a slow, deep breath. It was a fortunate thing her aunts had called out when they had, and that the viscount had swiftly departed. Her legs had been trembling so much, she couldn't have gone a step. If he'd actually kissed her, she'd probably have slipped right down to the ground, regardless of her lovely gown. She had hardly been able to breathe as it was.

She'd allowed herself to play with fire, for heat was exactly what the viscount inspired—an exciting, delicious and very dangerous heat that had forced her to use all her self-control to keep from revealing his effect on her. She hadn't because she was quite sure he would think her a silly, hen-witted female with an extremely exaggerated sense of self-worth if she did. She was, after all, plain Diana, which meant that his real motive for acting as if he found her attractive was to intimidate her, or discomfit her at the very least.

It had very nearly worked, until she'd realized just how ridiculous their embrace would look if anybody had happened upon them. She'd laughed as she'd pictured the stunned expression that would surely come over Aunt Calliope's features.

Mercifully, they hadn't been caught together. It would have been awkward to explain, and could have led to scandal, as she was certainly well aware.

But she wouldn't have married him if it had. She'd meant what she'd said to her aunts: such men were all very well in fiction, but the reality was surely not so pleasant. He would probably never be faithful, for one thing. Judging by some of the gossip Aunt Calliope eagerly told her, and the tales of London society her father had used to illustrate why he preferred to stay away from it, a handsome, titled nobleman like the viscount surely lacked the moral rectitude—and even the intent—to remain true to his wife.

Although certain aspects of a life married to such a man might be wonderful, it couldn't make up for the years of living with an adulterous, un-trustworthy husband.

Not that he would have married her anyway, as he'd so colorfully informed her.

He was so frustrated with her at the last, poor man. Perhaps he would have felt better if he'd known how his retort that he wouldn't marry her if they were found naked together had affected her. She'd never seen a naked man, but she'd seen enough classical statues to have some idea of the male form unclad, and she was quite sure the viscount would not disappoint.

Indeed, the viscount was too dangerously seductive, and if she was wise, she would observe him from a safe distance in the future, no matter how tempting getting close to him might be.

Ignoring the gaggle of females gathered around Brix, Edmond stalked up to his friend and grabbed his arm, then tugged him toward the bridge over the Kennet canal. "We're leaving," he declared. "In my barouche."

Mercifully, he hadn't encountered Adelina or her duenna. He was in no mood to talk and certainly in no mood to flirt with Adelina, or have her flirt with him.

Brix planted his feet and shook himself free. "Good God, man, are you ill?"

Edmond glared at him. "No."

"But I've just met—"

"I don't care if you've met the Infanta of Spain and she's utterly enamored of you," Edmond snarled. "We're leaving."

Brix shrugged his shoulders. "All right."

Edmond marched onward, Brix tagging along behind.

"Don't tell me," Brix offered, slightly out of breath. "Your apology went awry and you quarreled with Adelina Foxborough."

"No, it didn't. *I* didn't. I apologized very nicely and all is forgiven."

"Then what's the matter?"

Edmond came to a halt and let his breath out slowly. Brix would probably never believe what had just happened. Hell, *he* hardly believed it. Edmond Terrington running away from a woman and her two maiden aunts!

It was really too embarrassing to discuss.

"It's nothing. I'm sorry. I've been a pig."

Brix eyed Edmond with a truly serious expression. "What happened to upset you? I've never seen you so annoyed."

Edmond never lied to Brix, tempting though it might be in some rare circumstances, like tonight's. "I ran into Lady Diana Westover again, that's all. Or rather, she ran into me. In the labyrinth. I suspect she could use a pair of spectacles. Maybe that's why she stares."

"Damned unsettling, I'm sure. And then Lady FitzBurton chastised you royally for being a bounder," Brix concluded. "No wonder you aren't in the mood for company."

Edmond wished he'd never mentioned Lady Diana. "No. Lady FitzBurton wasn't there."

"Well, thank God for that. Lady Harbage is more sensible, or at least hides her dislike better."

"She wasn't there, either."

Brix stared, agog. "Do you mean to tell me Lady Diana Westover was *alone*?"

Edmond regretted giving even Brix any inkling that Lady Diana had done something scandalous. "Your newfound friends are getting impatient."

He studied them a bit more, noting their low-cut dresses and the rouge on their faces. Sometimes Brix could be a little naive, like certain young ladies who didn't know better than to wander around Sydney Gardens at night without an escort and who would then be insulting to a man who was only trying to make her see the dangers—

He commanded himself to forget Lady Diana and think about his friend's possible peril. "Are they—?"

"They're actresses," Brix genially supplied. "Have no fear, my friend. I will not be spending my money on *that*. Some wine, though, and coins for their company will not be amiss, for they're certainly lively and amusing. No false modesty from them, either, which is really quite refreshing."

As long as Brix was going to be sensible—and Edmond was sure he could trust his friend on that point—he wouldn't interfere. "I'll send my coachman back with the barouche after I've gone home."

Brix looked over his shoulder, to see that the gaggle of young women were staring in abject fascination—at Edmond. "I think the blonde really likes you." He frowned with mock gravity. "Actually, I think they all really like you. Maybe you *should* go home. They'll probably ignore me entirely if you come back with me."

"You always manage to hold your own with women," Edmond reminded him, "but I wouldn't be good company tonight. I'm going home to have a stiff drink, read a little and then go to bed."

Brix looked as if Edmond had announced he was locking himself in a dungeon for a decade. "That makes you sound positively ancient."

"Well, I'm not as young as I used to be."

"If I had your looks, there'd only be one reason I'd go to bed."

"If you want nothing more than a series of shallow, empty couplings, Brix," Edmond said wearily, truly tired of the comments people made about his looks, "continue on the path you're treading. That may not be nearly as pleasant as you think it will be, though."

An expression of sudden understanding dawned in Brix's eyes. He grinned and waggled his finger. "Don't tell me. That new book you've been awaiting with breathless anticipation has finally arrived here in the far reaches of Bath."

Edmond smiled. "Sadly, no. I'll have to content myself with *The Haunted Hall of Halton*. It promises to be quite bloodcurdling, though."

Brix shook his head in despair. "I give up. I really give up. You're worse than Lady Kentisten." He clapped Edmond on the shoulder. "Go home then and curl up with your book, but if you have nightmares about dungeons and ghosts and giant helmets falling on your head, it'll be your own fault and I won't pity you a bit."

"Each to his own, Brix. You enjoy yourself with your charming companions. Just don't be too free with your money. I'd keep my eye on my wallet, too. Remember that time in Bristol."

Brix laughed. "Yes, I will. I won't get drunk, either. Good night, Hades."

"Good night."

Brix turned on his heel, while Edmond headed for home.

Where he poured himself a whiskey, opened *The Haunted Hall of Halton* and never read a word. Instead, he thought about meeting Lady Diana in the labyrinth, and what he *should* have said, until the clock struck 5 A.M.

Chapter 4

Evangeline's heart nearly burst with longing. Rodolpho, dear Rodolpho! How she yearned to be held in his strong arms again, safe and secure. How much she wanted his sweet, tender kisses.

How she desired to be with him, to run her hands through his thick, dark wavy hair—

From the first draft of
The Castle of Count Korlovsky,
The Westover Papers

Setting down her quill, Diana rubbed the back of her neck. Outside, the light rain that had been falling on the pale yellow ochre buildings and cobblestone street for the better part of three days was subsiding. The weather had kept most people indoors and given her the opportunity to work on her novel, something all too rare now that she was living with her aunts. However, it seemed to be clearing, and soon she would be back in the social whirl of Bath, with little time to write.

She looked down at the page before her, then she stared as if the last line had been written by su-

pernatural locomotion. Rodolpho, the young man
destined to win Evangeline, didn't have dark hair.
He was fair.

She blushed, for it was as if she had written for
all the world to see: *I am not thinking about my
story. I'm thinking about the viscount.*

She crumpled up the page and began again, determined to concentrate and only use the memories of that night in Sydney Gardens when and
how she needed them, to add romantic verisimili-
tude to her books.

*How she desired to be alone with Rodolpho, like
the last time they had been together, standing under the willow tree on his father's farm, as if it
were Mother Nature's own chapel. The scent of
the leaves filled the spring air. Nearby, the water
of the river cascaded over the rocks, hiding the
cave where Rodolpho had first kissed her.*

*His strong arm around her, he had put his fin-
ger beneath her chin and tilted her head upward,
bringing his lips to hers so gently, yet so passionately. She had relaxed in his arms, feeling safe and
beloved. He had whispered tender endearments . . .*

Diana paused. If only she could have gotten a
little closer, to hear what the viscount had said to
Miss Foxborough as they stood in the grotto.

A twinge of guilt returned as she thought of
what she'd done. It hadn't been right to follow

them, and spying on a couple at an intimate moment hadn't been her intention when she'd managed to get away from her watchful aunts' supervision before Lord Fallston and his stern mama arrived. She'd merely wanted to admire the beauty of the gardens on her own for a little while, in silence.

Then she had seen the viscount and the beauty. By the couple's haste and furtiveness—at least on Miss Foxborough's part—she'd realized they were sneaking off somewhere together.

Since she had no personal experience when it came to what a man would say to a woman when they were alone, following them had seemed a good idea.

After all, she told herself, she wasn't watching them for a salacious purpose. Her interest was purely academic, for research.

She hadn't bargained on being discovered, chased and caught by the viscount after making a wrong turn in the labyrinth. She'd been sure she'd eluded him, only to crash headlong into his muscular body.

If she'd been sensible, she would have fled from him without a word. Instead, she hadn't been sensible.

She knew why, of course. Nothing so exciting had ever happened to her in her life. The feel of his grasp on her arms, like the prelude to an embrace, had immediately made her want to linger, no matter what the consequences.

Evangeline would be horrified when Count Korlovsky tried to kiss her. She surely wouldn't feel her heart race with unfamiliar excitement, and heat flash all the way to her toes. She wouldn't feel any desire.

She wouldn't laugh before a kiss, either, because it wouldn't be ridiculous for a man to want her.

Diana sighed. At least now, if she managed to capture the viscount's undeniable appeal on the page, she could be fairly hopeful that her readers wouldn't question Evangeline's decision to accept Count Korlovsky's offer of refuge in his castle. Indeed, if she could truly pattern the count after Lord Adderley and do him justice—the way he spoke and moved and thrilled—she would really have accomplished something.

She picked up her quill and dipped it in the ink, ready to resume her scene. Alone in a tower room in the count's crumbling castle, Evangeline was longing to resume her journey to meet Rodolpho so that they could be married. However, mysterious things were happening, things that prevented her departure and that would eventually convince her that the count was not the kind gentleman he seemed—

The sound of familiar footsteps outside her bedroom door interrupted her and she recognized Aunt Calliope's footfalls.

She shoved the pages of her scene into her writing desk, grabbed a sheet of plain vellum and hastily began to write to an acquaintance in Lincolnshire. Aunt Calliope could be rather trying at times, but she was glad she had gotten to know her aunts better during this time together. After her mother's death, there had been a breech between the sisters and her father, one that he had rarely discussed, although she knew it stemmed from their dismay at his decision to live exclusively at his country estate.

The siblings had never completely lost contact, but they had never been invited to visit, and she had never been allowed to visit them when she was a child. When she was older, her father's health had been poor, and she hadn't wanted to leave him lest he worsen. After his death, however, she'd sought out her closest relatives, and been rewarded for her efforts with a wise, compassionate friend in Aunt Euphenia. If Aunt Calliope's enthusiastic opinions and love of gossip could get a bit wearing, Diana never doubted that she loved her niece just as fiercely.

She didn't wish to upset either one of them in any way, with one exception. She was determined to write her book and try to get it published. She'd spent so many delightful hours reading, she yearned to give some other, unknown girl the same pleasure a well-told, exciting story had always given her.

"Here you are, Diana," Aunt Calliope exclaimed as she entered Diana's bedroom, although there were few other places Diana would be at this time of day. "Put that away. Lord Fallston has come to call." She spied the ink on Diana's fingers. "Oh, dear, that won't do."

Diana obediently set aside her letter and went to the basin.

"I can get most of it off," she said, "and I'm sure Lord Fallston won't begrudge me writing to my friends."

"You certainly seem to have a large correspondence," Aunt Calliope noted as she glanced at the scrawl upon the paper, "especially considering how your father . . ."

Flushing, she fell silent and wandered toward the walnut armoire on the other side of the room.

"Papa didn't like to leave the house, but he wrote to people often," Diana replied amicably. "I also enjoy writing. To my friends back in Lincolnshire," she quickly added.

"I must say that your friends are very indifferent correspondents. Considering the amount of time and effort you spend writing to them, I should think they would write back with more frequency."

"Most of them have more to occupy their time than I do," Diana replied, telling herself that wasn't strictly a lie. Most of them did; what Aunt Calliope could not know was that the vast majority of her niece's writing remained in her desk.

Aunt Calliope's pale blue eyes filled with tears and she sniffled. Tugging free the thin white silk scarf that went around her neck and tucked into her bodice, she used one end to dab her eyes.

"You must have been so lonely. We always wanted to have you visit, but poor dear Cyril would never hear of it."

"Papa said he would miss me too much," Diana replied as she continued to scrub her hands, "and I really think he would have. But I did know of and appreciate the invitations, dear Aunt Calliope." She smiled at her plump relative. "I'll also never forget how happy you made me by sending me a new gown every year. And the slippers and wraps from Aunt Euphenia were always a great joy, too. Papa and I didn't visit much, but it was always comforting to know I had at least one pretty, fashionable gown, and suitable slippers and a wrap to wear should the occasion arise."

Aunt Calliope dabbed her eyes once more and tucked her slightly damp scarf back into place. "Well, let us not speak of the past while a young gentleman waits downstairs. And let us hope Lord Fallston will not mind inky fingers."

He may not have minded them, but he certainly noticed them, for Diana saw him glance at them more than once as they exchanged the usual greetings before Aunt Calliope muttered something about her sewing and took herself off to the farthest corner of the room.

She couldn't have made her approval of a potential match between them any plainer if she published a notice in *The Times*.

"I was writing letters," Diana explained as she sat beside Lord Fallston on the camel-back sofa.

"Then I trust you have recovered from your fright."

"Fright, my lord?"

"Why, when you got lost in the labyrinth the other night, of course," he replied, giving her the sort of patronizing smile her old nurse used to give her when she told Diana not to be afraid of the dark.

She'd never liked Nurse Jones. And did he honestly expect her to be prostrate with the vapors over such a little thing? "I am quite recovered, my lord."

Aunt Calliope, who had been diligently pretending to ignore them, began to cough. Loudly.

Diana realized she was being chastised, and dutifully put a genial, bland smile on her face.

Lord Fallston returned her smile. Neither spoke, and it seemed as if the conversation had dried up like a spring in a drought when Aunt Calliope suddenly jumped up from her chair with an alacrity that Diana hadn't known she possessed. "Diana spends entirely too much time indoors, I think. She keeps up a prodigious correspondence, you know."

"And I read," Diana couldn't help adding, wondering what had prompted this particular observation from her aunt.

"I was wondering, Lord Fallston, if you'd be so good as to accompany Diana on an errand for me this morning? She needs the fresh air and exercise."

Diana had a vision of traipsing around the main shopping thoroughfares of Bath, list in hand and Lord Fallston trotting at her heels like an over-eager puppy. She could barely refrain from grimacing, but she didn't offer any objections to her aunt's request. Indeed, if she could have been alone, she would have welcomed the opportunity with enthusiasm.

Lord Fallston fairly beamed. "Nothing would give me more pleasure. I shall be delighted to escort Lady Diana on any errands she may wish to run."

Aunt Calliope suddenly looked a little less certain, perhaps, Diana suspected, because she now had to think of an errand for her niece. "Diana dear, would you be so kind as to get me the latest volume of poems by that fellow Keats at Duthney's Bookshop?"

Diana smiled with genuine joy. This was the one destination that met with her unmitigated approval, especially since she was anxiously awaiting *The Ruins of Rygellan*, which was due to be at the bookshop any day now. Indeed, the day before, Diana had told her aunts she would crawl on her hands and knees for a copy of that book, much to Aunt Calliope's chagrin, until Diana had explained she wouldn't really do anything so shocking. "I'll just fetch my bonnet and shawl and Sally, and then we can be off."

Lord Fallston looked a little confused.

"Sally's my maid," she explained. She couldn't

prevent the mischievous little smile that bloomed on her face at the memory of a conversation about proper behavior in the labyrinth. "We have to observe the rules of propriety, do we not, my lord?"

As they began to walk toward Broad Street, Sally following behind like a slender shadow, Diana waited for Lord Fallston to initiate a conversation. This time, she would follow society's rules, even if it meant a long and silent walk.

It did mean a long, silent walk, despite the many interesting things they passed by. Military men, naval officers, shops, horses, carriages, even a street performer swallowing a sword didn't elicit a comment from the young man beside her.

Maybe she should take the first conversational step, demure ladylike behavior notwithstanding. But what could she discuss without risking censure? So many subjects were deemed unsuitable for women, and she didn't dare mention books again. There was always the weather, she supposed, but she was weary of talking about the rain.

Mercifully, before the silence could become overwhelmingly oppressive, they reached the bookshop. As she entered, Diana breathed deeply, loving the scent of the leather and binding glue and paper. She had once told her Papa, to his delight, that she hoped heaven was like a big bookshop.

She immediately excused herself to speak to Mr. Duthney, the gray-haired proprietor, while her escort wandered over to examine a particularly large and fine atlas open on a stand. Sally hurried over to the periodicals illustrating the latest fashions from London and Paris.

As she neared the counter, Diana noticed several copies of the latest literary sensation, *The Spider's Web*, displayed on the counter. She'd enjoyed the account of an aristocratic scientist's expedition to study spiders in the Far East very much.

"The Keats we've got, and plenty, too," Mr. Duthney responded to her query, "but as for *The Ruins of Rygellan*, I regret to say I sold the last copy not five minutes ago, to that gentleman over there."

Following his gesture, Diana looked toward the other end of the shop, where three rows of shelves approximately five feet apart formed what looked like oversize stalls lined with books.

She blinked and looked again, but there could be no mistake. Holding a book-shaped package wrapped in brown paper, Lord Adderley stood talking with a gentleman who appeared to be approximately the same age.

The other man was well dressed, the cut of his coat excellent, the dark fabric very fine, and he was as broad shouldered as the viscount. His visage was not so astonishingly handsome, yet he was a good-looking fellow for all that, with a nose and fair complexion that instantly proclaimed him an Englishman. The viscount stood silent and still, regarding his companion with what looked like tolerant amusement, while his friend did all the talking.

Who was this other gentleman, and what were they talking about? That's assuming they *were* friends, for the other man seemed somewhat agitated. Perhaps this was not a friendly meeting at all. Maybe this man was an enemy of the viscount, accusing him of who knew what.

She slid a glance at Lord Fallston, who was busy contemplating Africa. Would he notice she was no longer at the counter if she moved away?

She surveyed the viscount and his associate, and the stall on the other side of theirs. She could pretend to be examining books while getting close enough to discover if the unknown man was the viscount's friend or not.

What business is it of yours?

She silenced that little voice of reason. It would harm no one if she listened just a little, to hear how a man like the viscount responded to hostility.

Checking to make certain Lord Fallston was still occupied with the atlas and Sally with the periodicals, she sidled toward the alcove.

Once there, she couldn't hear much at all, for the books muffled their conversation.

Another surreptitious glance at Lord Fallston proved he had not noticed she had moved. Holding her breath, she eased out a book of sermons by the Reverend Hamish MacTavish. Then she carefully shifted the books on the other side so that there was a very narrow gap. Lowering her head, she pretended to be reading the book by Reverend MacTavish while she listened.

"I really think you've gone too far this time, Edmond," the viscount's companion said, obviously exasperated.

What on earth had he done? Lost a wager? Proposed a duel?

"You didn't have to offer Duthney twice the price," the stranger continued. "It's only a book."

Were they talking about *The Ruins of Rygellan* or some rare first edition?

"I can afford it, Brix, and it was the last copy," the viscount replied, his tone amused and full of a patient acceptance of his friend's dismay. "I've been waiting for over a month, and I wasn't about to let Lady Kentisten read it before I did. She'd corner me at her next party and tell me the whole story. Then it truly would be a ruin for me."

They must be friends, and it sounded as if this wasn't the first time they'd had this sort of argument.

Nor could she blame the viscount for wanting to read a popular book as soon as possible. She hated it when somebody told her the ending of a book before she'd had a chance to read it. She was also rather sorry she hadn't thought of offering Mr. Duthney more than the listed price for a copy of *The Ruins of Rygellan*. Maybe he would have saved her one if she had.

"But that's theft . . . or piracy . . . or extortion . . . or *something*," the man with the unusual first name replied, still upset.

"I told you, I don't mind, as long as I get to read it before somebody spoils the plot for me."

"But you're a *man*, Edmond."

"I'm well aware of that."

She could well imagine the little smile of amusement on the viscount's face when he said that.

"Men don't read that drivel."

Diana was sorely tempted to throw her book at the speaker. She might have, if a gap between the books hadn't been so narrow.

"One man's drivel is another man's delight, Brix," the viscount replied. "You like the stimulation of gaming hells and consorting with women of a, ahem, carefree nature and I like reading about crumbling castles, mysterious happenings and assorted banditti."

"Or you like to impress women by reading them," his friend charged.

She could believe that.

"Do you honestly think I have to discuss my choice of reading material to impress a woman?"

Diana shook her head, then remembered how impressed she'd been when he'd known who Mrs. Radcliffe was. But surely Lord Adderley had felt no need to impress *her*.

"I won't disagree that some of the plots are a little much to bear," the viscount continued. "I'm not particularly enamored of the supernatural elements. The giant helmet in *Otranto*, for instance, made me want to laugh at first, which I'm sure is hardly the sensation Walpole wanted to produce. I think human beings can be frightening enough all on their own."

Diana's book hit the floor with a thud. That was exactly what she thought, too, and that was the kind of book she was attempting to write—a thrilling tale with elements of the gothic but instead of the suspense and danger coming from the supernatural, she would have them come from Evangeline's situation, and the count.

Whoever would have thought that a man like Lord Adderley would share her sentiments? she thought as she bent down to retrieve the volume of sermons. She hoped she hadn't damaged it; otherwise, she would be buying a book today, after all.

She was still crouched down checking the spine when a pair of Hessian boots appeared in her field of vision.

Lord Fallston wasn't wearing Hessians.

Still crouched, Diana slowly raised her eyes and found herself staring at the viscount's apparently amused face. On closer inspection, however, his lips were smiling, but his eyes definitely were not.

She wasn't about to admit she'd been eavesdropping, so as she straightened, she gave him a very bright smile. "Good day, Lord Adderley."

"Lady Diana." He nodded at his friend. "Allow me to present the Honorable Brixton Smythe-Medway, youngest son of the earl of Furnival.

Smythe-Medway, Lady Diana Westover. I believe
I've mentioned her."

"Lady Diana, a pleasure," Mr. Smythe-
Medway said as he doffed his hat, while she wondered exactly what the viscount had said about
her.

His friend colored. "At least, it is for me."

She inwardly chided herself for staring, but it
was easier to study Brixton Smythe-Medway's
pleasant face than encounter the viscount's dark-
eyed glare. "I'm delighted to meet you, too. Now,
if you'll excuse me . . ."

The viscount moved to block her way. His dark
brows lowered just as the count's would when
Evangeline questioned his intentions or tried to
escape his castle. Yet when he spoke, his voice
sounded calm and even good-natured. "You seem
to have a penchant for turning up wherever I happen to be, Lady Diana."

"That's not so surprising, is it?" she countered
with all the aplomb she could muster. "Bath isn't a
large town, so I suppose one should expect to encounter the same people frequently."

"Especially if they're dead bores," Mr. Smythe-
Medway genially interjected.

The viscount ignored him and nodded at the
book in her gloved hands. "You enjoy sermons by
obscure Scots clerics, my lady?"

"I have a broad taste in reading, my lord."

"As do I."

"So I understand." She gestured at the book in his hands. "You have the last available copy of *The Ruins of Rygellan,* I believe. I must confess I'm surprised a man of your tastes would read such a book."

His answer was a devastating smile. "I have many ways to enjoy my leisure hours."

"Of which you have so many," she noted, trying not to sound defensive or let him have the upper hand.

"Not enough that I would waste any reading the metaphysical musings of Scotsmen."

"His metaphysical musings might do you some good."

"Or it might only put me to sleep, especially since I have already plowed my way through Reverend MacTavish once. It was a form of punishment when I was child."

She was aghast that any parent would use reading in such a way.

"No need to look so upset, Lady Diana," the viscount coolly observed. "As I'm sure you'll discover, there are a few gems of wisdom among Reverend MacTavish's many, many words." His smile became a smirk, as if he thought he'd put her in her place.

Diana bristled and fired back. "The gems of wisdom would seem to have had little influence on you, my lord."

Her charge didn't seem to trouble him a bit.

"How would you know, my lady?" He regarded her as if he expected her to explain right then and there.

His mouth a thin, grim line, Lord Fallston appeared behind the two men. "Lady Diana, are these *gentlemen* bothering you?"

She should have been relieved by his arrival, especially at that precise moment. But she wasn't. She would rather have thought of something clever to say to Lord Adderley.

Then she realized that despite the obvious scorn in Lord Fallston's voice and manner, the viscount barely acknowledged his presence, while the Honorable Smythe-Medway looked as if he'd discovered something disgusting stuck to the sole of his shoe.

"I'm surprised to see you out in the rain, Fallston, old chap," Mr. Smythe-Medway drawled. "Your feet might get wet and you'd have to go crying home to mama. Hardly a way to impress a young lady."

Fallston's expression grew positively murderous as he glared at the two men. He subdued it somewhat before he looked at her. "Come along, Lady Diana."

Despite her escort's annoyance, she didn't like being summoned like a servant.

"Did you bring your valet to the shop?" the viscount asked, ostensibly scanning the store. His tone was even, but there was an undercurrent of irony as he brought his steely gaze back to Lord Fallston. "You can't be addressing Lady Diana in that rude way."

Lord Fallston flushed. "I don't need a lesson in manners from *you*, Adderley," he muttered.

"Apparently you do," the viscount replied, still unperturbed.

Lord Fallston's lip curled. "Of course, you have so much more experience speaking to women—all kinds of women."

"So you seem to ardently believe. I suppose I should be flattered by your blind faith in my apparently boundless virility."

Diana gulped as she stared at the brown leather cover of the book she held. If she'd ever met a man who seemed boundlessly virile, it was the viscount.

"You haven't changed a bit since Harrow, Fallston," Smythe-Medway noted with that same hint of disgust. "I recall you used to bark at the servants just the same."

"I did not!"

Heads swiveled in their direction.

Determined to end this confrontation, for she could easily imagine how people would describe it to her aunts, Diana intervened. "I was merely remarking to the viscount how fortunate he is to have obtained the last available copy of *The Ruins of Rygellan*," she said to Lord Fallston.

She took a step toward the earl. If the viscount

tried to stand in her way, she was quite prepared
for a judicious use of her elbow. "Now, gentlemen, I give you good day."

Fortunately, the viscount stepped aside, but as
he did, he gave Lord Fallston the most fiendish
smile she'd ever seen and held out his package to
her. "My lady, please accept this with my compliments."

The Ruins of Rygellan! She halted so abruptly,
she nearly fell over. She shouldn't take it—and yet
it might be the very last copy in Bath. Who could
say when Mr. Duthney might get another? Her
hand slowly rose to take it—

"She most certainly will not accept any gift
from you," Lord Fallston snapped. "No woman
of good breeding would."

Breeding be damned—but how would she ever
explain the present to her aunts? "Thank you, my
lord, but Lord Fallston is right," she said, trying
to hide her disappointment. "I couldn't accept it."

Good God, was it possible? Was that a flash of
regret in his eyes? The viscount was sorry she
hadn't accepted his offer?

If it was regret, it didn't last long. In another
moment a slyly seductive gleam brightened his
dark eyes. "I was thinking only of your pleasure,
my lady."

The images that statement conjured up . . . !
Her heart hammered like a piston and her throat
went dry. Her gaze was drawn to his lips, and she
wet hers.

Reality intruded. Surely he was being outrageous only to shock her and upset Lord Fallston.

Annoyed at her own gullibility and his successful attempts to annoy the harmless Lord Fallston,
she said the first thing that came into her head. "I
can take care of my own pleasures, my lord."

Mr. Smythe-Medway coughed as if he had
something stuck in his throat. Lord Fallston's face
turned bright red, and even the viscount looked
rather taken aback.

The implication of what she'd just said hit her
and she wanted to sink through the floor, prefer-
ably all the way to China, where they wouldn't
understand a word she said.

It was now absolutely imperative that she leave.

"Good day, my lord, Mr. Smythe-Medway,"
she said with all the dignity she could muster. She
marched past the viscount, her head high and the
book of sermons still in her hand. "Come along,
Lord Fallston. My aunt will be waiting for her
book."

*And I should probably consider never setting
foot in a public place again.*

"She certainly is an odd woman," Brix mused as
he watched Lady Diana pay for her book and leave
the shop with Lord Fallston and her maid trotting
dutifully behind her. "What a thing to say—her
pleasures indeed! I think I stopped breathing right
about then."

Edmond had, too. The most astonishing vision

had come to him at that moment, and it hadn't quite loosened its hold on him yet.

"Of course, you were just as bad."

Edmond forced his attention back to Brix. "Fallston makes me want to say things like that. He's such a prissy fellow."

"Isn't he, though? And she reads the same ghastly stuff you do," Brix noted as they ambled toward the door. "Did your father really make you read a book of sermons for punishment?"

"Yes. He said it ought to do me some good."

"Just as she did, eh? Hardly something to elevate her in your estimation, is it?"

"No, it's not." Except that her eyes had sparkled with defiance, not righteous zeal.

"I think I'd rather be on the run from the natives, like poor old Buggy was in Borneo, than read a book like that," Brix reflected as they exited the shop and walked toward George Street. "You're right about the way she stares at a fellow— definitely unnerving. Now I know precisely how Buggy's spiders must have felt."

"At least they didn't eavesdrop. I'm sure that's what she was doing, not searching for a book of sermons."

Indeed, he'd think she harbored some sort of fanatical desire for him, like the scandalous Lady Caroline Lamb had for Byron, except for what happened when he confronted her. She certainly seemed immune to his charm then. He doubted

Caroline Lamb had ever overpowered Byron with a jab to the throat, either.

"If she *was* eavesdropping, I wouldn't blame her," Brix said. "We're probably a lot more interesting than listening to that nuisance Fallston whine all the time. Still, he'd be a good catch for her. His mama would be delighted if he landed a duke's daughter."

Edmond cut him a glance. "So would yours."

Brix laughed. "You know full well I'm going to be a bachelor until I'm at least fifty. By then I won't give a damn if my wife is as boring as our old Latin master. A large dowry, a face that doesn't actually make me cringe, a decent figure and the ability to provide an heir—that's all I'll ask. As for old Fusty and Lady Diana, they'll probably marry and lead very boring lives and be perfectly content."

Edmond didn't think Lady Diana would ever be boring. She was frustrating, annoying, brazen, shocking, but definitely not boring, and he didn't want to think of the sparkle in her bright blue eyes snuffed out by marriage to Fusty Fallston, who'd been boring since he was twelve years old.

But Lady Diana's fate was really none of his concern, and if she wanted to throw herself away on Fallston, he wouldn't try to stop her.

Chapter 5

The count closed in on Evangeline, a gleam of displeasure in his dark eyes. "Where are you going, Evangeline?"

She summoned her courage and hid her dismay at being caught trying to sneak into the other wing of the immense building. "Do I not have the freedom of your castle, Count Korlovsky? Or have you been lying to me? Am I a prisoner here?"

His lips turned up in a smile that only increased her dread. "Of course you are free to wander as you will, my dear. But as I have told you, there can be unforeseen dangers in a castle as ancient as this."

The Castle of Count Korlovsky

Standing beside Lord Fallston as he conversed with an elderly gentleman at Lady Kentisten's party, Diana stifled a sigh. She enjoyed riding, but she had little interest in horse racing or breeding, which her current companions obviously did.

Unfortunately, Aunt Euphenia and Aunt Calliope were firmly ensconced in a corner with some friends, animatedly discussing the latest news from London. Aunt Euphenia had a healthy interest in politics and the machinations of government. Aunt Calliope was fascinated by politicians, particularly their personal quirks and foibles. Between the two of them, Diana doubted there was a motion in parliament or stand by the government they couldn't anticipate or discuss as thoroughly as any journalist or political satirist.

Meanwhile, Diana was deliberately avoiding being anywhere near the evening's hostess, Lady Kentisten. Lord Adderley's comment in the bookshop proved to be true: the woman, who was holding court across the drawing room, had proceeded to reveal the entire plot of *The Haunted Hall of Halton* when the ladies had retired after dinner, a book Diana had yet to read.

She cast her gaze around the crowded room. She'd much rather be at home, writing. Evangeline had discovered that the count was not the kind benefactor he pretended to be. First he kept making excuses for the delay in providing her with his carriage. Then she realized her bedchamber door was being locked from the outside. Now she was sure he was trying to drug her wine. She had decided to flee that very night, sneaking out of her window, along the ledge to the next room, then down the stairs, only to be caught by the count—

Who came sauntering into Lady Kentisten's drawing room.

No, not the count, but she was just as shocked to see Lord Adderley, breathtakingly handsome in his evening dress, cross the room toward their hostess. Lord Adderley hadn't been at dinner so she'd assumed, despite his comment about Lady Kentisten's parties, that he hadn't been invited or had declined to come.

She shrank back against the draperies, trying to be inconspicuous. Meanwhile, Lady Kentisten spotted him.

With a delighted exclamation, she darted toward him, taking his arm with familiarity and dragging him back to her little group, all of whom smiled at him with open admiration.

Whatever she thought of the man personally, it must be invigorating for him to be the object of so much female fascination, Diana thought as she watched him smile and nod and answer their questions. She didn't think she'd particularly enjoy that kind of attention, if it had been possible; having her aunts watch over her was proving more onerous than she had ever imagined.

Of course her aunts' overseeing was a different kind of surveillance than the viscount was enjoying. These women, of various ages, seemed utterly enamored of him. Clearly whatever tales they'd heard of the villainous viscount, they either didn't credit, or didn't care about.

Perhaps the stories even added to his fascination. There was certainly an element of mystery to him that made one wonder which were true and which were false. She'd tried to add that air of mystery to the count's introduction to Evangeline and hoped she'd succeeded.

Apparently Lord Adderley wasn't missing the lovely distiller's daughter, who hadn't been at dinner, either. After kissing Miss Foxborough the way he had, she had assumed their relationship was headed toward the altar, lowly birth on the part of the bride or not.

She glanced at Lord Fallston, who openly scowled at the viscount until Lord Ramsbottom asked him about a brood mare, once more claiming his undivided attention.

Suddenly, Diana wanted to be out of the crowd, away from the perfumes and scent of candle wax, and discussions of horses and watching flirtatious people flirt. If her aunts or Lord Fallston noticed her absence, she would say she felt a headache coming on and wanted to find somewhere quiet to rest, which was perfectly true.

She sidled toward the door closest to her leading to the corridor, a different one from that the viscount had used, and slipped out. After setting her wine glass on a side table, she wandered down the corridor, looking at the portraits hanging on the walls.

She reached the end of the corridor and heard voices approaching. Although it was likely only servants, she thought it best not to be discovered wandering the halls, so she cautiously opened the nearest door and stole inside.

She looked around the dark room lit only by the moonlight, then sighed with pleasure. She was in Lady Kentisten's library, a vast chamber lined from floor to ceiling with books. A huge globe stood in one corner, and two sofas and several chairs were distributed about the room. A round mahogany table stood in the very center; on it was a pile of books.

Like a mouse to cheese, Diana went forward to examine the books. She picked up the first one— *The Haunted Hall of Halton*!

Surely she wouldn't be missed for a few minutes, or even half an hour, she decided, and eagerly pulled the nearest chair over to the window. Moonlight wasn't the best illumination for reading, but she simply couldn't resist the opportunity. Soon she was lost in the perils of Thomasina Cheddington, haunted by the ghost of Halton Hall.

Until she heard a latch moving. With a gasp of dismay, not sure how long she had been there, she quickly closed the book and put it back on the table. As the door opened, she realized she didn't want to have to explain her absence from the drawing room to anyone, and impulsively crouched behind the globe.

As she waited, hardly daring to breathe, Lord Adderley walked into the room as if he owned the house and closed the door behind him.

Now effectively trapped, she tried not to think how uncomfortable her position was while he strolled past the shelves, a lit cheroot in his expressive mouth. As he slowly walked along, the fingertips of his right hand brushed the spines of the leather-bound volumes like a lover's caress.

Good God, why had she thought of *that* comparison?

She should be worried about him finding her there, especially in such a ridiculous position, rather than thinking about his long, elegant fingers or noting the lithe grace of his prowling walk.

She certainly didn't want a repetition of previous confrontations, and surely that was why her heart was pounding so hard.

Yet her back was starting to ache, and her aunts or Lord Fallston might be looking for her. If she was found here, in the same room as the viscount, alone . . . well, it would be far better if she wasn't.

Lord Adderley was on the other side of the room. This side was more in shadow and—oh, thank God!—there was a second door not far from where she was hiding. If he kept his attention on the books, she might be able to get out without being discovered.

Keeping her eye on Lord Adderley's slow progress by the glowing tip of his cheroot, she carefully inched out from behind the globe toward the other door.

She made it to the door undetected. Her hand was on the latch. . . .

"Lovely perfume you're wearing, Lady Diana. Rather unique, too."

A curse slipped out before she could stop it. She whirled around, to find the viscount only two feet away. Leaning back against the door, glad of its solid support, she wondered how he had managed to cross the room so silently.

"That's rather colorful language for a young lady," the viscount coolly noted. He tossed his cheroot into the empty hearth. "Are you here all by yourself?"

He seemed taller in the darkness, too, and more menacing, as if he were the ghost from Halton Hall or some other medieval manor come to haunt her. She commanded herself not to be so fanciful and tried to get her erratic breathing under control.

"Or might I find Lord Fallston hiding beneath one of the sofas?"

That brought her to her senses. "No, of course not!"

"Then why are you here hiding in the dark? I hope you weren't lying in wait for me."

His tone implied that he thought she was.

"I most certainly was not!" She wasn't some silly, moonstruck schoolroom miss. Her interest in Lord Adderley, such as it was, was purely scholastic.

"Fallston being a bore, was he?"

She didn't want to give him the satisfaction of being right. "I wanted to see Lady Kentisten's library."

If she'd known what it was like, she would have, she silently added in excuse.

"Ah, of course," he replied skeptically.

"I was reading."

"Reading? At a party?"

"I like books."

"All kinds, apparently," he noted with the hint of mockery as he finally moved away toward the table, "including self-righteous sermons by small-minded clerics."

She wasn't going to submit to being interrogated as if she'd been caught trying to pilfer the silver. "What are *you* doing here, my lord? I do hope I haven't disrupted an assignation with a lady."

His dark brows lowered. "No. As it happens, Lady Kentisten was being a bore and I sought refuge. I had no idea anybody was in here."

"Well, I was. I *am*."

"And now it is time for you to be on your way like a good girl, Lady Diana."

Of all the patronizing, supercilious—! She wouldn't leave now if the room was on fire. Instead, she lifted her chin and marched up to him, hands on her hips.

"What's the matter, my lord?" she demanded, looking into his cold, handsome face. "Afraid of a little scandal?"

"We've had this discussion before, my lady, or have you forgotten?"

"Not at all. Perhaps I simply don't care what people may say."

His brows lowered and he was silent a moment before replying. "Whether my dastardly reputation is deserved or not, perhaps you should."

"You aren't going to frighten me away, my lord," she said, meaning it, and at the same time very aware that they were alone, standing close together, and that his imperious tone had definitely softened. "If you are so frightened of scandal, *you* may go."

He laughed softly, the sound low and unexpectedly melodic in the dark room. "I'll go when I decide, my lady. But shouldn't you be returning to your aunts, and your doting admirer? He and Lord Ramsbottom might be finished talking about their stables by now."

"I *don't* want—" She fell silent, mentally berating herself for revealing even that much.

"To be around Fallston?" Lord Adderley finished, strolling around the table, his movement leisurely. "I can't say that I blame you. For a young lady who seems to enjoy reading, I'm having difficulty imagining you getting along with him. I don't think he's read a book that he didn't have to in his entire life. I have it on good authority he doesn't even subscribe to the *Times*. His library is strictly for show, so that people believe he is more learned than he is, like this one."

"But this is a wonderful library," she protested, appalled to think of books as mere decoration.

The elegant man snorted as he reached her. "Wonderful it may be, but I doubt our hostess has read anything except the latest gothics for the past ten years."

"There's nothing wrong with gothic novels, is there?" Diana countered. "I seem to recall that you purchased such a novel yourself not long ago."

"I'm not saying there's anything wrong with that," he replied, leaning back against the edge of the table, his arms crossed over his broad chest. "I'm simply saying you shouldn't be overly impressed by the number of volumes in a person's library. Many of them are strictly for show, collected by the previous generations for the same purpose."

His face was more visible now, all angles and planes and centuries of aristocratic heritage. Despite his casual pose, it wasn't difficult to imagine him dressed in chain mail like one of Arthur's knights, or enthroned in regal robes.

"How much of your library is for show, my lord?" she asked, the force of her retort lessened by the way her body responded to the pictures her mind conjured up.

"I've read all the books in my library," he replied. "Over the years, I've kept only the books I enjoyed." He straightened and his voice hardened. "None of them are my father's."

To her surprise, he gestured abruptly at the door. "You'd better get back to the others before they realize you're gone and come searching for you."

Despite his action, his tone wasn't commanding or patronizing; it was weary and sad, like her father's when he was thinking of her late mother.

Even if she didn't love this man the way she had her father, and although he surely didn't need comfort—or at least not the kind that she could give—she didn't want to go, not right away. "I assume, then, that you no longer have a copy of Reverend MacTavish's sermons?"

She thought he wasn't going to answer her, but he did, with a single quiet word. "No."

Heartened that he had responded at all, she drew closer. "What had you done that you were forced to read a book of sermons?"

The corner of his mouth lifted in a smile that seemed more of a grimace than any expression of joy. "I'd been born."

She eyed him warily, all the while noting how sorrowful he seemed. Was it possible this man who seemed to have everything the world had to offer had suffered in ways that had nothing to do with material want, but that cut deeper and wounded longer? She had enjoyed a parent's doting love; he, apparently, had not.

"Tell me, are you always so stubborn? Do you never do what you're told?" he asked, his voice low in the intimate darkness.

She stepped back, putting distance between herself and his muscular body, and the magic of his deep voice. Whether real or only imagined, he possessed a power that tugged at her deepest, most secret desires and brought them surging to the surface. "It all depends, my lord, on who is asking me, and how they do it. Like most people, I don't enjoy being ordered about."

He cocked his head and regarded her studiously, as if she were some sort of scientific experiment. "Did you act this way even when you were little?"

That was better. She could breathe normally when he regarded her that way. "Yes."

"What did your parents do then?" He sounded sincerely curious, and because he did, she replied just as sincerely.

"I never knew my mother. She died when I was born. My father would try to convince me I was wrong and if that didn't work, I got sent to my room without supper. It wasn't such a terrible punishment, though. I always had lots of books to read while I was banished."

He nodded slowly, deep in thought, and when he spoke, it was more to himself than to her. "Yes, books can be a great comfort. I remember once when—"

He suddenly straightened as if he'd been called to attention. "Good night, Lady Diana."

"My lord?" she began, wondering what memory had prompted his abrupt change of manner.

He marched out of the room without another word.

Diana stared after him, puzzled and confused by what had happened.

Yet as she tried to sort out his reactions and her own, to make some sense of their conversation and its meaning, one thing was certain: Lord Adderley was a much more complicated man than she had ever imagined.

From his position beside the entrance of the lower assembly room two nights later, Edmond's gaze swept over the audience gathering to hear a noted Italian soprano perform. Thirty shield-back gilded chairs with scarlet brocade seats had been arranged in rows for the audience. In front of the chairs, a small orchestra mustered with the usual bustle. Talking quietly among themselves, they opened their cases, removed their instruments and set the music on the stands before them. Candelabra provided the light, along with candles attached to the music stands themselves.

Among those arriving were the people he expected to see, the ones who either truly enjoyed and appreciated music, or those who wanted people to think they did.

Brix fell into neither category. He was at their club, playing cards. Edmond had no desire to spend a night in a stuffy room swirling with tobacco smoke, nor was he particularly skilled at cards. Since he didn't enjoy losing anymore than the next man, he didn't regret begging off to attend a concert, even though Lady Diana might be there.

Not that he'd heard she would be, and he certainly didn't want to see her, or be drawn into another verbal duel, or find himself revealing things about his past he hadn't even told Brix.

At Lady Kentisten's party, he'd gone to the library for a bit of peace and quiet after a conversation with his hostess and her gaggle of women friends. Then he'd heard a little noise, no more than a whisper of fabric, and turned to find Lady Diana at the door, bent over like a thief trying to pick the lock.

Shocked, he then feared he'd been wrong about her all along, and that she was like so many other easily impressed young women who wanted to spend a few exciting moments alone with the handsome and notorious Lord Adderley.

He was relieved to discover she wasn't, but that didn't make her company any less disturbing. It had to be the way she looked at him with those big blue eyes, as if she were truly interested in him as a fellow human being, that made him want to tell her about his lonely, miserable, loveless childhood.

A hand touched his arm.

He started, then realized it was Adelina Foxborough at his elbow—and either he was imagining it, or he could make out her nipples through the thin, cream-colored silk of her gown. Very little of the tops of her breasts were covered at all.

He had thought Lady Diana brazen? Good God, she was a model of modesty compared to this overt display that had, he supposed, achieved the goal of getting his undivided attention.

"Are you expecting someone, my lord?" Adelina asked with a quizzical look.

"No." That wasn't exactly a lie, for Adelina's tone implied he was *hoping* to meet someone.

Three naval officers who'd been on a little up-spirits of their own and then blundered into the wrong place began to debate—loudly—how this mistake had been made and what they were going to do about it.

The interruption distracted Adelina for a brief moment, but her attention quickly returned to him.

"I am all astonishment to find you here, my lord," Adelina went on archly. "I didn't know that you appreciated music."

He focused on Adelina's conventionally beautiful face. The musicians were all in place, and so were most of the audience. Surely Lady Diana and her aunts weren't coming if they weren't here by now. "I do, although I prefer to hear a love song in my native tongue."

He'd no sooner spoken when Lady FitzBurton and Lady Harbage entered the room. Lady FitzBurton saw him, frowned and cut him, heading directly to some seats in the fourth row; Lady Harbage noticed him, too, then followed after her sister. Her reaction was more muted, but it was fairly clear she didn't think highly of him, either.

There was nothing surprising about that. What

was surprising was that Lady Diana wasn't with them. It struck him as odd that they would have come to the concert without their charge, unless she was ill. She couldn't be seriously sick, though, or he doubted her aunts would be here.

Gad, maybe *he* was coming down with something, to be worried about a woman who aggravated him so much.

"There is a vacant seat beside mine, my lord," Adelina said, nodding toward the familiar shape of Mrs. Jesser in the third row and the two empty seats beside her. "Will you join us?"

Edmond realized that if he did, Lady Fitz-Burton and Lady Harbage would be directly behind them.

He hesitated—but not for long. He wasn't about to let their presence dictate where he was going to sit, or with whom. It was enough that he had stood at the door like some sort of sentry keeping watch for their niece, something he hadn't been willing to admit to himself before, but which he now silently acknowledged. He should forget Lady Diana completely and concentrate on the woman with him. "I shall be delighted. And perhaps you'll translate the Italian for me?"

"It will be my pleasure."

He followed Adelina to their seats and had the grim satisfaction of seeing the annoyance on Lady FitzBurton's face as he sat directly in front of her, all five-foot-ten of him to her petite five-foot-two, or thereabouts.

He nevertheless shifted his chair a little to the left, so that she could see the orchestra and the soloist. That also got him a little further away from the coy Adelina and her overwhelming perfume.

The musicians lifted their instruments and straightened, and the babble about them died down. Madame Nostromo, a large woman dressed in a gown of blue satin, white silk overskirt with scarlet trimming, and wearing a very garish necklace of what had to be paste rubies, sashayed out of the side door and took her place. The first violin nodded, and the music began.

Madame Nostromo's voice wasn't bad, but she emoted as if she were playing to a crowd in the coliseum, not a small gathering in the lower assembly room at Bath, all seated within easy range of hearing.

Meanwhile, Adelina proceeded to demonstrate her rudimentary knowledge of Italian.

Edmond didn't pay much attention. Her whispering in his ear was too much like the drone of a small insect.

After several minutes, he couldn't stand it. If he didn't do or say something, he was going to go mad.

When Adelina stopped to draw breath, he leaned toward her, let his gaze drop for an instant, then murmured, "Lovely gown, Miss Foxborough."

She smiled and ran her fingertips along the edge

of the neckline. Gad, she was good at drawing attention to the most astonishing part of her anatomy. "My dressmaker is French. Madame Voisey's fits are not to be excelled."

He tried very hard not to betray any extraordinary interest. "Madame Voisey? I don't believe I've heard of her."

"She is only lately come to Bath from London. She was a refugee from the Terror. She tells me she wants to return to Paris as soon as she's earned enough to live in some comfort, perhaps even set up her own shop."

It couldn't be the Madeline Voisey of his past. Madeline couldn't sew, he didn't think. He'd never seen her so much as sew on a button.

Besides, if Madeline were in Bath, she would certainly have made her presence known to him. She would have come to him for money, at the very least. At that realization, he began to breathe more easily.

"Do you mind? *Some* of us are trying to listen," Lady FitzBurton complained in a harsh whisper.

Lady FitzBurton would have another sin to add to the list of his transgressions.

Well, he didn't care. Let her.

Her program covering the lower half of her face like a fan, Adelina leaned closer and, in a shocking and unwelcome display of familiarity, put her hand on his knee. "What a harpy!" she whispered.

Edmond stifled a curse that had nothing to do with Lady FitzBurton. He was going to tell Adelina to remove her hand in another minute if she didn't.

She did. Thank God.

The song ended and the crowd clapped politely, except for the boisterous group at the back.

Swiveling, he glared at the three drunken naval officers, who had obviously and mysteriously decided to remain. The people nearest them tried to shush them, and two rather brawny attendants in livery near the door moved in closer. They would have the officers removed shortly.

He was swiveling forward again when it happened.

He saw her.

Lady Diana Westover. Seated near the back of the room, with Fallston beside her, as cozy as a couple could be. They must have come in after he had taken his seat.

Now they were whispering together like two children at play. Or rather, she was whispering, nodding at the disruption, and saying something that was making Fallston smile like a besotted idiot.

He could believe she would have some piquant comment voiced in that smooth dulcet voice of hers that made him think of sparkling water tumbling over rocks.

Then she stopped talking and turned her head

in his direction. Her gaze met his for the briefest of moments and in that instant, something flared in her bright blue eyes, something that gave the sharpest of shocks to his equanimity, like the dart of an arrow directly into his heart.

What was it? Curiosity? Interest? Pleasure?

Whatever that expression was, it was damned disconcerting and nearly as bad as her staring. He hastily faced forward.

"There is no need to be so angry, my lord," Adelina said as she, too, faced forward again. "The attendants will take care of the interruption."

He nodded and as the liveried men duly bustled the noisy officers out the door, he commanded himself to forget that Lady Diana was there, probably staring at the back of his head in that disconcerting way of hers.

"I don't know how such persons ever came to be allowed in," Adelina continued with disdain.

"Apparently they allow in anybody who can pay the price," Lady FitzBurton said quite audibly behind them.

Edmond's head snapped around like a cracked whip. "Miss Foxborough was not addressing you. It's rude to eavesdrop, although it seems to be a family failing."

Lady FitzBurton had the grace to blush and look away, while Lady Harbage regarded him quizzically. Obviously, Lady Diana had not in-

formed her relatives of their encounter in the
bookshop. He was still certain she had been listening to his conversation with Brix, just as she
was surely staring at him again with those big,
blue, shining eyes.

He resumed his position and discovered that
Adelina was regarding him as if he'd won a major
battle single-handedly. "Thank you for coming to
my defense," she murmured, inching closer.

He wanted to move away, but what would the
watchful Lady Diana make of that? Instead, he
moved a little closer. Adelina flushed and smiled
sweetly, while the first violin lifted his bow in
preparation for the next piece. Madame Nostromo
began to sing, in a much more subdued fashion.

Edmond tried to concentrate on the music and
pretend Lady Diana wasn't there sharing a program with Fallston, heads together, close enough
to kiss. Her mere presence wouldn't upset *him*.

In spite of his resolution, it was all he could do
not to look back over his shoulder at them as the
concert progressed. However, it finally, mercifully,
came to a conclusion.

The instant Madame Nostromo turned to exit,
with many kisses of her plump fingers to her audience, he rose. "It's been a delight, Miss Foxborough," he lied as he took her gloved hand
and pressed the lightest of kisses upon the back
of it.

The first time he'd taken Lady Diana's slender

hand in his, he'd been impressed by the lack of limpid lifelessness usually evident in the touch of genteelly raised young ladies which was, he assumed, intended to convey grace and good breeding.

He'd discovered he preferred Lady Diana's firm vigor, as if her vibrant personality energized her very flesh and bones and sinews. Enjoying that novelty, he'd wanted to hold her hand for as long as he could, until she'd annoyed him.

Adelina frowned with more than a touch of petulance and recalled him to the present. "Must you hurry off *again*, my lord?"

"Alas, I must," he answered with feigned reluctance, ignoring the glaring presence of Lady FitzBurton rising from her seat behind them. "Another engagement calls me away."

Lady FitzBurton sniffed with audible disgust and muttered something about gamesters.

Unable to disregard his annoyance, Edmond turned toward the woman and gave her a glare of his own. They stood thus for a few seconds, until he realized how ridiculous he must look glowering at an overdressed middle-aged woman.

Immediately turning back to Adelina, he gave her his very best smile, while Lady Harbage whispered something to her sister and they made their rustling departure.

"I regret that it is so, Miss Foxborough," he said softly, glad that they were gone. "I hope to see you again soon."

Adelina smiled as if nothing at all was amiss. Perhaps she'd reconsidered revealing her frustration, which would hardly be considered ladylike among the *ton* and those who would join it. "I look forward to it, my lord," she murmured, dropping her eyes demurely.

Whatever hopes Adelina harbored, he felt liberated as he headed toward the door, except for the necessity of keeping his gaze on that objective and not letting it veer to see where certain other parties might be. That proved rather difficult, but he managed it.

Once out of the assembly room, he retrieved his hat and cloak, then marched through a slight drizzle to his waiting carriage. Once inside, he rapped on the roof and ordered his coachman to take him to his club. Brix would surely still be there, for it was early yet by gentlemen's standards. At the moment, he felt the need for a good friend's company.

He found Brix in one of the smaller card rooms, a dimly lit, walnut-paneled chamber containing tables covered in green baize, mahogany chairs with seats upholstered in dark blue and windows shrouded with heavy velvet draperies to shut out the noise of the street, or daylight if the games went past dawn.

He waited impatiently for the game of *vingt-et-un* to finish, and the wagers paid, then motioned for Brix to join him.

"Changed your mind and come to play?" his friend asked good-naturedly.

"The stakes are too high tonight," Edmond replied, having just watched Brix lose fifty pounds when the dealer made twenty-one. "Have a brandy with me, will you?"

"Since I've shot my bolt this evening, I'll be glad to," Brix said.

As he bade his card-playing companions good night, they expressed their boisterous regrets, Brix being a most genial and sporting player.

Edmond and Brix went to a larger room, which was mercifully less smoky and, at this time of night, deserted except for the servant who brought the brandy. Like the other rooms in the club, it was decorated in a decidedly masculine style, with aged oak trim, dark walls and heavy, yet comfortable, chairs.

"So, my friend, what brings you here this evening? Concert canceled?" Brix asked as he sank lower into his chair.

Edmond told him about meeting Diana in Lady Kentisten's library, as well as seeing her at the concert that night. He didn't tell Brix *all* about it; he kept his more distraught feelings to himself.

"I tell you, Brix, Lady Diana Westover's like a bloody ghost out to haunt me," he complained when he was finished. "Every time I turn around, there she is."

Instead of voicing some sympathy and agreeing

that something odd was going on, Brix shook his head mournfully. "I warned you that reading all those novels was going to damage your brain. Next thing you'll be telling me you see dead people, levitating helmets, walking portraits and maidens running about in nothing but their nightclothes." Then he grinned, the irrepressible Brix once more. "Which, come to think of it, wouldn't be half bad."

"My reading has nothing to do with Lady Diana," Edmond replied, in no humor to find anything amusing about what was going on.

Brix sobered. "I didn't see any signs of obvious infatuation in the bookshop. She didn't throw herself into your arms when you encountered her in Lady Kentisten's library, did she?"

"No, thank God," he admitted, wondering what he would have done if she had.

"She hasn't ever addressed you first, has she?"

"No."

"Nor sent you any *billet deux*?"

"No."

"Or hung about your house at all hours like Caroline Lamb chasing after Byron?"

"Mercifully, no." The gossips would have a merry time discussing something like that.

"Well, then!" Brix cried, slapping his hands on his knees in triumph. "I think you're making *much* too much of simple coincidences. I can more easily believe she was hiding from Fallston in Lady Kentisten's library, and I wouldn't blame her a bit. In fact, I don't think I've ever met a woman who seemed *less* attracted to you."

Edmond darted a sharp glance at his friend.

Brix's eyes widened and a mischievous gleam came to the emerald-green orbs. "Is *that* it? Is that what's got you so upset? The chit seems completely immune to the famous Adderley charm?"

Edmond shifted and stared glumly at the portrait of the club's founder immortalized on the wall before him. The pose was intended to be imposing, but the expression always made Edmond think the man must have suffered from indigestion his entire adult life. "Gad, Brix, you couldn't be more wrong. I'd be delighted to think she wasn't interested in me. It would be a bloody relief."

Brix rose and strolled toward the nearest window. He set his brandy glass down on the sill before addressing Edmond. "Tell me, do you see her every time you go out?"

"No." He didn't tell Brix he'd started expecting her to pop up any time he went out in public, though. That morning when he was riding along the riverbank, he'd pulled a muscle turning too quickly when he'd spotted a bonnet like the one Lady Diana had been wearing in the Pump Room.

Brix's shoulders slumped with relief as he leaned back against the sill. "Thank God! I confess you were starting to scare me there for a moment, Edmond. I was afraid you were beginning to harbor some sort of mania for her."

"I'm not mad, Brix."

"I agree that it's not time to haul you off to Bedlam." Brix began to pace like a barrister giving his final summation before a judge. "So we'll take it as a given that it is as you say. This lady is following you around or lying in wait for you. But it's not because she finds you attractive, as so many women do." He halted and shook his head while his voice—and his hand—rose dramatically. "No! Her purpose is deeper, darker, more mysterious, so very gothic—"

"Brix, sit down and be quiet," Edmond hissed. The staff here was discreet, but he couldn't completely trust them. He didn't want any more rumors spread about him, or Lady Diana. "You may find this all very amusing, but I don't."

Brix gave him a sympathetic smile and threw himself back into the chair. "I still think you're making too much of Lady Diana's activities. Besides, she seems destined for Fallston, and you haven't told me anything that makes me suspect otherwise. Ignore her and leave her to Fallston, fool that he is."

Edmond sighed. Perhaps he *was* getting too upset about a few coincidental meetings. As for the revelations of his past he'd made to Lady Diana, surely he could control himself now that he was aware of Lady Diana's effect on him.

"You know, Edmond," Brix proposed, "if she bothers you that much, we could always go to

Brighton and stay there until she's married."

Edmond sat up as if somebody'd pricked him with a pin. "What? Run away like a coward?"

"We're not talking about a duel or a battle, and if you're going to let that woman get under your skin this way—"

A devilish smile blossomed on Edmond's face as a brilliant idea bloomed in his head. "She's not getting under my skin. Not anymore."

"What are you planning?" Brix asked warily.

"Perhaps it's time Lady Diana Westover got a taste of being haunted herself," Edmond replied, excitement replacing frustration and annoyance and whatever other emotions Lady Diana aroused.

Brix did not look as if he thought this the best idea Edmond had ever had. "I thought you didn't want to have anything to do with her."

"I don't. But I refuse to live my life dreading her appearance, so I'm going to do to her what she has done to me. Let's see how Lady Diana enjoys being followed and ambushed."

Brix frowned like a reluctant boy who doesn't want to play.

"What's the matter?"

"I think it's going to cause more trouble than it's worth. Lady Diana seems generally harmless, and I wouldn't risk upsetting Miss Foxborough and her twenty thousand pounds if I were you."

"You obviously have no idea how disturbing it is being dogged by a woman."

"Fanny Epping's been chasing after me for years," Brix reminded him.

"But she's a harmless little thing. When it's Lady Diana doing the haunting, it's annoying, and I'm not about to let her get away with it another minute."

"I should point out, Edmond, that you could do a lot of damage to a woman's reputation by 'haunting' her. I know most of what they say about you isn't true, but the majority of the *haut ton* doesn't know you like I do."

Brix was, unfortunately, right. If he didn't want to ruin Lady Diana's reputation—and he didn't, because that would be going too far—he would have to be careful. "All I'm going to do is stare a few times, and perhaps speak to her once or twice. That's all."

"When it's you doing the talking and the staring, that might be enough."

Again, Brix was right. Edmond thought a moment, curiously reluctant to give up his plan of retaliation.

"I know," he said as an idea presented itself. "You always know all the gossip, thanks to your mama. If you hear something that makes it seem I'm going too far, you can warn me off. I'll even swear that I'll cease before there's any serious harm to Lady Diana's pristine reputation, if you like."

Brix reflected, then shrugged. "Swear it, then."

Edmond got to his feet and put his hand over his

heart. "I, Edmond Terrington, Viscount Adderley, swear that I will not ruin Lady Diana Westover's reputation."

Brix frowned. "I hope you can keep that pledge."

"Rest easy, my friend. All I plan is a few skirmishes that shall prove to Lady Diana she is not dealing with a mollycoddle like Fallston, and then I shall retire." He gave his friend an insouciant wink. "In triumph."

Chapter 6

The count approached Evangeline slowly, his gang of bandits behind him, his gaze frightening in its intensity. She backed away as far as she could.

"Why do you resist me, Evangeline?" the count whispered. "You feel as I do. I can see it in your eyes."

"No!" Evangeline cried, holding out her hands to stop him if she could. "No, I do not! It is only your own arrogant vanity you see reflected there."

The Castle of Count Korlovsky

As she sat in the darkened theater in a box Lord Fallston had procured and that now contained herself, her aunts and their host, Diana frowned with disappointment. She'd expected better acting at the Theatre Royal in Bath than she had found in Lincolnshire provided by a traveling troupe of players. Unfortunately, these actors were *not* better, and some were very poor indeed, their voices hardly audible, although it might be that the audience was responsible for some of the trouble. Many of the people who should be watching apparently preferred to whisper to one another and look around the theater, paying as little attention to the play as they had to their companions in the Pump Room. On the other hand, perhaps if the play were more entertaining, the actors would have the audience's full attention.

Rather than talk or look around, Aunt Calliope had fallen into a light doze. Aunt Euphenia, on the other hand, loved the theater, so her attention was firmly on the stage. That didn't mean she was enjoying the play, though. Diana had discovered, from her descriptions of other performances she'd seen, that Aunt Euphenia could dissect a poor performance the way an anatomist did a corpse.

As for Lord Fallston seated on her left, she avoided looking at him at all. She dreaded encountering more of his admiring looks, for she was finding his obvious esteem more tedious than she had ever supposed such a thing could be. Although she didn't want to reveal the cause of her frustration, he was also forever interrupting her writing these days.

Well, that, and thoughts of her encounters with the viscount. He had seemed so different in Lady Kentisten's library. Not mocking or charming or worldly, but serious and sincere, as if he really wanted to know about her parents, her childhood, and was telling the truth about his. Why? Why would a man like him want to reveal such things to her, or hear about her past?

He had said books were a great comfort and he spoke as if he knew that for a fact. Why would such a man—titled, rich, handsome—ever need the comfort of books?

His parents must not have been the sort to offer comfort, if he had to find that by other means. They couldn't have been like her beloved father, who had always been ready to offer words of solace and advice, and a warm hug if words would not suffice.

How she missed him and their conversations about anything and everything! He hadn't liked women who simpered, either, like the viscount. . . .

Good God, why did Lord Adderley keep intruding into her thoughts?

Because he was the most exciting, intriguing man she'd ever met, came the obvious answer, and she mentally shook her head at her pitiful attempts to ignore that fact. It would be better to acknowledge it frankly, and just try to stay away from him.

That wasn't going to be easy. He kept appearing wherever she happened to be. The bookshop, Lady Kentisten's party, and now here at the theater.

Keeping her face toward the stage, she surreptitiously slid a glance at a box on the second level near the center of the house containing Lord Adderley, the beautiful Miss Foxborough, Miss

Foxborough's ineffectual duenna, Mr. Smythe-Medway and a tall young man in a naval uniform.

Miss Foxborough was dressed befitting a woman of great wealth, in a shimmering green silk gown that left much of her shoulders bare and with several rows of delicate embroidery at the hem. Small puffed cap sleeves gave way to long kid gloves. Diamonds and emeralds shimmered at her throat and in her ears, and a string of pearls had been woven in her ornate hairstyle.

For a moment Diana envied her beauty, until she considered how long it must have taken to achieve that hairstyle. Likely the better part of three hours, and it must be very dull sitting for so long. *She* had barely endured the length of time it took for Sally to get her hair in this relatively simple Grecian style, and she'd been regretting the colossal waste of time, thinking she could have written a few pages instead.

She turned her attention to the rest of the party. Mr. Smythe-Medway looked quite dashing in his evening dress and grinned as if the performance were a great joke presented solely for his amusement.

While not as conventionally handsome as the other two men in his party, the naval officer was a comely fellow who suited his uniform—or perhaps the indigo coat with buttons polished to a golden sheen, impeccable linen, white breeches and stockings that showed a muscular shin, suited *him*. He held his cocked hat beneath his arm, and his saber dangled at his hip. His skin was tanned, from his time at sea, no doubt. Brushed back and tied in a tail, his hair, probably a shade similar to her own, had been lightened by the sun.

She would have liked to be in the box beside them. Their conversation was surely far more entertaining than the play, which she really should be paying attention to after Lord Fallston had gone to the trouble and expense of buying the tickets.

She tried again, but not only was the acting bad, this sort of pastoral farce wasn't at all to her liking. If only they could be watching *MacBeth*, or *Othello*. She had a sneaking admiration for Lady MacBeth, who certainly did not lack for energy and determination. Neither did Iago.

The viscount would make a good Iago, all lean and hungry and secretive, and with such a persuasive voice. Yes, she would cast him in that part without hesitation.

Instead, she was watching a troop of actors pretend to be in love, or not in love, or partly in love, traipsing about the stage spouting supposedly witty speeches about passion and marriage that bordered on the ludicrous. Love was not a farce—or at least, it shouldn't be. Love should be joyful, of course, and bring happiness. It should not be treated as a joke.

She mentally abandoned the silly couple on the stage. Instead of the actress in a peasant's costume, she saw herself. She kept the set, which was supposed to be a forest glade, but rather than meeting a young shepherd—whose sheep would all have wandered off under such an indifferent guardian—she saw the viscount standing beside her under a shady oak. Even her vivid imagination couldn't clothe him in peasant's garb of yoked shirt, brown breeches and boots. No, in her mind, he wore evening dress and a long black cloak.

They would be lovers, meeting in a secluded glade because she was a peasant and he was of noble birth. His parents, a stern, undemonstrative couple, would never approve of their marriage, so it was a blissful, passionate secret, comprised of brief moments to kiss and embrace, his strong arms about her, his soft lips upon hers.

But now, because of duty and honor, he was going away to war. He would tell his parents about their engagement the day he returned, and then they would wed, with or without their approval. This would be the last time they would meet before he left, perhaps never to return.

He would not chatter inanities about passion and marriage. No, he would say very little. He would just . . . look . . . with those dark, passionate eyes. She had seen cocoa beans once, and his were just that same color. Rich and dark, and in a similar way, exotic.

Her secret lover would wordlessly sweep her into his arms and kiss her with all the fervent longing of a desperate man. He would hold her tightly in his powerful embrace, as if he simply could not bear to let her go. The salty dampness of her tears would flavor their kisses.

Running her fingers through his dark locks, she would relax against him, loose-limbed with longing. As he held her with one strong arm, he would untie his cloak and throw it to the ground, then together they would sink down upon it on the soft grass. Their kisses would deepen. Lips would part. Tongues would touch, then entwine.

With anxious fingers, she would tear at his cravat until she ripped it from his neck. She would attack the buttons of his shirt, seeking the warm flesh beneath, pressing her lips to his hot skin while his hand slowly, slowly slid up her naked leg, her thin skirt bunching—

"Are you ill, Lady Diana?" Lord Fallston whispered. "You look quite flushed."

Fanning herself with her program, she glanced at the man beside her. She certainly wasn't going to explain to Lord Fallston that she'd been imagining making love with his enemy, which she shouldn't have been doing in the first place. Unfortunately, she had to give some kind of explanation for her state.

"I'm a little overheated," she said at last. "This theater is rather warm. And I may be more tired than I thought. Aunt Calliope and I were walking a long time this afternoon." She nodded at her relative. "As you can see, she's quite worn out."

"You need not have come if you were fatigued," he said. "I could have gotten a box for another night."

He reached out to place his gloved hand over hers and she started when his knee touched hers.

Still fanning, although not quite so rapidly, she shifted a little and reached up to pat her hair. "No, no, I shall be all right if we get a breath of air at the interval."

He smiled, nodded, mercifully withdrew his hand and turned his attention back to the principal actress, who was showing a rather shocking amount of leg.

When the curtain finally closed for the interval, Lord Fallston immediately rose and offered her his arm, then addressed her aunts. "Lady Calliope, Lady Euphenia, would you care to accompany us for some refreshments?"

"No, thank you," Aunt Euphenia said as she got to her feet with her usual alacrity. "I see some friends I would like to speak with. Calliope?" She gave her slumbering sister a little poke. "Calliope!"

Aunt Calliope awoke with a snort. "Is it the interval already? My goodness! What a charming play! Absolutely charming!"

"Lord Fallston wishes to know if you would like some refreshment," Aunt Euphenia repeated.

"Oh, no, I am quite content to remain here. You all may go on."

Lord Fallston bowed, and with no further ado,

Aunt Euphenia headed for an adjoining box, while Lord Fallston escorted Diana toward the sound of tinkling glasses and the buzz of conversation in the rooms adjoining the theater.

Lord Fallston frowned as he looked over the number of well-dressed people pressing forward in front of them as they neared the foyer. "This is a larger crowd than I expected."

Diana nodded. "Perhaps we should return to our seats. It is enough refreshment to walk about a bit."

"Very well."

Diana turned—and found Lord Adderley and his party right behind them. His brow rose, his eyes gleamed with a devilish glow and his lips curved up into a fiendish smile. "Well, well, well, my lady, we meet again. What a charming coincidence."

This meeting wasn't any kind of coincidence. His eyes gave the lie to that excuse.

What a change from the last time she had seen him! Now it was easy to believe he was a rake and a scoundrel, a gambler and a lothario keen to seduce any woman he could. Yet he had seemed so sincere in Lady Kentisten's library, she wasn't willing to believe he had been as good as lying to her then.

She studied his handsome face, seeking the truth. Why would he be one way tonight, and another when they'd been alone?

Perhaps that was it—company made the difference. Maybe this was his *public* face and his private was another. Maybe now he was playing a role, just as those actors on the stage were performing a part. If so, what did it mean that he had revealed even a small portion of his true self to her?

"Aren't you going to introduce us, my lord?" Miss Foxborough asked as she gave Diana the sort of pitying look beautiful women give women who are not.

Diana's pride sprang to attention, and she stopped pondering the mystery of the viscount's behavior. "Yes, my lord, please do me the honor of introducing me to your friends."

Lord Fallston made a little noise in his throat.

She'd forgotten he was there.

If Lord Adderley had found her scrutiny disturbing, he gave no sign. "My lady, allow me to introduce Miss Adelina Foxborough and Lieutenant Charles Grendon of His Majesty's Royal Navy."

The viscount fairly emanated command, but so did the lieutenant. She could easily picture him amidst the swirl of smoke on the bridge of a man-of-war engaged in battle, coolly issuing orders above the din of cannons and the cries of wounded men.

Perhaps in her next book, if there was a next book, the heroine could be captured by pirates and saved by some dashing naval officer—

"You already know Mr. Smythe-Medway, of

course," Lord Adderley continued. "Miss Foxborough, Lieutenant Grendon, this is Lady Diana Westover." He made a dismissive gesture at her companion. "Oh, and that's Lord Fallston. You remember him, Charlie, I'm sure."

Charlie obviously did, for a cool look froze his sapphire-blue eyes.

"Fallston, you know Brix and Charlie, of course."

"Yes, I do."

Lord Fallston spoke as if he'd like to strike them down on the spot. They must have been in on the infamous prank, or perhaps any friend of the viscount was an enemy of his.

"I didn't think a pastoral farce quite to your taste, my lady," the viscount observed, giving her another mocking smile.

Whatever his game was, she would play it. "And I'm sure love is a subject with which you are completely unfamiliar."

"You think I know nothing of love?"

The viscount's two friends exchanged wry glances, while Miss Foxborough tittered behind her fan. "Then I would say you don't know Lord Adderley," she said. "He is quite the conqueror of ladies' hearts."

Diana regarded Miss Foxborough steadily. "If he is the lothario rumor paints him, no, I don't think he knows anything about love—the emotion, that is. I'm sure he performs the physical act quite competently."

As Adelina Foxborough's eyes widened and Lord Fallston bleated like a startled sheep, the other two young men turned away, their hands over their mouths to stifle their laughter.

Diana began to blush furiously. Thank heavens Aunt Calliope hadn't heard what she'd just impulsively said.

"I'm delighted that you believe I'm competent," the viscount calmly replied. "As for falling in love, surely you wouldn't expect me to admit to a moment of weakness."

She forgot her embarrassment. "I gather from your prevarication that you haven't."

"The heart can be a dangerous battleground."

"So you are admitting that you have never been in love?" she charged, surprisingly anxious to hear his answer.

"Once I was fool enough to think I was. It proved to be nothing but a fancy, an attraction, a lust that was as false and fleeting as a will-o'-the-wisp."

Miss Foxborough looked as dumbfounded as Diana felt, and the beauty was not nearly so attractive with her mouth agape.

The viscount smiled and neatly changed the subject. "I confess I was shocked to see you here, Lady Diana. I would have thought opera more your style, and the bloodier the better. Plenty of corpses on the ground and supernatural creatures, like a gothic novel. Is that not your favorite sort of story? Why else would you sneak off at a party to read a tale of ghosts and maidens in distress? He dropped his voice to a low, deep murmur that seemed to wreck havoc on her common sense. "And you seemed so desperate for *The Ruins of Rygellan* I thought you would grab it out of my hands right there in the bookshop."

Miss Foxborough looked even more baffled, as well she might, and a swift glance at Lord Fallston revealed his blush, and his dismay.

On the defensive, Diana smiled sweetly and let the sarcasm drip like honey in the sun. "Accepting *The Ruins of Rygellan* would have meant touching you, my lord, which I was loathe to do. I can live without the book for awhile. I'm sure Mr. Duthney will be getting other copies soon."

Lord Adderley shook his handsome head. "Not for another six months. I inquired."

"Oh no!" she cried. Then she hoped he was saying that simply to get a rise out of her—as he had.

The viscount eyed Fallston. "Tell me, Fallston, do you share Lady Diana's taste in novels?"

"Lady Diana and I do not discuss reading material," he haughtily replied, obviously pleased to finally get a word in.

"No? Well, how could you, when you haven't read a book in the past ten years? What *do* you discuss? The weather?"

As Lord Fallston colored even more, Diana decided she'd had quite enough of this conversation, and the baffling, upsetting viscount. "What we choose to discuss is none of your affair." She took firm hold of Lord Fallston's thin arm. "It's been an interesting experience talking to you, my lord, as always. A delight to meet you, Miss Foxborough, Lieutenant. And you, too, Mr. Smythe-Medway. Good evening."

Turning and taking Lord Fallston with her, she marched purposefully back to their box. Whether Lord Adderley was a cad or a man with a past that aroused her sympathy, she was not going to waste any more thoughts on him. He was too disturbing, too confusing, too handsome, too interesting, too upsetting, too attractive.

She hoped she never met him again, not even for the sake of her book.

A few days later, Diana studied the volumes on the shelf of the circulating library that were at her eye level, as well as those below, then sighed with disappointment. She'd read every single version of the Greek myths here, or tried to. The fiction section was woefully lacking in books that looked appealing, too.

She supposed she could always reread a few of her favorites, like *The Spider's Web*, if she couldn't find something interesting here today. Perhaps she could try to figure out how the author had managed to infuse his scenes with such action and movement, so that she'd felt she was right beside him in the jungle or on the deck of a ship caught in a raging storm at sea.

Ever since she'd started *The Castle of Count*

Korlovsky, she'd been discovering how difficult writing was. She'd naively assumed she could simply put pen to paper, and the drama would unfold. Instead she'd been faced with all she didn't know, about trying to capture the pictures her mind created, how to make those pictures lively and exciting, how to describe a man who turned out to be the villain in a way that would enable her readers to believe Evangeline would go with him without seeming like a fool.

That was one good thing to come from her confrontations with the viscount—the only good thing, she reminded herself. She was still determined to stay away from him, no matter how tempting it was to engage in verbal battles with him, or how intriguing the hints about his past. He puzzled and confused her, and she didn't need that.

Unfortunately, while Lord Fallston was the very epitome of a safe, acceptable future husband, he rarely said anything interesting, while she couldn't deny she found talking with the viscount stimulating. Afterward she might regret it, but at the time . . .

She was doing it again! She simply had to stop thinking about the man!

She wandered a few more feet along the aisle. At least it was quiet here, and she wouldn't be disturbed. Her maid, Sally, was sitting back near the entrance, quite willing to wait and rest her feet while her mistress tried to find something enjoyable to read. At this hour of the morning, not very many other people had arrived, so she had this section all to herself.

Or so she thought.

"That sigh seemed to come all the way from your toes, Lady Diana. Tell me, are you weary, disappointed or disgusted?"

She whirled around to find Lord Adderley standing not three feet away, leaning casually against the stacks, as smug and self-satisfied as a cat who'd imbibed a saucerful of cream. With his polished boots, tight trousers and dark jacket, he looked more like he should be riding to hounds. He must have ridden his horse—a fine, lively gelding, no doubt—to the library, or come here directly from the stables.

"No need to look so shocked to see me here, my lady," the viscount said in a low voice as he pushed off and strolled closer. "I do know how to read."

"Nevertheless, you don't seem the sort of man to frequent a library," she noted as she inched backward, toward the door.

"I do prefer to purchase books I like," he replied, apparently not the least bit nonplussed by either her scrutiny or her remarks as he strolled closer, so that the same distance was always between them, "but there's something so calming about a library, don't you agree?"

Normally, yes, she did. But not at present. Right now, she felt anything but calm. However, she wasn't about to let him see her discomfort. She wouldn't add to his satisfaction. "Libraries are generally very pleasant places," she allowed,

"And as you put it once, Bath is a small place, so naturally we must expect to encounter one another. It's not as if I were lying in wait to see which way you went when you left your aunts' house this morning."

She'd never had an attack of the vapors, but as she imagined him doing just that, like something out of a novel, she had an inkling of what the vapors must be like.

Surely he hadn't *actually* done that, though. He was probably just saying that to disturb her.

She never should have spoken to him so boldly. She should have played the demure duke's daughter, curbed her tongue, fled the labyrinth and run out of the library, even if every particle of her pride and self-esteem argued against it.

"Since we are both avid readers, it seems highly likely that we would meet here eventually," he continued. "I've come because, having finished *The Ruins of Rygellan*, I need something fresh. How about you, my lady?"

How was he able to make what should have been an innocuous statement so pregnant with hidden meaning?

And more importantly, was *The Ruins of Rygellan* as exciting as she hoped?

She longed to ask him, but didn't. For one thing, she wanted to get away from him. For another, what if it was? She was already anxious to read it and knowing it was going to live up to her expectations would only increase her desire.

To read the book.

And what if he hadn't enjoyed it? She would be so disappointed . . . assuming they shared the same taste in plots and characters, of course.

"Ancient myths and legends hold some appeal for you, do they?" he inquired quietly as he pulled out a book and flipped through it, mercifully taking his dark-eyed gaze off her face. "I confess I enjoy the tales myself, particularly Homer's versions. I like a good battle scene."

Good God, just as she did. But she wouldn't admit they had anything in common.

As he returned the book to its place, she continued to back away.

He ambled forward. "Despite their supposedly exalted status, the gods and goddesses seem so very human—indeed, almost childish sometimes, don't you think?"

If anybody saw them, they'd appear to be engaged in some sort of strange dance, or perhaps even a mating ritual. It would be better if they simply looked to be having a conversation, so she came to a halt. "I suppose that's why *you* enjoy their antics."

He gravely shook his head as he, too, stopped moving. "Ah, once again, you wound me, my lady. I don't think I'm at all childish, but their humanity appeals to me. We cannot all be paragons."

Fortunately, they were nearly at the door, and relief began to replace her dread of discovery—and being alone with him. "We can all try."

"Like Fallston?"

"Yes," she replied as she turned to leave. "Now, I must beg leave to be excused, my lord."

He deftly intercepted her. "Which is your favorite?"

"I beg your pardon?"

"The gods, which is your favorite?"

It was an interesting question.

"Let me guess," he said as she hesitated. "Hermes, with his little winged feet? Or Cupid with his bow? Having an invisible husband would have some advantages, I suppose. I daresay there are times you wish the very attentive Lord Fallston would disappear for a while."

This was so close to the mark, she blushed. To cover her embarrassment, she blurted out the truth. "Hades."

A slow smile spread across his features. "The god of the underworld? Why, my goodness, Lady Diana, this gives me a whole new perspective on your character."

She marshaled her wits. "I feel sorry for him, and I'm not surprised he felt the need of a woman's company. Of course, abducting the daughter of a goddess wasn't a very wise way to get it."

The viscount smiled. "Don't you think it was a case of love at first sight?" he proposed. "Surely, as a woman, you can give Hades credit for that."

"Indeed, I don't," she said firmly. "I don't think he loved Persephone, certainly not at first. I'm sure he never gave any thought to her feelings when he abducted her, which he would have done had he loved her. He simply lusted after her, so he took her."

"Can you honestly picture Hades courting a girl with flowers and pretty speeches? Perhaps a song while playing his lyre? And would her mother have encouraged the match even if he had? I doubt it. It's my opinion that Hades saw no other way. It was the action of a desperate man— or god, as the case may be."

She'd never thought of it from that perspective. But still . . . "He should have courted her regardless."

"In secret, perhaps? Rendezvous in the night and that sort of thing? I can't see that her mother would have approved of that, either."

"He should have managed to communicate with her somehow, rather than just grabbing her and taking her away."

"Some women enjoy being swept off their feet."

"Not literally."

"How would you know?"

"*I* wouldn't."

During the moment of silence that followed, she was sure she'd won her point. "Who would be your favorite among the goddesses, my lord? Aphrodite?"

"For a woman with an imagination, that's a dull guess and as it happens, quite wrong. Try again."

"If you say Diana, I will say *you're* lacking in imagination."

"I agree, and I happen to prefer Athena. I like intelligent women."

"Who do not guard their virginity?"

Surprise flared in his eyes, and she immediately wished she'd said something—anything!—else. Yet as embarrassed as she was, she didn't move. She felt captured by the intensity and interest of his gaze. It was as if he found her a fascinating woman.

"If you don't feel any sympathy for Hades, why do you like him?" he asked, as serious as he'd been in Lady Kentisten's library.

"I didn't say I *liked* him, particularly," she replied, compelled to try to explain her decision. "I find him interesting. It must be very difficult living in hell."

"Nearly as difficult as trying to avoid it."

She felt in her bones that he was being completely honest with her; that here and now, she was seeing the real Lord Adderley, and he was not the charming scoundrel her aunt believed him to be. "You sound as if you know all about that."

Whatever had clouded his thoughts, it either

disappeared or he hid it better. "Well, I don't claim to have led a faultless life."

"Can that be said of anyone?"

"I suppose it could be said of you." He smiled and she had the sudden sensation that he was trying to summon the mask he usually wore.

She knew she must leave, and yet she couldn't without trying to discover a little more about him. "I suspect that whatever you did, it's not as bad as people claim, is it?"

She held her breath as she waited for his answer, desperate to know whether he was truly a scoundrel or not, and quite certain, deep in her heart, that he would tell her the truth.

He met her gaze steadily, and resolution glinted in the dark depths of his eyes. "I confess that I have, in my time, done things that I am ashamed of, but I don't think I should pollute the ears of an innocent like you with the details."

She wasn't ignorant of the world and human nature. "I wasn't raised in a convent, you know."

"As good as, or so I've heard."

She shook her head. "Not at all," she said, hoping to encourage him to reveal more about himself. "My father and I had very busy lives in Lincolnshire and many friends, albeit several I'm sure the *ton* would never approve of. My father didn't discriminate according to rank or wealth."

"An admirable quality, and one Lord Fallston doesn't possess," Lord Adderley replied. "He's inherited very limited ideas about what makes a person socially acceptable."

Why did he have to change the subject to Lord Fallston? "I am hardly a schoolroom miss, my lord. I can make up my own mind about Lord Fallston," she said, trying not to show her frustration.

"The man will have you bored out of your wits within a month of marriage. I spent years at Harrow with him and I'm sure he's not the man for you. Better to live a spinster than in a miserable marriage, or hasn't your unfortunately wedded aunt made that clear to you?"

It wasn't his place to tell her who she should or should not marry, or to consign her to spinsterhood. And then to mention Aunt Euphenia's disastrous marriage!

What motive could he have for doing that and warning her against Lord Fallston?

The goodness of his heart? *Perhaps.*

An interest in her well-being? *Maybe.*

His own attraction to her?

Ridiculous.

A man like the viscount could probably have any woman in England if he tried. He would never be seriously interested in her. She was too different, too homely, too odd and outspoken.

Out of that certainty another motive came to her, one distressing and cruel but sadly plausible and one that had little to do with her feelings or her happiness, based on an old enmity created long before she arrived in Bath. Maybe the only reason the viscount had distinguished her at all was because Lord Fallston had.

Hiding her dismay and burying her disappointment, she summoned her pride and defensive resolve. She wouldn't betray her feelings, and she wouldn't let him believe she would pay heed to anything he said against Lord Fallston. Instead she clasped her hands together and regarded him as if he were a hero come to rescue her from an ogre. "Oh, how very kind of you to care! And not just for me, but to feel for my beloved aunt and take such an interest in her welfare, too! I shall certainly tell her she has your sympathy and I'm sure she'll be thrilled beyond measure. For myself, naturally I am full of appreciation for your wise counsel. Of course, I shall listen and obey."

She couldn't keep up the pretense that he hadn't upset her, and her voice revealed it. "But should it come to pass that I remain a spinster because of your well-meaning advice, I trust you will be willing to spend an evening at whist with me as I while away my lonely days. Surely you will come to Lincolnshire and stand up with me at the county ball. Should I be on my deathbed, unloved and childless, you will come to hold my hand. And how foolish of me not to realize that you have not yet wed because you are selflessly setting an example to me and your friends by holding out until the perfect woman presents herself to you. You simply must let me know when you've found her."

He gave her the oddest look.

"Now, my lord, please excuse me and allow me to go home to digest this sage advice and recover from the pangs of gratitude your words have elicited."

With her head held high, she turned on her heel and marched away, leaving the viscount looking not unlike a man who'd washed ashore in a strange and unfamiliar country.

Which was the way Edmond was beginning to feel after every encounter with the mercurial, brazen, astonishing Lady Diana.

He fell back against the shelves and exhaled slowly. All he was supposed to do was discomfit her. He hadn't meant to get drawn into one of the most interesting debates about the gods that he'd ever had, or be charmed by her life in Lincolnshire with a man who sounded like the sort of father he'd always wished he'd had.

And then to bring her relationship with Fallston into it, even talking about marriage—he must have been temporarily deranged!

Or forgotten that her happiness wasn't his responsibility.

That concern, however fleeting, had to be a vestige of the mantle of responsibility he'd assumed all those years ago when he'd first arrived at school. His parents had let him go at last, finally convinced he was sufficiently prepared against the temptations and sins of the flesh to be allowed to go forth and set a good example to other sinful boys.

He hadn't felt prepared to set an example when he'd gotten to Harrow. He'd felt ancient and miserable, as if he were older than most of the other boys' fathers and never had a childhood at all.

In recent years he'd almost broken the habit of acting the wiser, more somber older brother, except sometimes with Brix, but every time he was with Diana, that urge to safeguard and protect came leaping out of some dark recess of his soul.

Obviously, that urge and his advice were quite unwelcome to her. He shouldn't bother trying to make her see that marrying Fallston was a mistake.

An elderly, bewigged gentleman dressed in clothes that had been fashionable twenty years ago when the king was hale and hearty came tottering into the room. He started when he saw Edmond and frowned as if he thought the younger man didn't belong there.

Edmond bowed politely. Then he launched into a long and formal greeting in perfect Latin before he sauntered out the door.

Chapter 7

❧

Evangeline held her breath as she crept through the dungeon beneath the castle. All around her was the stench of stale air and death. Rats rustled in the damp and fetid straw of the ancient cells, and she whispered a brief prayer for the souls of all the poor tormented men who had met their deaths in this terrible place.

But she would not go back. She would escape and find her way back to her beloved Rodolpho.

The Castle of Count Korlovsky

Aunt Calliope bustled into the sitting room, waving an opened letter in her right hand, the rest of the post, including a package, in her left. "Oh, Euphenia, Diana, I am so pleased! We've been invited to the earl of Granshire's reception for his son. I was so afraid we might be snubbed."

Diana looked up from her book. She was trying to make her way through Reverend Mac-Tavish's sermons, with little success. She should have been using this time to sort out the next episode of her book, but that was proving rather difficult. More precisely, the count was proving rather difficult, because he was turning out to be more exciting than villainous. Oh, he was doing evil things, but all out of his twisted love for Evangeline, and she was finding it very hard to give him the fate he deserved.

Which was ridiculous. She was the creator of the story, was she not? The count had no existence apart from her mind, and she should be able to control him, and what happened, but it didn't seem to be working out that way.

She probably wouldn't be having so much trouble if she hadn't patterned the count after Lord Adderley.

"I don't know why we wouldn't be invited," Aunt Euphenia said, interrupting her thoughts. "We are titled, after all, and the earl will surely invite every titled person within thirty miles."

"Including dear Diana! This is a great day, a very great day!" Aunt Calliope cried in triumph, as if Diana had scored a coup. She collapsed onto the sofa, the invitation pressed rapturously to her ample bosom, and put the rest of the post on the table beside her.

Since Diana had no idea who this earl was, or why his invitation elicited such pleased excitement, she couldn't share her aunt's unbridled enthusiasm.

"You're already acquainted with the earl's son, I believe," Aunt Euphenia said, noting her bafflement.

"I am?" Diana wracked her brain, but nobody

came to mind. "Did I meet him in the Pump Room or one of the concerts?"

"He's Lord Justinian Bromwell, the author of *The Spider's Web*."

For ten seconds, Diana was too stunned to reply. Then the thrill of meeting a real, live author—especially one whose book she'd so thoroughly enjoyed—animated her. Lord Bromwell had made what could have been a boring, dry discussion of tropical arachnids as thrilling as any novel; indeed, in some ways, more so, because the things he wrote about had really happened to him.

"When? When is the reception?" she cried, as delighted as Aunt Calliope had been.

Aunt Calliope consulted the embossed parchment edged in gold. "Friday week, at the earl's manor, which is outside the town." She smiled happily at Diana. "Oh, it's a most magnificent estate, my dear! He had the marble imported from Italy!"

Diana didn't care about Italian marble. "I wonder when Lord Bromwell arrives in Bath. Perhaps we'll have a chance to meet him before the reception."

Which was likely to be crowded, given the author's well-deserved fame.

"I doubt that," Aunt Calliope said, to Diana's dismay. "They say he's still not recovered from the illness he suffered on the voyage home."

"And no doubt his father will not want to dilute the sensation of presenting him," Aunt Euphenia remarked. "I daresay he'd despaired of

ever having cause to celebrate his son. I well remember the ruckus when Lord Bromwell announced that he was going to the Far East to study
spiders."

"His family didn't approve?" Diana asked.

"Not at all," Aunt Euphenia replied. "It sounded
too much like work, I suspect. The earl would consider that beneath his son."

"He must be very proud of him now."

Aunt Euphenia looked a little doubtful. "Of his
fame, at any rate."

"But not what he's learned?"

"I think the earl puts little stock in scientific
discovery."

"But the book. He must be proud of the book,"
Diana insisted.

Aunt Calliope and Aunt Euphenia exchanged
dubious glances.

"What if one of your relatives were to write a
book and get it published?" Diana asked, trying
to sound as if this wasn't fraught with significance
for her. "Wouldn't you be pleased?"

"Of one like *The Spider's Web*, of course,"
Aunt Euphenia replied. "It's a wonderfully educa-
tional volume."

"So much of what is published these days is the
most ridiculous trash," Aunt Calliope declared, finally putting down the invitation. "If someone in
my family were to write anything so embarrassing, so degrading—well, I certainly wouldn't acknowledge the relationship."

Although Diana wasn't surprised, she wished she hadn't asked the question at all.

Aunt Euphenia nodded at the package sitting on the table. "Who is that for, Calliope?"

"Oh, I forgot." Aunt Calliope picked it up and then frowned. "It's for you, Diana. Do you have any idea what it is?"

Diana studied it as she held out her hand. "I believe it's a book."

Hadn't she seen a package like that before, being held by long, slim, elegant male fingers?

No, it couldn't be. He wouldn't. Even Lord Adderley wouldn't do something so outrageous as send her *The Ruins of Rygellan*.

But in the library he'd said he'd finished it. . . .

No, no, she had to be wrong. Or if she wasn't, she really *ought* to wish she was. After all, such an act would put her in a very awkward position with regard to her aunts.

Aunt Calliope began to turn it over, examining the wrappings. "Did you order this from Mr. Duthney?"

Diana saw a ray of hope. "I was asking him about *The Ruins of Rygellan*. Perhaps he's gotten some copies in and remembered my interest."

"Ah." Aunt Calliope continued to examine the package, bringing it up to her eyes for a closer inspection of the wax seal.

Then she dropped it as if it had burst into flame and fixed an outraged and suspicious eye on Diana. "This package is from Lord Adderley."

A swift glance at Aunt Euphenia proved that she was likewise upset.

Diana hurried to explain as best she could. "Lord Fallston and I met him in the bookshop after he had purchased the last copy of *The Ruins of Rygellan*. I mentioned to him that I had hoped to buy a copy. He must think he's doing me a kindness to send it."

"*Kindness?* It's nothing of the sort. It's . . . it's rude impertinence," Aunt Calliope exclaimed. "Insufferable man! It will have to be sent back at *once*." She marched to the secretary desk in the corner of the room, and after opening and slamming shut most of the drawers, finally found her writing paper. "I shall write a note telling him what I think of insolent young rascals who presume to send gifts where they are not wanted!"

"This really is most improper," Aunt Euphenia said, her voice quieter, but no less condemning.

Blushing, Diana wished she'd never met the viscount. Indeed, at this point, she almost wished she'd never learned to read.

Nonetheless, her gaze drifted to the package like a compass needle drawn to the north.

Aunt Euphenia got to it first, picking it up off the floor and turning it over in her hands. She began to unwrap it with excruciating slowness.

The wrappings opened to reveal *The Ruins of Rygellan*.

Of course it must be returned to the viscount. Diana knew that. No unmarried lady could accept a gift from a man unless he was a relative or there were serious intentions of matrimony, which was certainly not the case here. And yet, if she could but read even the first page . . .

Aunt Euphenia held up a small white visiting card that had been tucked inside the cover. "It says, 'Far be it from me to deprive a lady of something she desires.'"

That really was . . . unpardonable.

With a sniff of disdain, Aunt Calliope stalked toward them bearing a much-blotted note as if it were a declaration of war. She thrust it at Aunt Euphenia. "Here. Put this with it, and then wrap it up at once."

Diana jumped to her feet. "Can't I just look at the book before you return it?" she pleaded without stopping to think. "It may be months before any more copies arrive in Bath, and the circulating libraries don't have any, because I've asked at each and every one and . . ."

She fell silent. Aunt Calliope couldn't look more shocked if she'd suddenly revealed a passionate interest in the viscount, and Aunt Euphenia . . . Aunt Euphenia's expression was a distressing mixture of suspicion and dread. "I only wanted to look at it," she murmured, sitting down.

"The sooner that is out of this house, the better," Aunt Calliope said. "Euphenia, send it with the footman at once."

"Would that be wise?" Diana asked, cautious but also desperate. "Surely your servant's livery will be recognized in Bath. What might people think if your footman is seen at the door of the viscount's home?"

"Oh dear, I hadn't considered that," Aunt Calliope murmured.

"Perhaps it would be better to send it back by some unknown lad glad to earn a shilling by running an errand."

"Diana is right," Aunt Euphenia agreed. "We shouldn't use one of our own servants."

"We can dispatch the footman to find a likely lad," Diana suggested. "He could take it first thing in the morning."

Aunt Euphenia nodded her acquiescence to this plan.

"Do whatever you think best, sister," Aunt Calliope said as she went toward the door. "I need to lie down. That man has given me a headache."

When she was gone, Diana looked beseechingly at her more reasonable aunt who was reading Aunt Calliope's note with pursed lips. "Please, can't I read just one chapter?"

Although her expression was not without sympathy, Aunt Euphenia shook her head. "It must go back, Diana, and why torment yourself with the first chapter if you cannot finish the entire book for months?"

Aunt Euphenia folded Aunt Calliope's note and set it on top of the book, then began to rewrap it. "Calliope's suspicions aside, I can't think what he meant by this." Aunt Euphenia cut her eyes to Diana. "Can you?"

Diana moved away a little more, as if the book might explode, and sat on the edge of the sofa. She could think of two possible explanations: either the viscount had done this out of generosity and sympathy for a fellow reader, or he wanted to upset her. Neither explanation was likely to please Aunt Euphenia.

"He wasn't very polite to me in the shop," she replied, avoiding a direct answer to her aunt's question. "Perhaps his friend put him up to it."

Aunt Euphenia went to the secretary and returned with fresh sealing wax. "Did he introduce this friend?"

"The Honorable Brixton Smythe-Medway."

"Ah." Aunt Euphenia took a taper and lit it in the fireplace. "Perhaps Mr. Smythe-Medway did suggest it. They were always together in mischief at Harrow, those two."

Diana watched her aunt seal up the package holding the precious book. "Were they very bad, Aunt?"

"I don't know that they and their circle of friends were the worst boys to attend Harrow, but judging by the stories, they were certainly high-spirited and not liable to consider consequences. However, that could be said of many boys."

"Aunt Calliope made it sound as if the viscount deliberately tried to drown Lord Fallston by enticing him into a leaking boat."

"Yes, so I've heard."

"Why would he want to do that?"

"Lord Fallston claims it was because he was a better scholar," Aunt Euphenia replied.

Lord Adderley hardly seemed the envious sort, especially of scholastic ability. She could more easily believe that Lord Fallston would envy *him*, for his charm and his looks and his conversational skills.

Aunt Euphenia gave her a little smile. "Exactly—nobody else quite believes that, either. I think that's why Adderley and his friends weren't expelled, despite Lord and Lady Ellis's best efforts and her son's claims. Of course, Lord Adderley's parents saw that he wasn't, either."

Diana immediately envisioned a stern, majestic couple intimidating a bewigged and regal head of Harrow, demanding that their son remain at the school. "They're formidable, are they?"

"They *were*. They both died some years ago. But long before, they got involved in some sort of strict sect started by a Scots clergyman and left London—Sodom and Gomorrah combined, his father said in a letter to *The Times*. He was always writing denunciations of London to *The Times*. I do believe he would even have renounced his title if he could. He gave most of his income to the church. Fortunately, his property and a considerable sum for its maintenance were entailed, or his son would have been left with nothing *but* the title."

A Scots clergyman? The Reverend Hamish MacTavish perhaps? That might explain the book of Reverend MacTavish's sermons Lord Adderley had been forced to read.

Reverend MacTavish preached a life devoid of anything that might tempt one to the sins of the flesh. A parent's task, he believed, was to ensure that their children weren't tempted, either. No frivolities, no laughter, no music, no celebrations. No demonstration of love. It was all duty and watchfulness against the least sign of sin.

It must have been very difficult to be a child growing up in such a household. Would it be any wonder if a man so raised rebelled, turning to the very things his stern parents spoke against?

The greater surprise might be if he didn't.

"I'm surprised they would send their son to Harrow," she reflected.

"So was everyone, but I gather people were reluctant to ask them why, in case his father went on one of his harangues."

"But if the viscount and his friends had really wanted to hurt Lord Fallston, wouldn't the headmaster have sent them down regardless of what his parents said? Surely for the sake of the school, he wouldn't have let really bad boys stay."

"Well, I do believe the incident has been blown out of proportion," Aunt Euphenia conceded.

"And other boys spoke up in their defense. Adderley was particularly well regarded, it seems."

Diana could believe that, just as she couldn't believe the viscount and his friends would deliberately try to drown anyone.

Her aunt cocked her head as she regarded her niece, looking more like her father than Diana had ever noticed before. "Diana, is there more to this business with the book that I should know about? You're a sensible and trustworthy girl, but a place like Bath can make even the most level-headed girl a bit giddy, and the viscount is one of the handsomest fellows I've ever seen."

"I've spoken to him, as you know," Diana admitted, determined to be honest, "but there is nothing that should give cause for concern."

At least, she hoped there wasn't. In the beginning, it would have been easy to disregard the viscount, to think of him as merely a handsome reprobate who made a good model for a villain. But the more she'd learned about him, the more complicated he was turning out to be, and the more confused her feelings for him had become, in spite of her resolve to have nothing more to do with him.

Her aunt reached out and took Diana's hands in hers. "I didn't think I had to warn you about men, my dear, but even the most sensible and trustworthy of women can sometimes be tempted by a fine figure and a handsome face." Her grip tightened. "When I met my husband, I was sure it was love at first sight, only to discover that as powerful as the feeling he elicited was, it was no more love than fool's gold is the true metal. I would not have you make the same mistake, Diana, and live to regret it, as I did. I don't think the viscount is the sort of man who could make a woman like you happy. He's not stable and steady, like Lord Fallston."

Appreciating that she spoke out of love, Diana embraced her aunt and held her close. "I know that you care about me, Aunt Euphenia, and it's not easy for you to talk about your husband and those terrible days when he was gambling away most of your fortune. I value your wisdom, too, so I'll stay away from the viscount."

Although it pained her to admit it, avoiding him completely really would be the best course of action. An elegant, handsome man like that should never be more to her than the model for Count Korlovsky, anyway.

Aunt Euphenia replied by hugging her beloved niece even tighter.

Like a predator stalking its prey, Edmond warily circled the desk in his study, his attention on the plain, brown-paper-wrapped parcel lying in the center of it.

The late morning light streamed through the muslin sheers, the edges defined by heavier velvet draperies. Prints of hounds and horses hung on the walls, and several books of various sizes, widths and ages lay about, basically wherever there was a flat surface.

The parcel had arrived, so his butler said, very early that morning, brought by a lad of unknown origin. Ruttles had been most indignant that the youngster would not give the name or the address of the party who had sent the package, not even when promised a shilling.

Edmond, however, had known what it was and who it was from the moment he'd seen it. He told himself he shouldn't be surprised to see that particular parcel again, nor the method Lady Diana had chosen to return it. She obviously didn't want anybody to realize that she had received anything from the notorious Lord Adderley.

Yet he was surprised nonetheless. In the bookshop she had looked at his purchase the way a greedy man would eye a chest of gold. He was certain she'd want to read it no matter what social strictures she might break. Surely any woman who wandered the labyrinth at night or hid in a darkened room at a party to read wouldn't suffer any guilty pangs when offered the chance to do something as harmless as read a book, regardless of who had sent it. He'd been so confident of that, he'd laid awake for a long time last night imagining her poring over the pages, just as he had, and wondering what she would make of the secret of the ruins.

He'd also wondered what she thought of the hero's efforts to rescue his beloved. During the fight with the heroine's evil stepfather, a swift jab to the throat would have come in handy, and he'd smiled as he imagined Diana thinking the very same thing.

There were other parts of the story that he would have liked to know her reaction to, as well. The parting of the lovers at the beginning. Their reunion. Their passion . . .

He halted and looked at the book again. She must possess more self-discipline than he had suspected. Or perhaps her aunts hadn't even told her it had arrived, if they had recognized his seal. He'd been so busy contemplating her reaction, he hadn't thought of that.

Sighing, he picked up the parcel and unwrapped it. A note in a large, scrawling hand dropped out. He read:

> *Sir (and I do not use your title on purpose, since you are deserving of only the bare minimum of respect):*
>
> *You are an insolent rogue and I am SHOCKED that you would have the gall and outrageous presumption to send my niece a gift! Have you no notion of the conduct becoming a gentleman AT ALL? Obviously not. Here is your book and I trust you will never speak to my niece again.*

It was signed Lady Calliope FitzBurton.

This haughty, offended missive was about what

he would expect from her. What he really wanted to know was how Diana felt about what he had done, if she knew of it. He hoped she didn't share that level of angry indignation, until he recalled that the initial purpose of this exercise had been to upset her.

He took the book and sat in his favorite wing chair near the window. He flipped through the pages, inhaling the beloved scent of ink and paper, an odor that reminded him of the quiet times when he had been alone with his books, and somewhat happy.

Another piece of paper fell from the pages, very small and much folded. He opened it out and read with increasing wonder.

Sir: I profess myself surprised that after chastising me for my lack of propriety more than once, you have elected to send a young lady you barely know such a marvelous gift. As my aunt is so correct as to observe, I cannot keep it and thus I return it. I trust this will end any social intercourse between us.

> *Yours sincerely,*
> *Lady Diana Westover*

P.S. And yet I must thank you, regardless of your motive. It was quite worth the loss of sleep.

He stared at the note. The sneaky little minx must have read the entire book between the time it had arrived and before it was given to the lad to return that morning. To confirm it, he hoisted himself to his feet and hurried to examine the brown paper.

There was the stain from his sealing wax, and the newly applied wax that he had pulled off. Now he noticed other stains, too, whose meaning was obvious. The parcel had been opened, rewrapped and sealed, and then opened and re-sealed again.

Lady Diana clearly *didn't* see a need to follow all of society's rules and conventions when her own desires were at stake.

He returned to his chair and contemplated the astonishing Lady Diana. At first glance, she seemed so very prosaic, not remarkable in the least, except for her habit of staring. Yet he was becoming more and more aware that she was unlike any other young lady he had ever met.

He could easily imagine her preparing for bed as usual last night, pretending that she absolutely agreed with her aunts' decision to return the book. Undressing, getting into a plain, white nightdress (of thin lawn perhaps), brushing her thick doe-brown hair while seated in front of her dressing table, the only light the glow of a candle.

Then, taking up the single candle and quietly and cautiously stealing her way to where the forbidden book had been put and carrying it off like a housebreaker with his booty.

He let his imagination linger for a while on the image of Diana clad only in a nightdress, wandering her aunts' townhouse like a gothic heroine. Wouldn't it have been amusing if he'd been there and leapt out at her?

What would she do then? Swoon? Not likely. Scream? He would have had to silence her before she roused the household. A hand over her mouth as he held her in his embrace?

No. A kiss. A long, lingering one.

He shifted in his chair, undeniably aroused by the scenario playing out in his head.

This was Lady Diana Westover, he reminded himself. She couldn't possibly be arousing, not when there was a Miss Foxborough to admire. Besides, Lady Diana wouldn't scream. She'd probably attack him.

That had a certain undeniable appeal, too. How her eyes would flash as they struggled.

Who would win? He honestly couldn't guess.

He shifted again and commanded himself not to be so ridiculous. If he ever did anything as ludicrous as jump out at Diana in the dark, she'd probably shout loud enough to wake the dead, bruise him severely with her martial skills, and have him thrown into jail.

"My lord?" the butler intoned from the door.

Edmond folded the paper, put it in his pocket and laid *The Ruins of Rygellan* in a shady spot on the windowsill. "Yes, Ruttles?"

"Mr. Smythe-Medway—"

"Is here!" Brix cried as he strode into the room. He tossed his hat and gloves to the sixty-year-old Ruttles, who caught them neatly, this not being the first time Brix had rid himself of those accoutrements in that manner. In spite of that, Ruttles's expression was a masterpiece of stifled disapproval.

"Thank you, Ruttles," Edmond said.

As the disgruntled butler departed, Brix crossed the thick carpet and sat in the wing chair opposite Edmond.

"You really ought to let the poor man announce you properly and you should hand him your hat," Edmond said. "I swear you take years off his life every time you do that."

"Oh, he enjoys it, really. Makes him feel young when he makes the catch and superior to me in every way."

Edmond realized trying to get Brix to change was a hopeless cause and gave up. "So, what brings you here?"

"I've come to drag you out of your lair. Drury's arrived."

Edmond didn't hide his surprise at their friend's unexpectedly early advent. "What, already? He hates leaving London. I thought he wouldn't come until the day of Buggy's reception."

"So did I, but he's already ensconced in the Fox and Hound, flirting with the maids."

If Drury had already come down . . . "What about Buggy? Has he arrived yet?"

"Oh, he's been here for a week."

Edmond straightened abruptly. "Why didn't you tell me? We could have gone out for a visit."

Brix shrugged. "Didn't see any point. Mama says they aren't accepting visitors yet. Seems the journey from London laid him low."

"Not seriously?"

"No, I don't think so. It's more likely his father wants to keep him under wraps until the grand unveiling."

Edmond relaxed against the soft back of the wing chair. "Ah."

"Amazing to think ol' Buggy's done so well for himself, eh?" Brix said as he slouched even lower. "Fellow of the Royal Society, and now a famous author. *The Spider's Web*—wonderful title for a book."

Edmond glanced at his well-worn copy lying on a nearby shelf. "Have you read it yet?"

Brix had the grace to blush. "No, I'm afraid not."

"I give *you* up," Edmond declared as he rose and fetched the box of cheroots from the top of his desk. He opened it and offered one to his friend. "I told you, it's really very good. Several hair-raising brushes with irate savages, a hint of heathen mating practices, a near shipwreck in a hurricane—something for everybody, including you. *And* good ol' Buggy makes it all very exciting, although there's not a ghost or levitating helmet in sight," he finished with a wry grin as he lit a taper from the hearth where a small fire was burning on this cool summer morning.

"What about the spiders?" Brix shivered as he exhaled a puff of aromatic smoke. "Nasty little insects."

"If you'd read the book, you'd know that spiders are *not* insects," Edmond said as he returned to his chair.

"Who the devil cares? They're still disgusting."

"Not to Buggy. He writes about them as if they're rare jewels, and he makes you believe that, too."

Brix did not look convinced. "Whatever he says about them, I never thought chasing spiders would prove so beneficial in so many ways. He's finally done something to make his father proud."

"I certainly hope so."

Remembering some late-night conversations at Harrow, neither spoke for a moment.

Then Brix frowned darkly. "I say, you're smoking!"

"Obviously," Edmond muttered as he tapped the ash of his cheroot into a small porcelain bowl at his elbow.

"But you only do that when you're upset."

Edmond immediately realized he'd betrayed more than he meant to and stubbed his out. "Or spending too much time in your company, perhaps?" he suggested with a grin.

His attempt at humor didn't fool Brix. "I suppose Miss Foxborough won't be invited to the reception?"

If Brix thought he was upset about that, he wouldn't disillusion him. He wouldn't lie, though, either. "Buggy's father's the worst snob in Bath, so I think we can be fairly certain a distiller's daughter will not be receiving an invitation to anything at his house."

Brix cleared his throat. "So that means you'll be footloose and fancy-free, and therefore, old friend, I have a favor to ask."

This time, Edmond's grin was real. "I thought so. That's the only time you ever clear your throat, unless you've got a cold."

Brix's eyes widened. "Really?"

"Really. Now, what boon have you to beg?"

"Gad, Edmond, can't you talk like a normal person?"

"What do you want me to do for you?"

"You don't have to be so bloody blunt."

Stifling a frustrated sigh, Edmond began again. "How may I be of assistance?"

"That's better," Brix noted with a fleeting smile. "If, as we suspect, Buggy's pater and mater have invited all the aristocrats in Bath to their party, Fanny Epping will be there."

Edmond began to smile. Brix's trials over

Fanny's unrequited affection were like a never-ending melodrama. He hoped Fanny would triumph in the end, because whether Brix realized it or not, she would be perfect for him. Besides, sweet, gentle Fanny was deeply in love with him, and what man wouldn't want that?

The amusing, genial Brixton Smythe-Medway also needed somebody steady and thoughtful in his flighty existence, should *he* be otherwise engaged with, say, a wife of his own.

Which was a thought that had never entered Edmond's head before. He wondered what had made him think so now.

He didn't have time to ponder, because Brix gave him a sour look. "Yes, yes, I know, it's my own bloody fault for kissing her in her mother's rose garden when we were twelve years old. But honestly, who knew she'd hold an infatuation even longer and stronger than Fallston holds a grudge? Surely you can be a friend and help me."

Edmond nodded. "Of course I will." He couldn't resist a little teasing. Brix had teased *him* often enough. "I draw the line at kissing her, though, in a rose garden or anywhere else."

"You won't have to," Brix said, his good humor restored. "Just talking to her ought to be enough to rid her mind of any thoughts of me."

Edmond studied his friend, who really must not understand the depth of Fanny's feelings. "I don't know why you react with such horror whenever she's around. She's a kind, gentle, pretty woman who's been in love with you for years. She's also got impeccable family connections and her lineage goes back to the Conquest. If you were ever to marry—"

"Edmond, you're my best friend, but there are some things I simply cannot tolerate, even from you," Brix declared with an aggrieved air. "One of them is any suggestion that I marry Fanny Epping."

"She'd be a very devoted little wife—"

"Edmond," Brix warned.

He gave up. "All right. I'll talk to Fanny Epping."

"Good! Say, I suppose Lady Diana will be there. Just imagine her meeting Buggy! Ought to be fascinating watching the two of them stare at each other."

Edmond had thought of that the moment he'd received the invitation. Not the staring, though, just the possibility that she would be there. "Fascinating."

"By the by, Mama says it's the talk of the town that Lord Fallston is going to propose to Lady Diana. Maybe it's time you stopped bothering her."

"I'm not bothering her." At least, that wasn't the word he would use. "Besides, even the slight appearance of some competition might be good for old Fusty—spur him to greater heights of devotion."

"Or it might remind him of Lucinda running off

with Sissingsby," Brix countered, "and farewell Lady Diana."

Edmond frowned. "If Fallston's devotion is so lacking that the sight of another man simply talking to his intended bride makes him believe she's as lacking in honor as his former fiancée, Lady Diana is well rid of him."

Brix's normally unworried brow furrowed. "Edmond, what's really going on between you and Fallston? He's no threat to you, and never has been."

"This has nothing to do with Fallston," Edmond replied.

And it didn't. In fact, he suddenly realized, when he was with Diana, everybody else in the world ceased to exist.

Shocked by the realization, confused by the implication, he decided he'd had enough talking about Diana, and thinking about her, too.

He got to his feet. "Come on, Brix. Enough of Fallston and his love life. Let's go see Drury and hear the latest news from London."

Chapter 8

"The heart can be a dangerous battleground,"
the count warned as he tugged Evangeline into
his arms.

The full scope of the count's evil threatened to
overwhelm her. As for what he wanted of her in
this isolated castle, that was all too clear.

"There is no battle here," Evangeline cried,
struggling. "My heart already belongs to another."

"Evangeline, Evangeline," the count chided as
his grip tightened, holding her as helpless as a
butterfly caught in a spider's web. "Forget that
boy Rodolpho."

She pushed against her captor, trying to break
free.

"No!" she cried, finding new strength. "I love
him!"

"You will forget him!" the count growled. "In
my arms, you will forget. You were meant to be
mine, Evangeline. You will be mine . . ."

The Castle of Count Korlovsky

Diana hadn't been this excited since . . . well,
she didn't want to consider the last time
she'd been excited.

173

What she was feeling as her aunts' carriage conveyed them to the home of the earl of Granshire was a different sort of excitement anyway. To think she was going to be able to meet the author of *The Spider's Web* in person! She wouldn't be this thrilled to meet the Prince Regent.

Aunt Euphenia smiled as she regarded her niece, who was clad in her favorite ball gown of pale lilac silk with a bodice cut as low as Diana would permit. Around her neck she wore a silver necklace of diamonds and amethyst, the last gift her father had ever given her. Silver earrings that had been her mother's dangled at her ears.

"You look like you could fly right out of this carriage," Aunt Euphenia said.

Diana smiled broadly back. "I wish I could. I'd be able to reach our destination quicker."

"So do I," Aunt Euphenia confessed with a little laugh. "I've never met a famous scientist."

"It's sure to be quite a party," Aunt Calliope noted with an approving little sigh. "The earl's wife will have invited all the nobility in Bath."

Including Lord Adderley?

Twisting to look out the window to see if she could spot their destination, Diana tried to subdue any reaction to that thought, especially when she felt Aunt Euphenia's questioning gaze.

She'd simply have to get used to seeing the viscount in public occasionally, as long as they were both in Bath, while managing to avoid speaking to him. That would be a good deal easier if Aunt

Euphenia would quit looking at her that curious way every time he was hinted at in a conversation.

They soon reached the long, sweeping drive leading to a massive house of pale yellow Bath stone ablaze with lights. Torches lined the approach, which was full of carriages, most bearing coats of arms. Aunt Calliope detailed their owners in a series of excited exclamations, and it did seem as if every nobleman and his family within the vicinity of Bath had been invited.

The viscount might not attend even if he was invited, Diana mused. After all, what could he possibly have in common with a famous scientific scholar and author? Of course, it was very possible he'd have read *The Spider's Web*, and if he had, he, too, might wish to meet the talented author.

She tried to put such thoughts out of her mind. She was here to meet Lord Bromwell, not him.

With that thought to bolster her, she stepped forth from her aunts' barouche and hurried up the steps behind them.

She gasped when she entered the enormous foyer of the country manor. Her slippers trod on a polished marble floor; more marble graced the walls in columns that wouldn't have been out of place in Caesar's palace. A white-domed plastered ceiling rose high overhead, intricate and lovely. The walls themselves were delicately painted in soft blue, the shade of the summer sky. Several side tables of polished mahogany gleamed, the surfaces reflecting the enormous, colorful bouquets of hothouse flowers set in vases upon them.

Her gaze swept the crowd as she divested herself of her cloak and handed it to a footman. The people gathered here, removing their wraps and handing them to a veritable army of liveried servants, were indeed the cream of Bath society. She recognized several from the assembly balls, the theater and the Pump Room.

Mercifully, the viscount wasn't among them, although she thought she saw his friend, Mr. Smythe-Medway, standing near the entrance to some sort of large room or gallery. He was talking to a dark-haired gentleman whose evening dress would have passed Beau Brummel's inspection. The unknown man's shirt was so white, it fairly gleamed, his cravat had likely taken an hour to tie in that complicated knot, his collar points were precisely aligned and the cut of his jacket made her wonder if it took two servants to get it on him without so much as a single wrinkle.

He looked to be of the same age as Mr. Smythe-Medway, so perhaps this was another of the viscount's friends from Harrow. If so, he was also probably an enemy of Lord Fallston. As she watched, and as if to confirm her guess, Lieutenant Grendon joined the pair, laughing and exchanging greetings.

The unknown man didn't actually laugh out loud, but there was something about his countenance that made her think he was glad to be with his friends.

Most of the people were headed in that direction, so she suspected the guest of honor must be in the large room beyond, which meant there might not be any way to avoid Lord Adderley's friends.

Provided she wanted to. It might be rather interesting to find out who the stranger was and where he fit in amongst the men from Harrow. Judging by his clothes, he was likely the most vain of them, and she suspected he could wreak even more havoc among the petticoats than the viscount. It wasn't that he was as classically handsome as Lord Adderley; indeed, considered dispassionately, his features weren't very attractive at all. Nor did he project that aura of power the viscount did, or the leadership of Lieutenant Grendon, or Mr. Smythe-Medway's good humor.

Before she could figure out just what the appeal of the man was—for the reaction of other women around her certainly proved she was not the only one who noticed him—Lord Fallston appeared. He passed Mr. Smythe-Medway and the others with a barely disguised scowl, then charged through the crowd like a very determined stag.

"Good evening," he said, bowing in greeting when he reached Diana and her aunts.

"My lord," Aunt Calliope said, "I was so hoping you'd be here. But then, you went to school with Lord Bromwell, so I suppose I shouldn't be surprised."

Diana turned to him. "You did?"

"Yes, he was at Harrow with me. The receiving line's in the ballroom." He took her arm and began heading toward the double door near the viscount's friends, glancing back to address her aunts as well as herself. "I don't think he's enjoying all the fuss, though. He always was a quiet fellow."

Given the connection to Harrow, perhaps the viscount *was* here . . . unless he'd played a trick that went wrong on Lord Bromwell, too. But if that were so, Mr. Smythe-Medway surely wouldn't have been invited, nobility or not, since he was apparently the viscount's partner in pranks.

The ballroom with gilded columns, ornate wallpaper and polished mirrors was even more crowded than the foyer. A dozen large chandeliers provided illumination and sets of French doors opened out to a terrace. At the opposite end of the room, an orchestra on a raised platform performed, although they could scarcely be heard above the din of excited babble. All around them people talked, laughed and gossiped, most about young Lord Bromwell, his recent illness and the sensation his book was making in literary circles, and among the general public, too.

She realized none of them seemed to be discussing the book itself. She also realized, with even more dismay, that Lord Fallston seemed to be deliberately trying to slow their progress. Her aunts were already in the receiving line, drawing closer to the person who had to be Lord Bromwell standing near a pair of open doors leading to the terrace. The young man's thin face was the color of lightly aged oak. His clothes seemed loose on his slender frame, but he had been seriously ill on his journey back to England, so it should be no surprise that his evening dress—probably kept here at home—did not fit him well anymore. An older man who looked so proud his chest might burst the confines of his vest stood beside him, smiling with regal condescension as a line of eager supplicants spoke to him before moving on to the guest of honor.

That must be Lord Bromwell's father, the earl of Granshire.

"What did you think of Lord Bromwell's book?" she asked Lord Fallston as they waited for a group of elderly gentlemen complaining about the younger generation to pass by. It seemed men like Lord Bromwell had it too soft, even in the jungles of Borneo.

He colored. "I haven't had a chance to read it."

"Oh," she murmured, hiding her dissatisfaction. "Well, it's very good. Very interesting and exciting, too. The part where his ship is caught in a hurricane—"

"My lady, I must speak with you alone," Lord Fallston interrupted with quiet intensity.

Startled, she took a moment to recover, and

suspected Lord Fallston had dawdled in order to make this rather shocking request. "I'm not sure—"

"*Please*. It is truly important, or I wouldn't dream of making such an impertinent request."

He really did look desperate. And he was generally a very proper young man . . . but that didn't mean she relished the prospect of hearing something he thought required solitude.

However, they hadn't moved a foot since he'd asked to speak to her. He might keep her out of the receiving line trying to convince her, and that she certainly didn't want. "If it can be arranged," she said at last, "we could go out on the terrace later, after I meet Lord Bromwell."

Lord Fallston sighed with relief.

Suddenly, Mr. Smythe-Medway and his friends appeared beside them. He raised a blond brow as if this was the most unexpected event of the year. "Well, Fallston, fancy meeting you here." He gestured at his companions. "Lady Diana, you know Lieutenant Grendon, and this is Sir Douglas Drury, baronet and barrister. Drury, this is Lady Diana Westover."

"My pleasure, my lady," Sir Douglas said in a deep voice nearly as attractive as the viscount's. His tone was polite, but he barely smiled as he ran a measuring gaze over her.

She finally recognized what quality he possessed: arrogance, far more than Lord Adderley, or any other man she had ever met. Yet that was hardly an attractive trait, so why did she and all these other women find him so? She stood puzzling, until Sir Douglas raised a questioning brow. "Something wrong with my cravat, my lady?"

"No, not at all. I beg your pardon."

"Just so long as my valet's efforts haven't been in vain," he replied, and then his lips lifted in a very small smile.

The effect of even that slight change to his countenance was astonishing. It was like drawing near a warm fire on a cold day, and just as suddenly, his effect upon women was absolutely understandable.

Lord Fallston, not unnaturally, was quite immune. "From your presence I assume that the king's court can easily spare you, eh, Drury?" he noted with more than a hint of a sneer.

"We're all expendable," the baronet calmly replied. "I've been hearing some very interesting tales about you, Fallston. I gather this is your bride-to-be?"

Diana stiffened, rooted to the spot. She was about to refute him when the blushing Lord Fallston did. "No, this lady and I are not yet engaged."

Diana had a horrible feeling that she now knew exactly why Lord Fallston wanted to speak to her, and she wished she'd refused his request. Perhaps she still could.

"Well, if you *do* become his fiancée, my lady," Sir Douglas said, his tone confidential, but his gaze sharp, "mind you don't run off with some cad like the other one did, or perhaps he'll take my advice—which he didn't do before—and sue you for breach of promise."

If this man was Lord Fallston's enemy, why would he have offered legal advice?

"I didn't sue because unlike *some* people, I have no desire to see my family's name trotted out in the newspapers," Fallston retorted.

"You would have won. According to every solicitor I asked, it was a simple case."

"You talked about my . . . my trouble . . . with *strangers*?"

"Since I'm a barrister, I don't know much about that sort of thing. Solicitors do. I was only trying to do you a good turn, old man."

"You shouldn't have bothered!" Lord Fallston said through clenched teeth.

Mr. Smythe-Medway shook his head. "Save your breath, Drury. He doesn't want your help anymore now than when you hauled him out of the river."

So, the baronet had been in on the prank, too. Perhaps his guilt compelled him to suggest legal remedies to Lord Fallston.

His eyes full of barely suppressed fury, Lord Fallston glared at Mr. Smythe-Medway. "I'm shocked you and your friends have the gall to come tonight. What was it you used to call Lord Bromwell? *Buggy*, wasn't it?"

His harsh words didn't seem to disturb Mr. Smythe-Medway or the others a bit. "So we did. Now he's really earned the name, hasn't he?"

"You've lived up to yours, too," Fallston charged. "So has Adderley."

Mr. Smythe-Medway grinned at Diana as if he were letting her in on a great, secret joke, and he made a jaunty little bow. "I'm afraid he's right, my lady. Middling I was, and middling I continue." He indicated his companions. "Grendon here we called The Captain because he was so enamored of ships and all things nautical. Used to talk our ears off about great battles at sea. Drury's Cicero because he's such a good debater. Give him a topic and, pro or con, he'll convince you he's absolutely right. He's never lost an argument yet, or a case at court."

The baronet's response to this praise was a very slight raising of one corner of his mouth in another mere hint of a smile.

"Can you guess what Edmond's was?"

"She didn't come here to play guessing games with you," Fallston snapped.

"You wound me, Fallston, you really do," Mr. Smythe-Medway replied with another broad smile, his eyes twinkling with mischief.

"Let me see," Diana mused, ignoring their war of words and contemplating the viscount's dark hair and commanding manner. Several names of gods, warriors and archangels came to her, but in the end, it was Mr. Smythe-Medway's lighthearted manner that prompted her response. "Was it Beelzebub?"

"Close, my lady!" Mr. Smythe-Medway cried, delighted.

"Hades," Lord Fallston said impatiently. "Adderley's nickname was Hades."

Diana's throat constricted as she immediately recalled the conversation she'd had with the viscount in the circulating library. No wonder he had pursued that particular topic. He must have enjoyed his secret little joke, at her expense.

"I gather Fallston never told you what we used to call him," Mr. Smythe-Medway asked merrily. "Fusty Fallston. He was a prig even then."

With a disdainful sniff, the earl gently tugged her forward. "Come along, my lady. I don't know how long Lord Bromwell's health will permit him to stay at the reception."

Afraid that he might be right about the guest of honor's health, she didn't protest. She was about to look back at the three friends and make a polite farewell when she encountered Aunt Euphenia's curious gaze and decided not to. It was obvious she and Aunt Calliope had already been through the receiving line and witnessed the confrontation.

"Since I know Lord Bromwell, I'll introduce you," Lord Fallston said, possessively putting his hand over hers.

She ignored that unwanted action and everything else that threatened to ruin this moment. In-

stead she focused on the famous author. To think
of the things he had seen and done! And then to
have written about them so clearly, so feelingly. If
she could but possess a half—a quarter—an
eighth of his talent.

She didn't say that when she was actually presented to the obviously not-completely-recovered
man of the hour, by a somewhat supercilious Lord
Fallston. She was too awestruck to say much of
anything, especially when Lord Bromwell kissed
her hand.

She didn't feel the thrill she experienced when
the viscount had done the same thing, or the
shock of disappointment when Lord Fallston had.
This time, she felt as if she'd received a benediction, from one author to another. He couldn't
know that, of course, but she felt it just the same.

"I enjoyed your book so much!" she said as he
regarded her studiously with his blue-gray eyes.
"Especially your descriptions of the storm—it was
as if I were on the ship with you. The pitch and
roll, the water washing over the side, the huge
waves, the howl of the wind! It was wonderful, my
lord, simply wonderful. And I don't think I'll ever
look at a spider quite the same way again, either."

Lord Bromwell smiled and continued to regard
her so steadily, it was easy to imagine him watching a spider's web for hours at a time. "I can tell
you mean that," he said, his voice surprising low
and rough for such a slim, well-educated young
man—a result of his illness, perhaps. He smiled a

little wistfully and slid a glance at his father, who was busily bragging to another guest. "I'm afraid not everybody who claims to have liked my book has actually read it."

Diana dared not look at Lord Fallston, who had been captured by the earl. The nobleman was loudly telling him the number of copies *The Spider's Web* had sold in Yorkshire.

Lord Bromwell's attention was taken by something past Diana, and he broke into a truly happy smile.

"I will be delighted to talk to you some more in a little while, my lady," he said. "No author dislikes hearing his efforts praised. However, I must beg leave to be excused. I must speak to Lord Adderley at once."

She followed his gaze, saw the viscount looking wonderful in evening dress standing with his friends, then quickly turned her attention back to Lord Bromwell. "Of course," she murmured.

Lord Bromwell took a step forward, then hesitated. His steadfast, intense gaze searched her face, as if he could silently force her to confess her innermost secrets by that means alone. "I hope you won't believe what you hear about my friend. He's really a very sober, modest, scholarly fellow who happens to be handsome. It's my theory that because so many women find him attractive, people assume he must take advantage of his looks, which I assure you, he doesn't. What's more, I owe my career to him. He told me I'd be miserable if I didn't pursue my study of spiders—which was quite right—and I wouldn't have been able to complete my work if he hadn't contributed as much as he did to my expedition. I wanted to dedicate my book to him in gratitude, but he wouldn't hear of it, so now I must thank him in person."

In the next moment, he was gone, striding through the crowd toward the viscount, who was talking to Mr. Smythe-Medway and his friends near the door.

Diana felt as if the floor had suddenly tilted. The viscount was a sober, modest, scholarly fellow? Was Lord Bromwell a fool—or a friend of long-standing who could be counted on to know the truth?

Lord Fallston returned to her side. "My word, how the earl does go on," he muttered. "You'd think his son had discovered a new continent."

Diana ignored his complaint. "Did you know that Lord Adderley contributed significantly to Lord Bromwell's expedition?" she asked as she watched Lord Bromwell go up to the viscount and eagerly shake his hand.

"Who told you that?" Lord Fallston said, as if she'd been tricked by an obvious cheat at a fair.

She straightened her shoulders and her chin jutted out a little. "Lord Bromwell himself."

Fallston clearly realized he'd offended her, for he immediately became the personification of remorseful apology. "I beg your pardon, my lady. I had absolutely no idea Adderley had even kept in touch with Bromwell, let alone provided funds for his research."

She was spared replying because the earl of Granshire left his place and silenced the orchestra in preparation for making a speech.

Beaming, the vainglorious man's chest puffed out even more as he addressed the assembly. "My lords and ladies, I beg the indulgence of you all as I introduce my son, who has recently returned from his journeys to the acclaim he so richly deserves."

Lord Bromwell's scarlet face and downcast eyes proved that whatever his father thought, the man himself was far more modest about his accomplishments.

"I well recall my son's fondness for his studies even from his childhood, which naturally I, as a proud parent, was glad to indulge," the earl continued.

She noted that the viscount and his friends exchanged knowing and skeptical looks, telling her that the earl's memory of his early encouragement of his son might be less than accurate.

Yet Lord Bromwell had persisted—an admirable act, and one that, having embarked on a risky venture of her own (albeit less fraught with personal danger), impressed her more than it would have before she started to write.

As his father continued to speak in praise of his son, and Lord Bromwell continued to look embarrassed, Lord Fallston leaned close and whispered, "This might be the best time for a quiet conversation. Nobody will notice if we slip out onto the terrace now."

She'd forgotten all about his request, and was about to say she'd reconsidered when an unexpectedly stubborn look came to his eyes.

Perhaps it would be better to hear him out at once and get it over with. If that were so, this might be the best time. Like everyone else, her aunts were listening to the earl or watching Lord Bromwell and his companions.

They did make a rather attractive group—the lean, worn man of science, the dark-haired Hades who fairly emanated virility, the commanding naval officer, the arrogant barrister and their fair-haired jester.

She didn't want to take her eyes off them, either.

"If anyone notices, we can always say you needed fresh air," Lord Fallston murmured, mistaking the reason she lingered.

She glanced at him. "Or you did, my lord."

He smiled. "Very well, or I did."

Stifling a sigh, Diana eased backward, then outside. The cooler air was indeed welcome, but while it was refreshing, Diana wasn't dressed for a long discussion in the evening air. She hoped that whatever Lord Fallston had to say, he would be quick about it.

He started down the steps to a formal garden

laid out in a geometric pattern of squares and circles. She wavered, not wanting to get far from the ballroom.

"Don't you trust me?" he asked softly.

"Trust is not the issue, my lord. As you know, being alone with you isn't proper."

"I promise it won't be for long," he pleaded, "and I don't want to be interrupted by anyone. Please, my lady. Just for a moment? You'll be back before anyone realizes you're gone."

He looked absolutely harmless in the moonlight, and she got the distinct impression that if she didn't hear him out at once, he would persist in trying to get her alone all night. Better listen to him now, and be done.

She followed him, but once at the bottom of the steps, she said, "This is far enough, my lord."

He nodded. Then he drew a deep breath. "My lady, I adore you."

He went on in a rush before she could speak. "I hope you won't hold my views about your taste in reading against me. I was wrong to be so critical."

Suddenly, he went down on one knee, wincing as it hit the flagstones. "Diana, darling, I love you! You must make me the happiest man in the world by becoming my wife."

Instead of feeling the sort of things she imagined she would feel when—and if—a man ever proposed to her, she felt ridiculous and annoyed. He looked like a fool down on one knee, and more importantly, what had made him think she would welcome his rather imperious request? She *must* make him happy? She *must* be his wife, when she'd given him no encouragement at all? Why, they barely knew one another. She knew more about Lord Adderley than she did about him. "Get up, my lord."

"I would gladly worship at your feet forever!"

She refrained from pointing out the obvious constraint that would put upon his future existence. "I don't want you at my feet." *Or anywhere else.* "Please, my lord, get up before somebody sees us."

He did—and then he threw his arms around her and swooped down to kiss her with his lips tight, his mouth firmly closed, as if he'd never kissed a girl in his life.

"My lord!" she cried, aghast, as she shoved him back.

She *never* should have come outside with him! He had totally misinterpreted her acquiescence— and apparently everything else she'd done.

He blushed and looked down at the ground like a remorseful little boy. "Forgive me," he muttered. He raised his sorrowful eyes and reached out to grasp her hand. "But if you only knew how I feel—"

"After that demonstration, I believe I can guess. Now let us return to the ballroom."

He took hold of her hands and looked as if he

was about to burst into tears. "Please, forgive my impulsive kiss, my lady. I was carried away by my feelings."

"I forgive you. Now we must go back."

He went down on his knee again, grabbed her hand and kissed it fervently. "Oh, thank you, my angel, for your forgiveness. Thank you." He continued to hold her hand and kiss it until her glove felt damp.

This was truly ridiculous. "Please, my lord, let go of me."

"Good God, what have we here?" a man's voice demanded.

Diana's breath caught as she raised her eyes and stared at the viscount illuminated by the moonlight as he stood on the steps above them, as commanding as a general on the field of battle, yet sophisticated and elegant in black evening dress.

Lord Adderley crossed his arms, leaned his weight on one long leg and raised a lordly brow. "Am I to assume by this shocking behavior that the banns will soon be read?"

Oh, why, of all the people in the world, did it have to be Lord Adderley who saw them? Blushing furiously, she wished she could dematerialize like a ghost.

Meanwhile, Lord Fallston scrambled to his feet, obviously more angry than anything else. "The lady and I—"

"No!" Diana cried before he said another

word. She ignored a bleat of protest from Lord Fallston. "The banns are not about to be read."

"Not very pleasant being watched during an intimate encounter, is it?" the viscount noted.

She knew what he was referring to, but she wasn't going to confirm his observation.

"Allow me to point out, my lady," he coolly continued, "that unless you want people to assume that either you are affianced, or wish to be, or that you're a woman of very loose morals, you shouldn't kiss young men."

"I wasn't!"

"It certainly looked like it to me. There's nothing wrong with my eyesight and the moon is very bright tonight."

"Adderley, you have no right—" Fallston spluttered, finally finding his voice.

"I have every right to take a stroll in the earl's garden without having my moral sensibility assaulted," Lord Adderley interrupted.

"As if you possess moral anything!" Fallston scoffed.

The viscount looked at Diana with calm equanimity. "My lady, would you please excuse us?"

Diana looked from one—calm, commanding, sure of himself—to the other—hot-tempered, angry, possessive. "Gladly."

She marched up the steps.

But instead of going back into the ballroom, she kept to the shadows and crept across the terrace until she was close enough to overhear their conversation. She was too curious about what the viscount intended to say to her erstwhile suitor to leave.

"I know what you're trying to do," Fallston charged the moment he thought they were alone, his voice low and full of venom. "You're trying to ruin my life! You've always been jealous of me! That's why you tried to kill me and—"

"For the hundredth time, Fallston, I didn't try to kill you at Harrow," the viscount replied. "It was an accident, and you couldn't have drowned in that shallow spot if you'd tried. And I assure you, I am not, nor have I ever been, jealous of you."

"Yes, you are! You were jealous of me at Harrow because I was better than you at Latin and Greek. And you're jealous of me now because of Lady Diana. She's worth ten of the sort of vain, silly creatures who are always trailing after you."

"I don't disagree."

Diana couldn't believe her ears.

"She does seem quite an admirable young woman," the viscount went on, "which means I'm rather mystified as to what she sees in you. Clearly, there must be something, or I daresay she would have slapped you when you presumed to kiss her."

"What we were doing is none of your business!"

"What if I had been her aunt, or one of those

meddling busybodies in the ballroom? What would have happened then? Did you ever stop to think of that?"

Lord Adderley had been worried about her reputation from the first. Surely if he really were a cad, her reputation—or the loss of it—wouldn't matter to him a bit.

"Nothing would have happened, because we're going to be married."

Diana gasped with dismay at Lord Fallston's confident retort, as if she couldn't possibly refuse him.

"You seem very sure of her affections, Fallston. However, I must point out that Lady Diana doesn't seem to share your conviction. If the woman I wanted to marry reciprocated that desire, I would expect her to have no qualms about saying so or allowing me to kiss her."

Diana was sure he was absolutely right about that.

"She *does* want to marry me, or as you are so good to point out, she wouldn't have let me kiss her."

Diana wanted to howl in protest.

"Did she? It looked like she was pushing you away to me."

"Yes, yes, mere maidenly modesty, which of course is something you know nothing about."

"You know nothing about *me*, Fallston. You never have. Like so many other people, you make assumptions based on very little evidence and then claim that's the truth—and invent your own 'truths,' too."

"I know what you did to me!"

"So do I," the viscount answered. "It was nothing much at all, although you've used it as an excuse to spread false accusations and rumors ever since. Don't you think it's about time you grew up?"

"Oh, yes, you'd like that, wouldn't you? The past all forgotten, your crime buried."

"*There was no crime*," Lord Adderley replied, for the first time sounding angry. "There was an accident, and I said I was sorry more than once to you, your mama, to anybody who asked me. Good God, man, what more do I have to do?"

"You could start by staying far away from me, and the woman I intend to marry."

"Is she to have no say in the matter?"

"Of course she is! Don't put words in my mouth."

Lord Fallston could protest all he wanted, but she'd seen the stubborn glint in his eyes, been subjected to his unwelcome persistence, heard his confident assumption. He did believe, without doubt, that she was going to be his wife, as if her opinion didn't matter in the least.

She held her breath as she waited to hear what the viscount would say next.

But his answer wasn't mocking, or sardonic or angry. He sounded thoughtful, like the scholarly young man Lord Bromwell claimed he was, and his question was completely unexpected. "Let's suppose you're right about her feelings and I'm wrong, do you think you can make her happy?"

He was concerned about her *happiness*? How many rakes and rogues cared about the future happiness of the women they were trying to seduce? If ever she wanted proof he wasn't a lascivious, selfish scoundrel, this was it.

Fallston straightened like a soldier on parade. "Yes, of course I can make her happy."

"Why do you think so?"

The softly spoken words hung in the air like dewdrops on a spider's web.

"I don't have to explain to you," Fallston muttered at last.

"No, you don't. But perhaps you should think about that. She's an unusual woman, Fallston. The rules that govern the normal sort of husband and wife relationship among the *ton* may not apply."

"What are you getting at?" Fallston's tone became even angrier. "If you're implying anything bad about her character, you—!"

"Not at all. It's *your* character I'm worried about."

Diana wanted to shout with triumph—and relief. Somebody was finally suggesting that Lord Fallston was not the perfect matrimonial prospect.

"There's nothing wrong with my character!" Fallston retorted. "And it's rather rich to hear *you* even dare to mention such a subject."

Lord Adderley ignored the mocking insult. "Are you sure you're worthy of her?"

Again, Diana was flabbergasted. The viscount was implying Lord Fallston wasn't worthy of *her*, when Aunt Calliope was doing all she could to ensure that Diana seemed worthy of *him*.

It was a delightful difference.

"Why wouldn't I be?" Fallston retorted. "I'm titled, I'm wealthy, I want her. What more could she desire?"

"I can think of a few things."

So could Diana, and the viscount's words made the most delicious shiver run down her spine, while the most amazing visions popped into her head, all of them featuring Lord Adderley.

"This is ridiculous!" Fallston declared. "Who I do or don't marry, and who Lady Diana does or does not marry, is none of your business. You're just doing this to upset me. Why can't you leave me in peace?"

"I've left you in peace for over ten years, Fusty. It's you who keeps bringing up the past and reminding everybody of a schoolboy prank that should have been forgiven and forgotten long ago."

With a muttered oath, Lord Fallston pushed past the viscount and hurried up the steps.

He would be looking for her back in the ballroom. Her aunts might be wondering where she was, too. She had better go inside.

Despite those possibilities, she hesitated, and as

she did, the viscount exhaled a sigh that seemed to hold the sorrow of the ages before he swiveled on his heel and strode up the steps.

She pressed back against the dew-damp ivy, making it rustle.

Lord Adderley checked his steps.

She sucked in her breath and tried not to move a muscle.

It didn't work. He turned toward her and marched right up to her without hesitation, then he barred her way like a sentry at Buckingham Palace.

For the second time that night, she wished she could disappear.

"So, my inquisitive young lady who insists she doesn't eavesdrop, are you pleased by what you overheard?" he demanded.

She flushed, but wasn't about to answer his question. "Is that true, about the prank? Was the water really shallow?"

If he was surprised by her question, he didn't show it. "At the place the punt sank, the river was about two and a half feet deep. You can ask any-body familiar with the place."

"Did you scuttle the punt on purpose?"

"No. Charlie didn't realize he'd torn off the strapping when he dragged it up on the bank the last time he'd taken it out for a row on the river at night."

"I suppose it was Mr. Smythe-Medway's idea to get Lord Fallston in the boat in the first place?"

"Whoever concocted the plan, I was the one who did the asking, so the fault for what happened, if fault there be, lies with me."

Her brow furrowed as she studied his handsome, impassive face. "Why, my lord? Why did you play the prank at all?"

He seemed to be struggling with something within himself before he finally answered. "Because he clung to us like a leech and kept offering us treats and money to be his friend. We were tired of him following us around all the time and insulting us with the implication that our friendship could be bought. He should have left us alone." He stepped forward, closing the space between them. "You seem very concerned about the man's feelings."

Refusing to be intimidated by his proximity—which she was sure was his plan—she continued to regard him steadily. "Because I feel sorry for him. Did it never occur to you that he might have been envious, or lonely, or simply desperate to be your friend?"

The viscount's brows lowered with puzzlement. "Lonely? Desperate for friends? He had scads of friends there."

"But not you and yours. I'm sure you were quite the merry band."

"He was a nuisance."

"Yes, I can understand that." Indeed, she certainly could. "Can't you try to understand him? He can't forgive you because you humiliated him.

How would you and your friends have acted had he played that sort of trick on you?"

The viscount crossed his arms. "I can tell you exactly. If Drury had a dunking like that, he would have crawled out on the bank, gone back to bed and never said a word about it. Charlie would have managed to steer the punt to shore somehow and Brix would have played a retaliatory prank the first chance he got. I would have been furiously angry and quoted passages from Homer about death and bloodshed at great, irritating length. But not a one of us would have accused the prankster of attempted murder and circulated nasty rumors for years afterward. Where do you think most of the tales of my many sins originate?"

Diana could easily believe his description of his friends' reactions and she could sympathize with his anger at Fallston's behavior, and yet she had to say, "Perhaps all this animosity could have been avoided if you'd acknowledged that you were in the wrong."

He stiffened, the vitality of annoyed impatience fairly pulsing from him, and his intense gaze once again locked onto hers. "My lady, even without the benefit of your perceptive explanation, I *have* tried to make peace with him. You heard me say I apologized. I did—many, many times, right afterward and then for days. So did Brix and Drury and Charlie.

"He wouldn't accept any apologies from any of

us. Instead, he accused us of trying to kill him, an accusation, I point out, he makes at fairly regular intervals to this day. He also tried to get all of us expelled from school. Drury nearly got sent to some godforsaken school in the wilds of Scotland. Charlie's stepfather whipped him within an inch of his life, only too glad to have an excuse. Brix lost a horse he'd been promised and, let me tell you, a gift from his parents was no common thing. He joked about it, but if you'd known how much he yearned for that horse . . ." He took a deep breath. "That's why we don't like Fallston."

He was so indignant for his friends' punishments, and yet from what she had heard about his own upbringing, she doubted he had been spared. "And you, my lord? How were you punished?"

She watched another silent battle wage within him and feared she had overstepped the bounds.

But then he told her. "During the next holiday, I was locked in my room every day with no books, no candle, no company, no clean linen. I had to live on bread and water, just as if I was in jail. That would show me the wages of my sin, my father said."

"I'm so sorry," she whispered, her heart welling with sympathy as she pictured him as a boy, suffering that horrible punishment, alone, and without even anything to read.

"You needn't look so upset, Diana. That experience may not have achieved what my father intended, but it did teach me to value my books and my friends even more."

He'd called her Diana. Not my lady, not Lady Diana, but Diana.

Even more miraculously, after the things he had endured, he spoke with little bitterness and no self-pity, as if those torments were simply his cross to bear.

It was true the past could not be changed, but what of the future? How long must he tolerate Fallston's spiteful behavior? "Yet after all this, my lord, you allow Lord Fallston to say whatever he likes about you. Why don't you make him stop?"

"What do you suggest?" he asked with a vestige of his usual mocking tone. "Cut out his tongue?"

"There must be *some* way."

He gave her a smile that didn't reach his eyes. "Since you persist, I'll confess that I won't give him the satisfaction of thinking he can upset me, in any way."

He was certainly a master of that. "Yet other people—"

"I don't care what people think of me."

"You should. And you seemed to care a great deal about what they say about me."

"While I appreciate your indignation on my behalf, our situations are not the same. I'm a rich and titled man. Whatever scandal attaches to my name, there will always be plenty of people willing to overlook it because of that."

She couldn't deny what he said, and yet . . .

"Do you really have any idea the sort of lies people are saying about you?"

"Yes, actually, I do, although I wouldn't be surprised to discover the most colorful tales don't reach my ears." He moved a little closer and when he spoke, the low timbre of his voice sounded like purring. "You seem to be a very intelligent woman, so I assume *you* know better than to believe everything you hear, even from your own esteemed relations."

Her blood thrummed through her veins, and a little frisson of excitement trilled along her nerves. "Of course I consider the source of the stories I hear. Unfortunately, other people don't."

He took another step forward, so that he was inches away. "Diana, my champion, I honestly don't care what most people say or think about me. If they choose to believe such things, let them. I only hope that *you* don't think badly of me."

She didn't know what to say, where to begin. Whatever she had thought of him before, she thought very differently now.

"Does this prolonged silence mean you don't believe everything you hear about me?" he murmured, reaching out to caress her cheek.

She wanted to say something, but her throat was dry and she could scarcely think of a reply that didn't end by throwing herself in his arms.

The clink of glasses near the French doors startled her and shattered the aura of isolation that had been surrounding them, as if they were miles away from anybody. Regrettably there were many other people nearby, people who might see them together. "We must go in."

"Not yet," he said, his intense gaze pinning her to the wall. He inched closer. "What about Fallston, then?"

What about him? At the moment, she could barely conjure up a mental image of the man.

But if she felt next to nothing for him—except anger that he could be so spiteful—should she tell Lord Adderley? Why? What could she hope for? He was still the handsome Lord Adderley who could probably have any woman in England, and she was still plain Lady Diana Westover who wanted to be a writer.

"I meant what I said to him, Diana," Lord Adderley said, dropping his voice to that low, intimate purr that made her body soft as silk. "I don't believe he's worthy of you, and I don't think he'll make you happy."

She was sure he wouldn't, either.

The viscount drew her into his powerful arms. "I believe I need to make my point somewhat more strongly," he whispered, "with a thorough demonstration of the difference between the way Fallston feels about you and the way I do."

In the next moment, his lips came to hers, softly seeking. This was no arrogant aristocrat sure that she must accept him, lunging like a hawk and nipping. This was the most wonderful, perfect kiss, from an amazing, passionate man.

An incredibly blissful relaxation stole over her as his mouth moved over hers, a sense that this was perfectly right and where she belonged. She gave herself up to the feeling, letting her mind drift along on waves of pleasure, warmed inside and out by his embrace.

He shifted, holding her close while he deepened the kiss. Willingly she parted her lips at the urging of his tongue. It slipped inside her mouth, thrusting, seeking and finding.

Not leisurely anymore. As a slack rope tightens when pulled, his yearning, anxious kisses pulled at something within her, creating a new and wondrous tension.

No longer was she aware of the possibility of discovery, the sound of glasses and muffled conversations, or the moonlight, or the music in the ballroom. All she knew was *him*—his lips, his mouth, his tongue, his touch, his body, lean and hard against her. She was willingly falling into an abyss, where all that mattered was being with him . . .

His hands moved gently over her body, skimming the silk of her gown as if it were her naked skin. She slid hers beneath his evening jacket, running her palms up the crisp linen of his shirt. Beneath, she could feel his muscles, taut and firm.

He gently pushed her back against the ivy. Then one hand came forward to cup her breast.

The shock of the new, overwhelming sensations brought her to her senses.

Breathless, she broke away, albeit as feebly as if she were drunk. In a way, she was, her mind lulled into bliss by his kisses and his touch. But she shouldn't be out here in the dark, kissing him. Kissing any man. What if somebody saw them? Her aunts. Lord Fallston. The viscount's friends.

She mustn't be with him, especially like this, no matter what she felt about him. Not even if she was falling in love—

The realization of the depth of her feelings for him struck her like the swipe of a saber—and so did her doubts.

What exactly did this man feel for her? Affection? Desire? Lust? Or something more?

And even if he sincerely cared for her, she couldn't forget the things her father had told her about the nobles of the *ton*. The loose morality. The adultery. The unfaithfulness. If she permitted herself to love this man, and he proved to be no different from the other men of his rank, her heart might shatter into too many pieces to be completely whole again.

"My lord," she stammered, trying to regain her self-possession, "we mustn't . . . that is, we shouldn't . . ."

"You aren't going to tell me you prefer being

kissed by a man who sees you only as a proper and suitable bride, not a man who desires you because you are a vibrant, passionate, fascinating woman?"

How could she? "No."

"Good."

Again his mouth found hers, only this time, there was a new and different urgency, something that tugged at her most basic desires, releasing primitive need from deep inside her. It throbbed through her body like the surge of the sea.

His hands caressed her and a host of new sensations danced along her skin, through her body, along her nerves, tingling down her spine. She clung to him, pulling him to her. She inhaled the scent of soap and starched shirt and felt the edge of his collar tickling her cheek.

He slipped his hand inside the bodice of her gown, his warm flesh against her softness. More anxious pleasure grew as his thumb brushed her hardened nipple until a moan escaped her throat.

"Shhhh," he murmured, his lips still on hers, reminding her again that they mustn't be caught like this.

Because no matter how she felt, or how he did, this was wrong.

She put her hands on his heaving chest to hold him away from her. "We shouldn't be doing this."

"Not in the earl of Granshire's garden during a reception, anyway."

Diana stared at him with disbelief. She'd just

had the most passionate, profound moments of her life, and he was making jokes? Did he feel so little, then? Was he indeed the sort of nobleman of the *ton* her father had detested, one who would never prove faithful?

Distraught, her eyes flashed fire. "I don't think that's at all amusing," she charged in a whisper as she pushed her way past him.

He hurried after her. "I didn't mean it to be funny!" he cried softly as she disappeared through the French doors.

He was about to follow, to tell her he was sorry for upsetting her, but caution checked his steps.

People would notice if he came inside directly after her, and wonder and speculate why Lord Adderley was in such hot pursuit. If he'd been almost any other man, they might simply have wondered if they had been alone together. Because of Fallston's lies about him, they would think he and Diana had definitely been alone, and that he'd probably seduced her in the garden.

If only he hadn't given that stupid response to her very genuine concern! But he'd been so happy and so full of desire, he'd said the first thing that came into his head.

He still didn't think they should have been kissing in the earl's garden. They should have been somewhere warmer, more comfortable and more private, where there was no danger of discovery.

In spite of that, he should have responded better to her reasonable distress, not sounded as if he took her fear lightly. Her loss of reputation was of great importance to him although, he had to admit, when she was kissing him and he was experiencing the most amazingly passionate moments of his life, that danger had not been uppermost in his mind. Hence, his inconsiderate answer, and he didn't blame her a bit for being upset.

Frustrated, wondering how he was going to get the chance to apologize to her—tonight, if possible—he walked toward the balustrade and leaned upon the railing, looking out over the earl's moonlit garden.

He could no longer deny that a powerful, passionate feeling for the bold, intelligent, sympathetic, incredibly arousing Lady Diana Westover had been steadily developing ever since that very first encounter in the Pump Room. It was as if she'd shaken the core of his heart, and he would never be the same again.

His life would never be the same again. If she were not in his life, he would have none at all.

Brix strode onto the terrace, spotted Edmond and made a beeline for him, coming to a halt with his arms akimbo. "Where the devil have you been?"

Smiling and trying to stifle ruminations about his relationship with Lady Diana lest he betray his feelings prematurely, Edmond faced his friend. "Right here, getting a breath of fresh air."

"You were *supposed* to be saving me from Fanny Epping."

"Oh, gad, I'm sorry. I forgot."

Brix fixed Edmond with a suspicious stare. "Who were you with out here? Miss Foxborough wasn't invited. I asked Buggy."

Edmond gestured at the terrace. "Do you see any women here?"

His friend frowned, as serious as Edmond had ever seen him. "You're acting very odd these days, Edmond."

Edmond wasn't about to try to explain his feelings or what had just happened with Lady Diana, not even to Brix, not even if he wanted to.

"Too much reading, probably," he replied lightly. Then he grew serious. "Do you ever think that maybe if we'd been a little more lenient with Fallston back at Harrow, he might not have borne such a grudge all these years? Perhaps he was just desperate to be our friend and we totally humiliated him, at least in his eyes. You or I or the others might have reacted just the same."

"No, we wouldn't," Brix said without hesitation.

Brix was right. Although Lady Diana did have a point, she hadn't been there. And she wasn't the one who'd been living with Fallston's lies.

A young woman's dulcet voice drifted out of the closest French door. "Have you seen Mr. Smythe-Medway?"

"Gad, that's Fanny searching for me," Brix said anxiously. "Are you going to help me, or not?"

Edmond clapped his hand on his friend's shoulder. "Of course I am. What else are friends for? But I stand by what I said before. I won't kiss Fanny in the garden."

There was only one woman in the world he wanted to kiss now, and it most certainly wasn't Fanny Epping.

Chapter 9

"Rodolpho!" Frantic with joy and relief, Evangeline ran down the hillside toward the lone man standing on the road and rushed into his welcoming arms. "Oh, Rodolpho, I was afraid I'd never see you again!"

He held her close. "I've been searching everywhere. Oh, Evangeline, did he hurt you? Are you injured?"

"I'm fine now," she said, clinging to him. "How did you find me?"

"I've been searching everywhere. When I got to the village nearby and told them I was looking for my fiancée and they heard me describe you, they got such a look! I knew they had something to tell me. It took me hours, until finally an old woman told me of the count and his castle. She told me to leave this place, that if he had taken you there, I should forget about you. But I wouldn't. I couldn't. I don't care what he's done, my beloved Evangeline. All that matters is that I have you in my arms again."

"I escaped before he could do his worst," she whispered, looking up into Rodolpho's wonderful, open face, incapable of sly deceit. "We must hurry before—"

"Before I find some boy running away with my prize?" the count declared, appearing on the ridge like the embodiment of evil as his black cloak swirled about him.

　　　　　　　The Castle of Count Korlovsky

Aunt Calliope burst into Diana's room like a force of nature. "Are you still asleep?" she cried, horrified, as she halted at the foot of the bed.

Diana hoisted herself on her elbows and looked at her aunt with sleep-befuddled eyes. Although they had left the reception early when Diana had pleaded a headache, they had not arrived home until well after midnight. "What time is it?"

"It's ten o'clock," Aunt Calliope declared as she swiftly tugged open the drapes, letting the sunlight pour in. "You must get up at once! I'll send my maid to you. Hetty's faster than Sally, who's lollygagging in the kitchens, I have no doubt."

"I haven't rung for Sally yet," Diana said with a yawn. Indeed, two minutes ago, she'd been asleep, after finally dropping off some time after dawn.

She'd lain awake for hours contemplating what had happened with the viscount.

What he'd said.

What they'd done.

She refused to regret kissing him, or feel ashamed, or wracked with guilt. The experience would benefit her literary efforts, or so she told herself.

Despite that, it did gall her to think that she had been as foolish as all the other women who found the viscount titillating, and as vain as any of them if she believed that he found her attractive despite the evidence of her own reflection in a mirror, if only for a little while.

". . . so I told her you'd be down directly."

Diana forced herself to focus on her aunt, who was now bustling about the bedchamber like some sort of demented maid. Diana had to lean to the left to avoid being smacked by the hair brush Aunt Calliope tossed her way. "Who's downstairs?" she asked.

Aunt Calliope threw a chemise onto the bed. "Lady Ellis."

Diana had no wish to see Lady Ellis this morning, or her son. Especially her son. "Lord Fallston is waiting, too, then?"

"No. She came without him."

Diana sighed with relief.

Aunt Calliope whirled around, a pair of Diana's stockings in her hand. "What are you doing still in bed? Get up! Get up!"

Since she really had no choice, Diana scrambled out from under the covers. "I take it this visit is significant?"

"Significant?" Aunt Calliope cried, throwing her hands—and the stockings—into the air. "It's momentous! Lady Ellis hasn't paid a morning visit in years! And to think, she's come *here*. To see *you*. And you're still abed!"

Her aunt's maid, the gaunt, fifty-three-year-old Hetty, appeared, mercifully putting an end to Aunt Calliope's exclamations. She quickly set about getting what Diana required while Aunt Calliope collapsed into the chair by Diana's dressing table.

"He's going to propose, of course," Aunt Calliope declared, fanning herself with her hand and wiping her brow with the edge of her scarf. "That's what this means. His mother is making an effort for that reason, I'm absolutely certain."

In that case, Lady Ellis was going to be disappointed, for her effort was in vain. She wasn't going to marry Lord Fallston. Still, there was no reason her disappointment had to be today, especially when she—Diana—was so tired. The last thing she needed this morning was a conversation with Lady Ellis about her son. "I would rather not be home to anybody today."

"That's what comes of all this gallivanting about," Aunt Calliope charged, as if she were not the one constantly encouraging Diana to go out and attend any and every social function possible. "I'm sure you'll feel better after you've had some tea. Or perhaps some smelling salts will help."

"Just the tea, please," Diana quickly replied. She addressed Hetty. "Please ask Sally—"

"You can have your tea with Lady Ellis."

Diana stifled another sigh. Apparently nothing

short of a life-threatening illness was going to be considered a suitable excuse to remain in her room. Well, what couldn't be helped had best be endured with as good a grace as possible, her father always said.

So Diana soon found herself sitting in the drawing room, very hungry because she hadn't had anything to eat since yesterday's dinner, but looking well enough turned out to suit Aunt Calliope, given the time constraints.

Opposite her, Lady Ellis perched on the edge of the gold brocade sofa, rigidly upright, as if her stays were made of iron. Aunt Calliope sat nearby, just as upright. Only Aunt Euphenia seemed remotely at ease.

Lady Ellis fixed her stern gaze upon Diana as if she was about to examine her for entrance to an exclusive academic institution.

Despite her mien, Diana greeted her politely. "Good morning, Lady Ellis. A fine day, is it not?"

It could not be said that Lady Ellis's response was a model of good breeding, for she immediately launched into the purpose of her visit. "It is not my habit to prevaricate, so let me be blunt, Lady Diana. My son likes you."

Diana slid a surreptitious glance at her aunts. Aunt Calliope looked both petrified to move and anxious to speak, while Aunt Euphenia appeared utterly calm and only slightly surprised.

"It's my understanding he wishes to marry you."

It suddenly occurred to Diana that she hadn't definitely refused Lord Fallston's proposal last night. Her words could have been considered a refusal to admit only that the banns were not about to be read, not that they *never* would. Otherwise, she had been too concerned about being seen with Lord Fallston and his unwelcome, impetuous embrace to refuse in a way that left no doubt that he should not continue to believe she would accept him.

That was her error, in a way, so the kind thing to do would be to speak to him first, in person, to tell him his suit was hopeless, not send word by his mother, who didn't seem like the most sympathetic woman in Bath. "We are not yet formally engaged."

The woman's eyes narrowed. Meanwhile, Aunt Calliope started to fidget as if she had bugs down her back.

"I know for a fact that my son wants to marry you and if he hasn't asked you yet, he will very soon. I, however, have some reservations. Your father's mental condition—"

Despite Lady Ellis's brusque manner, Diana had harbored some pity for what the woman might feel when her son's offer of marriage was refused; that pity disappeared the moment Lady Ellis implied that there was something wrong with her father's mind. "My father was perfectly sound in mind and body until his final illness, Lady Ellis."

"I had heard—"

"What must have been idle gossip, rumors and speculation." Diana smiled in a way that would have been a warning to a more perceptive person. "I can procure a letter from the physician who attended him and our solicitor, if that would set your mind at ease," she went on sweetly, although she had absolutely no intention of doing so.

"I also understand all your father's property, with the exception of his Lincolnshire estate that was part of your mother's dowry, is entailed to a distant relative," Lady Ellis continued.

Diana's annoyance at the woman's incredible audacity grew, as did her appreciation for Lord Adderley's ability to ignore what people said about him. She was finding it impossible to keep a rein on her temper. "Although I have no idea how you came by such knowledge, those details are none of your business, my lady."

"I don't agree with the notion of entailing property only to male heirs, unless there is a problem with the female who is to take possession upon one's death."

The implication was unmistakable. Lady Ellis was wondering if her father had not trusted her judgment and so settled the estate on her distant cousin.

Diana's rage burned hotter, yet again she smiled. "You seem very sure that I will accept your son's offer of marriage."

This time, Lady Ellis seemed to get the hint that Diana's smile was not necessarily a good sign. It had obviously never occurred to her that Diana might refuse her son's hand, or that she wouldn't immediately divulge her financial situation. "You speak very boldly for one so young."

"I speak as I am spoken to, my lady."

Lady Ellis's already narrow, beady eyes narrowed even more. "Disturbing rumors have also reached me concerning you and Lord Adderley."

Aunt Calliope was fidgeting so much, she looked about to launch herself into the air, but she remained silent, even when Diana coldly said, "I'm surprised you pay heed to idle gossip, my lady."

"It is not idle and not gossip. Several people have seen you speaking to him."

Diana inclined her head in acknowledgment. "I have no doubt been seen speaking to your son, too. Do people suspect he's trying to seduce me, as well?"

Lady Ellis gasped, Aunt Calliope squeaked in protest, but Aunt Euphenia stifled a smile.

Lady Ellis's lips thinned. "If you think Lord Adderley's attention to you is flattering, it is not. He has paid attention to you only because he knows that would upset my son, and I must tell you, an insult to my son is an insult to *me*."

Apparently the viscount's actions were aimed at everybody *except* her. "How does the viscount know about your son's feelings? It's my understanding they're not on friendly terms."

"No, they are not—and with good reason."

"Very good reason, I should say."

That deepened the frown on the woman's face. "Be that as it may, it's quite clear my son wishes to marry you."

"Then I am surprised he didn't accompany you this morning."

Unexpectedly, the woman's demeanor softened. "He doesn't know I've come." She swallowed and sat up even straighter. "I'm sure my son will soon reveal his intentions, and I wanted to warn you that if you do not cut the viscount, he may reconsider."

Diana wasted a brief moment wondering why Lady Ellis was so keen to promote the match if she had such serious reservations about the potential bride, until she realized that what Lady Ellis thought about anything—and her most of all— was utterly immaterial.

She rose and gestured toward the door. "Thank you for coming. Good day, my lady."

If Lady Ellis thought her dismissal rather sudden, she made no sign. Her lips twitched again in what passed for a smile as she got to her feet. "I'm delighted we have reached an understanding, Lady Diana."

With that, she swept out of the room, while Diana sat heavily on the sofa. The only understanding she'd reached was that she wanted nothing whatsoever to do with Lady Ellis and her son ever again.

Aunt Calliope jumped up and hurried to her.

"Oh, Diana, how could you say such things? Why wouldn't you want Lord Fallston for a husband? Isn't he nice? And charming? And good-looking? What more could you want?"

Excitement. Passion. Independence, or at least as much as possible. Respect.

A man who likes books so much, he'll pay double the price for one he particularly wants. A man who has suffered and hasn't become vindictive and bitter. A man who needed her love.

She could never marry Lord Fallston, just as Aunt Calliope would probably never understand what she sought in a husband. Even Aunt Euphenia, who was sympathetic to her, might question her niece's quest for excitement, passion and independence. Passion and excitement hadn't made her life easy.

When Diana didn't answer, Aunt Calliope's expression grew determined. "My dear, let us speak frankly. I couldn't love you more if you were my own daughter, but there is no denying that you are not a beauty. And you have certain defects of character that do not make it easy to attract a man."

"Calliope," Aunt Euphenia warned.

Aunt Calliope swiveled and glared at her, then spoke with a fervent fierceness. "You can't deny that what I'm saying is the truth." She faced Diana again. "I don't say this to be cruel, Diana, but honest. Nor do I blame you."

"No, I can't help how I look."

Aunt Calliope flushed. "It's Cyril's fault. He shouldn't have kept you secreted away in Lincolnshire all those years. He should have allowed you to be more in society, to give you some manners and polish and—"

Diana sprang to her feet, all her passionate pride roused. She could endure hearing her own faults listed. She knew she was not pretty, that some of her opinions seemed outrageous and that she was too outspoken. But she would not sit idly by while her beloved father was disparaged, especially this morning, after the visit from that horrible woman and a sleepless night spent wondering if Lord Adderley truly admired her and found her attractive, or if he was only using her to upset Lord Fallston.

"I'm *glad* he raised me that way," she declared. "This society you're so fond of is nothing but a collection of shallow hypocrites. They don't even look at each other when they talk! They look beyond, to see who else of more consequence might be nearby. All they do care about is clothes and carriages and fine houses and money, and marriages that will give them more. When they speak of love, they don't mean a genuine emotion. They mean a sport, a game, a physical act. There is no sincerity, no trust, no love. And yet this is the society whose opinion is supposed to matter to me. These are the people I'm to try to impress.

"Either I will just as I am, or I will not. I really don't care which!"

With that, she turned and strode from the room, slamming the drawing room door behind her. She hurried up the stairs, brushing past the startled footman whose visage told Diana she probably looked like a hysterical female, something that upset her in a different way. She'd always prided herself on being able to maintain some semblance of calm.

By the time Aunt Euphenia joined her a few minutes later, she was seated by her dressing table, cool and composed, or at least outwardly so.

Aunt Euphenia toyed with a silver-handled hairbrush while surreptitiously studying her. "I'm sorry if we've upset you, Diana."

"I'm sorry I lost my temper," she replied, meaning it. She shouldn't have let Lady Ellis bother her so much, and her aunt's opinion as to her faults, or those of her father, was hardly new.

Aunt Euphenia left the brush alone and looked down at her niece. "Like most mothers, Lady Ellis assumes her son must be the apple of every young woman's eye."

"He's not the apple of mine," Diana replied, keeping her tone light, but determined.

"So I gathered," Aunt Euphenia said with a wry smile. "Poor Calliope must learn to bear her disappointment, too, as must he."

"Sometimes I think I'd rather be a spinster than get married," Diana confessed with a sigh as she unnecessarily rearranged her toilet articles. "Finding a husband seems such a troublesome, upsetting business."

"I fear we dwell too much on the mercenary aspects these days, my dear," Aunt Euphenia replied as she watched her. "There are other things to consider that make marriage something to be sought, or at least not dismissed completely. Some parts of the first few months of my marriage were very pleasant indeed."

Diana stopped rearranging things and looked at her aunt, surprised by this unexpected revelation. Aunt Euphenia colored, then went gamely on. "It was only afterward, when I realized Donald had no head at all for money and seemed to truly believe it would spring from the ground if he wished hard enough, when I understood that he loved to gamble more than he loved me, that our lives became a misery."

Diana rose and went to the window. It wasn't easy for Aunt Euphenia to broach this subject, and Diana appreciated the effort, and the concern for her welfare and happiness that had caused her to raise it.

She ran her hand down the edge of the sea-green velvet drapery. "I thought you said you didn't really love him, either."

"In hindsight, no, I didn't," Aunt Euphenia replied as she joined her, looking out into the street.

Aunt Euphenia was usually well spoken, but her next few comments came awkwardly, be-

speaking her reluctance to discuss intimate matters. "However, Diana, there are some experi-
ences that, even without a true emotional
commitment, can be enjoyable. I imagine that
with an emotional commitment, they would be
even better. That is not something to be dismissed
out of hand, especially if the prospective groom's
mother is the biggest problem between you."

How much Diana wanted to be honest with
her, about Lord Adderley and Lord Fallston and
everything else, but she feared that if she spoke
about the viscount and what had happened between them, she might upset her aunt a great deal.

She could be honest about her feelings for Lord
Fallston, though. "I don't love Lord Fallston, and
I'm surprised he thinks I care enough about him to
accept a marriage proposal. I've been pleasant to
him, but no more. I also don't believe I could ever
be the type of wife that would best suit him."

Aunt Euphenia visibly relaxed. "Thank you for
being so honest with me, my dear. If that is the
way you feel, no, you shouldn't accept his proposal." She smiled sympathetically. "I must confess the thought of having Lady Ellis for a
mother-in-law seemed rather daunting."

Diana breathed a sigh of relief. Aunt Calliope
would undoubtedly take longer to get over her
disappointment, but if she had Aunt Euphenia on
her side, she could better bear her other aunt's ex-
pressions of dismayed disappointment.

"However, perhaps you should modify your

behavior a little, in some circumstances," Aunt Euphenia reflected. She raised her hand for silence before Diana could respond. "I don't mean you should change what you think, only that you should learn to make your comments in more acceptable form."

Aunt Euphenia regarded the miniature of Diana's father that she kept on the table beside her bed. "I loved your father very much, Diana, but there is no denying that in some ways, he did you a disservice by raising you as he did. Unless you want to live like your father did, in relative isolation, you should have been exposed to society, and the people who comprise it, earlier on. As the daughter of a duke, you should have mixed among the rank to which your birth consigned you, so that you would have been prepared when it came time to think of marriage."

Diana picked at the hem of her sleeve. "Perhaps I should have stayed in Lincolnshire."

Then she never would have met the viscount. Her life would be what it was. Safe. Secure.

Bland. Dull. Lonely.

"Is there nothing about Bath you would miss?" Aunt Euphenia asked gently.

Diana slid her a sidelong glance and wondered what had prompted the question. "What do you mean?"

"There is nothing here you have enjoyed? The play? The concerts? The balls? Encountering a certain viscount in the bookshop and the theater?"

Diana sucked in her breath and flushed, feeling as guilty as a child caught stealing sweets from the dinner table. "I didn't think you knew about that," she confessed without thinking.

She looked at her aunt, fearing to see anger and a loss of trust, but instead she encountered her aunt's usual serenity. "You should know that Calliope hears everything, one way or another. She told me."

Diana wondered why she was just discovering this now. It would have been more likely that Aunt Calliope would have railed at her immediately after learning of these events. The fact that she hadn't, and Aunt Euphenia's calm, rallied her spirits. "I would have told you if there was anything you needed to be concerned about," she said. "I didn't mean to upset you."

Aunt Euphenia gave her a little smile. "I'm sure you didn't, just as I'm sure you're innocent of any improper behavior, which is what I told Calliope and why I asked her not to chastise you. I also said I was quite sure these encounters were merely coincidences, and that you were too sensible to encourage him." Her expression clouded with a pain that added to Diana's guilt. "I am right, am I not, my dear?"

Remorsefully grateful that they didn't know about her private encounters with Lord Adderley, telling herself there really was nothing to worry about, Diana still couldn't meet her aunt's steadfast gaze. "Although I haven't encouraged him,

I'm beginning to think the viscount has been misrepresented."

"Oh, Diana!"

Diana raised her eyes to regard her distraught aunt. Perhaps she shouldn't have said even that much. Yet she wanted Aunt Euphenia to know that some things said about Lord Adderley were not necessarily true. "It's possible he's not as bad as they say, isn't it? Gossip exaggerates things, and then rumors grow. Isn't it possible he's a finer man than we've been led to believe?"

With a look of anguish in her eyes that tore at Diana's heart, Aunt Euphenia took her niece's hands in her warm grasp. "Anything is possible. It's possible that my usually levelheaded niece has been swayed by a handsome young ne'er-do-well's attention. It's possible she's fallen in love with such a man. It's even possible she might do something truly foolish, like elope with him. It's *very* possible she might live to regret a young woman's infatuation."

"Aunt Euphenia, I'm not planning on eloping with the viscount, or letting him seduce me," she said firmly. Indeed, she wasn't planning on having anything more to do with him, a vow she was determined to keep this time.

"I didn't plan on such a thing, either, once upon a time, but believing oneself in love has a way of making the impossible plausible." Aunt Euphenia looked straight into her niece's eyes. "I don't want you to make the same mistake I did."

Diana embraced her. "I know, Aunt Euphenia, I know. I won't. I give you my word of honor as the daughter of the duke of Dilby that I won't let Lord Adderley seduce me, and I won't elope with him. There is nothing between us."

From this moment on.

Horror-stricken, Lord Fallston stared at his mother, who was seated at the far end of the gleaming walnut dinner table set with bone china, crystal and shining silver. Two candelabra and a centerpiece stood between them, so he was really glaring at the top of Lady Ellis's head.

"You did *what*?" he demanded, ignoring the footmen standing behind him and his mother, the servant serving them and the maid waiting by the door.

"I went to see Lady Diana this morning to make sure she realized she might be injuring her chances with you if she didn't cut the viscount," Lady Ellis repeated.

Fallston hit the table with his fist and swore.

His mother's stentorian voice, which would have stood a drill sergeant in good stead, rose. "Crispin, that language belongs in the gutter, not my dining room."

The knuckles of his clenched fist whitened. "You shouldn't have done that, Mama."

She continued to eat her roast mutton with perfect calm. "I did it for your sake, Crispin."

"Has it escaped your notice that I'm twenty-six years old? I can look after myself."

"Of course you can."

"I mean it, Mama. You didn't have to interfere." He swore again. "What must she be thinking?"

"Language, Crispin, language. I'm sure she's thinking that your family is not to be trifled with."

He began to ball his napkin in his left hand. "Or I'm not man enough to handle my own affairs and so must send my mama as my emissary."

"Really, Crispin, there's no need to get overwrought. The meeting went quite well. I'm absolutely convinced she will cut Lord Adderley completely the next time she sees him."

"What did you say to her about Adderley?" he demanded through clenched teeth.

"Modulate your tone, Crispin. I merely said enough for her to understand that if she paid any heed to him, she might be jeopardizing her chances with you. I'm sure you have nothing to fear from the viscount now."

"I've never been afraid of him," Fallston retorted.

"You know what I mean. He won't interfere in your courting of Lady Diana."

Fallston eyed his mother suspiciously. "You seem very anxious to promote the match."

She took a sip of wine before answering. "I

want to see my son happy, and you've given every indication that Lady Diana is your choice."

"She is—but I still don't understand why you're being so helpful."

"She *is* a duke's daughter, and a wealthy one."

Another suspicion entered his head. "Mama, did you ask her about her inheritance?"

His mother attended to her mutton. "As a matter of fact I did, and she was not at all forthcoming. So I asked our solicitor, who knows her solicitor, and he assures me that while the bulk of her father's estates were entailed, her fortune is not meager. It's not as large as I would like, but adequate. Therefore, if you decide to marry her, you will have my blessing."

"If I marry Lady Diana Westover, it won't be for her inheritance."

"I know that, dear, but one of us must be practical."

Fallston picked up his fork and began to eat again, chewing slowly and methodically.

No, he didn't want Lady Diana for material gain. He had quite another reason, one that his mother might never understand, but any man of pride would.

Chapter 10

Looking around the dank, dark cell illuminated by the moonlight, Evangeline shivered and nestled closer to Rodolpho.

"Don't be afraid, my love," he murmured as he, too, surveyed their grim surroundings. "We will find a way to escape."

"I'm not afraid of anything, now that you are here," she said. "If we can but open the door, I know a way out of this dungeon. I found it before when I tried to escape the count. We must go up and through the tower. The other way will be guarded."

Rodolpho gazed down at her, smiling. Then he bent his head to kiss her, his lips brushing against hers gently. "How I love you, Evangeline," he murmured as he held her close. "Even these circumstances cannot dim your spirit."

The Castle of Count Korlovsky

Partly hidden by a conveniently placed potted fern, Edmond stood near the corner of the upper assembly room, where a fancy dress ball was already underway. From this vantage point, he could watch Lady Diana without being seen by her aunts.

It had been over a week since the reception at the earl of Granshire's and, incredibly, he hadn't seen Diana since. Not in the Pump Room, the library, the concert featuring a very thin alto and very plump soprano, on the street or in Sydney Gardens.

He couldn't loiter around Laura Place all day hoping to see her, so he had kept his ears open for mention of her name. Once he'd even ventured to ask Brix if she'd left Bath altogether. His mama thought not, and he'd never dared to ask again, lest he raise suspicions in Brix's mind that something of a more serious nature was developing between him and the lady. Until he could be certain he hadn't ruined his chances with Diana, he didn't want to say anything, not even to his best friend.

How lovely Diana looked tonight! She wore a gown of rich burgundy velvet, with cap sleeves and long white gloves. The dress was cut to leave the nape of her slender neck and a wide expanse of her back exposed. Her hair was done up on top of her head, and a simple, yet elegant, ostrich plume of matching burgundy, along with some gold ear bobs, were her only ornamentation.

Lady FitzBurton, dressed in the height of fashion, appeared to be giving a running commentary on the company, while Lady Harbage's gaze darted about the room like a hawk seeking a mouse. Or a woman guarding her beloved niece.

At least Fallston was nowhere in sight, giving Edmond the hope that not only wasn't he coming, he'd realized he had no chance of obtaining Diana's hand in marriage. Also mercifully, Adelina Foxborough, who'd barely left his side all evening despite his less than enthusiastic attitude, was being distracted by a bevy of soldiers, resplendent in scarlet and gold braid. That left him free to indulge in speculation and watch Diana, his heart beating like a war drum or as if he were a schoolboy again.

He instantly recalled the heated desire that had coursed through him when he had kissed her and felt the soft weight of her breast in his hand. Even better had been her gasp of pleasure and the sensation of her relaxing against him as he brushed the pad of his thumb across her pebbled nipple, hard beneath the fluid fabric of her gown.

Simply watching her from afar wasn't enough. He wanted to be near her, to speak to her, to listen to her fascinating, unexpected answers spoken in her lovely voice. He yearned to touch her, kiss her, take her in his arms and hold her close. He ached to whisper endearments in her ear while uncoiling her beautiful hair and running his fingers through the thick cascade.

Most of all, though, he wanted to be alone with her and tell her how he felt about her. Somehow.

What would happen if he simply walked up and asked her to dance?

Her aunts would be annoyed, but that would be nothing if Diana accepted. It would not be nearly as good as meeting with her in private, but for tonight, it might have to do.

He glanced at Adelina Foxborough, who happened to look at him at the same time. She gave him a brilliant smile and was clearly expecting him to ask her to dance, despite the group of soldiers gathered around her.

If he didn't, what would she think? More importantly, what would she say, to anybody who would listen, about his dancing with Lady Diana Westover? Somehow, he didn't think it was likely to be flattering.

Then the Honorable Brixton Smythe-Medway arrived in the room. He smiled genially to everyone and casually strolled toward Edmond's hiding place. Edmond didn't think Brix had seen him; by his attitude he was simply walking around the room enjoying the sight of so many pretty, well-dressed women, especially Adelina Foxborough.

A plan popped into Edmond's head and the moment Brix was in range, he darted out from behind the plant. "Brix, what a pleasant surprise!" he cried as if they hadn't seen each other for years.

Brix gave him a befuddled look, which grew more befuddled as Edmond pulled him behind the plant.

"What the devil's going on?" Brix demanded. His eyes narrowed. "What's in the punch?"

"The usual," Edmond answered. "Listen, Brix, old friend, you remember how I assisted you with Fanny the night of Buggy's reception?"

"Finally. Thank God her family's gone back to London, or I'd have to go into permanent hiding."

"Well, tit for tat. Tonight I want *you* to help *me*."

Brix's brows shot up. "Oh?"

"Engage Adelina Foxborough for the next dance, will you, if one of those soldiers doesn't? They all seem too stunned by her beauty to do much more than stare. I tell you, I'm really beginning to fear for the state of our military."

His friend was not amused. "Why do you want me to dance with Miss Foxborough?"

"I'm going to ask Lady Diana. If you dance with Miss Foxborough, she won't be looking around for me."

Brix put a finger between his neck and his cravat and tugged as if the knot was too tight. "So you still mean to bother Lady Diana? I thought you'd given that up."

"I'm *not* bothering her," Edmond replied. "I daresay it'll be a thrill for her to be asked to dance by somebody who actually knows how. Fallston's a clod and I haven't seen any other young man asking her."

Both of these explanations were perfectly valid. Brix, however, still looked doubtful. "You seem very excited by the prospect of dancing with her."

A silent alarm sounded in Edmond's head. He was betraying too much of his feelings, so he gave his friend a charming smile. "I enjoy dancing."

"You know I don't, particularly. Besides, Miss Foxborough barely knows I exist. She wouldn't notice me at all if I weren't your friend."

Edmond couldn't refute that. "Then it's time to make her notice you, isn't it?"

Brix frowned. "What, are you setting me up to compete for her? If so, I won't take that bait. I wouldn't stand a chance, and I'd rather be spared the useless effort, thank you very much."

"It's just one dance, Brix," Edmond pleaded, trying to keep a rein on his growing frustration at the delay. "I only want Miss Foxborough to be engaged for the next little while, so I can dance with Lady Diana before Fallston shows up and makes a nuisance of himself. I'd ask Charlie or Drury if they were here, but Charlie's halfway to Plymouth by now, and Drury's left for London. Hell, I'd even ask Buggy, but he's ensconced in his laboratory with some new specimen of spider."

"I don't think you should ask her at all. In fact, I believe it's time you stopped your little game. According to Mama, people are already speculating about when Fallston will call you out."

Edmond's heart sank. "So soon?"

"Blame Lady FitzBurton. She claims you're out to ruin her niece's chances with Fallston." Brix regarded him with astonishingly serious speculation. "Are you?"

"Why would I do that?" Edmond asked, appalled.

"Because he's still telling people we're guilty of attempted murder."

"I don't give a damn about that," he replied, and he really didn't.

He *did* care about Diana's reputation, as well as his promise to Brix to cease and desist if it seemed his attention was going to cause trouble for her. He simply hadn't foreseen that what had started out as retaliation might turn into an entanglement, and one he didn't want to end. "The gossip's already begun, has it?"

"Mama is certain, and you know she spends hours gathering the so-called news about town."

Indeed, she did. Brix's mother had always been much more interested in the goings on among the *haut ton* than her own household. Brix had once joked—and not without a hint of hidden pain—that his mother knew more about the king's children than her own.

"You haven't forgotten your promise, have you?" Brix asked warily.

"Not at all."

"I hope this'll really be the end of it," his best friend replied, more serious than Edmond had ever seen him. "I don't like where this is going. End it, Edmond, before Lady Diana gets hurt."

Or he did, Edmond silently added, which would be the outcome if he couldn't convince Diana of the sincerity of his feelings.

Brix didn't give Edmond more of a chance to reply before he rolled his shoulders like a bareknuckle prizefighter preparing for a bout and strolled toward the swarm of officers surrounding Adelina, who was looking extremely lovely—and wealthy—in a silk gown of Nile green, with ropes of pearls in her hair and at her alabaster throat.

Edmond headed toward Diana and Lady FitzBurton soon spotted him. When she did, her expression couldn't have been more annoyed if he'd been coming to haul her off to prison.

Now determined to dance with Diana, he marched up to the small feminine group and bowed. "Lady Diana, would you please honor me with a dance if you are not otherwise engaged?"

Lady FitzBurton looked like she wanted him dead on the spot and would gladly pull the trigger if someone would but hand her a pistol. "My niece—"

"It's all right, Aunt," Diana murmured, her voice soft but her eyes alive with the bold, determined resolution that was so much a part of her. "I shall be happy to dance with the viscount."

He hadn't been so pleased to have a lady accept his offer of a dance since . . . well, ever.

Lady FitzBurton spluttered, and her sister didn't look particularly pleased, either, but he ignored them and held out his arm. Diana laid her hand lightly upon it, and he escorted her to the middle of the room where the line was forming for a reel.

"Have you been ill?" he asked as the music began and they circled each other.

"Not at all. I'm rarely sick."

"I haven't seen you anywhere."

"I've been trying to avoid you."

Dismayed by her blunt response, he didn't get a

chance to say anything more before they had to switch partners and he found himself dancing with a middle-aged woman who looked as if she couldn't believe her luck, until he grinned in a way that showed most of his teeth. She was as glad to leave him as he was to be rid of her when they returned to their original partners.

"You were avoiding me, my lady?"

"Yes. But I've decided that's the coward's way out."

Coward's way out of what? he wondered as they turned.

"I must speak with you tonight. Alone."

A host of possible reasons for her request ran through his head, from the mundane to the extremely titillating.

As they passed by one another again, she leaned closer and whispered, "Will you meet me in Sydney Gardens tonight? In the grotto by the willow? When the watchman calls two?"

He hadn't been this shocked since he had seen Fallston's punt sinking near the bank of the river. "You wish to meet with me in the middle of the night in Sydney Gardens?"

"Yes."

As tempting as it was—and it was *very* tempting—and as anxious as he was to speak to her alone, her suggestion was impossible. "It's too dangerous for a woman—"

"It's *necessary*. Will you be there or not?"

She didn't sound like a woman making an

assignation with a man she cared for. She sounded like a general issuing orders before a battle.

"Yes, I'll be there."

Pulling the cap down further over her face and holding the ill-fitting men's jacket tight about her, Diana flitted down Great Pulteney Street toward Sydney Gardens. She carried a lantern, its shutter open enough to allow a narrow beam of candlelight to illuminate her way. She wanted to be as invisible as possible, so that neither the watchmen nor any servants waiting by the door for their masters or mistresses still out upon the town would notice her.

The mist rising from the Avon had thickened in the chill of the night, just as she had hoped. She could barely see twenty feet in front of her, yet she was glad of the mist, for as long as she kept clear of the watchman, she should be able to come and go with relative ease and impunity.

Despite her serious purpose and the risk she was taking, her whole being was alight with excitement. This was so vastly different from what a lady was supposed to do—look decorative, embroider and gossip. It was undeniably romantic to be hurrying through the deserted streets in disguise.

She focused on how different everything sounded tonight, the drip from the houses more melancholy and the slightest sound more mysterious. Even the familiar seemed strange and forlorn.

She must remember this for that scene in her book. Evangeline wouldn't be running through the fog to meet the count, though. She would be running away, and her heart would be pounding with fear.

Evangeline would not have cobbled streets, either, but gorse and bracken and stones to stumble over, and she would have no lantern. The count would, and the beam of light could seem like his evil minion, seeking her out the way ferrets went after rats.

A black carriage rolled along the street, accompanied by a ragged linkboy, whose torch provided some additional illumination in the misty dark. The lamps beside the coachman's seat feebly flickered, and the driver was hunched over so much, she could easily imagine that he was asleep. Or dead.

In another few moments, the carriage and linkboy disappeared into the night as if the mist, like a living being, had swallowed them up. She shivered, both from the chilly damp and her own macabre thoughts.

Panting slightly, she slipped into the gardens unnoticed and, keeping off the gravel paths so that her footfalls would be silent, made her way to the well-remembered grotto beside the huge willow tree. She closed the lantern, shutting out the light, and shuffled her feet to try to keep warm without making a lot of noise.

Despite her discomfort, she didn't regret being

there. She had to speak to Lord Adderley where she would be sure they wouldn't be seen, or interrupted.

For a week, she'd tried avoiding him in the belief that would solve her dilemma. If she didn't see or hear him, she would be free of him, and the danger he posed to her equanimity. She'd thought being forced to stay home and not venture far would enable her to get more writing done, too, but she'd discovered that the opposite was true, and hiding from him only seemed to make her think about him more. She wondered where he was and what he was doing, and with whom. She continually thought of their conversations, the hidden meaning behind some of his statements, the looks he'd given her, the kisses they'd shared.

She'd tried to deny that she harbored any deeper feeling for him than a simple attraction to an attractive man. But as the days passed, she realized she wasn't being honest with herself. She did feel something more for the viscount than a fleeting admiration, and it wasn't lust. To be sure, physical desire was wound up in it, but there was more to her sentiments than that.

She cared about him, very much. She wanted to know what he felt about everything: his life, his friends, the things he'd endured, the things he wanted, the things he feared. She wanted to be a part of his world.

Sometimes, when she thought of their embraces, she could believe he felt the same and that he cared for her deeply. Yet other times, she was convinced he was doing so just to come between Lord Fallston and her.

She'd decided she couldn't go on wondering. Whatever he felt, she had to know.

To find out, she would reveal her feelings—or at least enough of them to gauge how sincere his were without compromising her pride.

If she couldn't, she would be no worse off, and she would make it clear that she was on to his game. She wouldn't let dread of him determine where she went or what she did anymore.

In the distance, a cat fight broke out, the mewling and caterwauling like something out of hell.

What if Lord Adderley was late? How long should she wait here in the darkness, frightening herself with visions that came solely from her own imagination?

She simply must try not to imagine too much. Or recall his kisses and his passion. If ever she needed to keep her wits about her, it would be tonight.

Footsteps sounded in the distance. A man's stride, if she wasn't mistaken. She peered out of the shadows, to see a lone man approaching.

It was the viscount. Even in the dark and fog, there could be no mistaking his athletic grace or aristocratic posture. He strode down the path like a king accepting the accolades of a grateful nation.

He halted and looked about in a leisurely fashion, taking his bearings before proceeding.

She didn't want to call out or open the lantern until they were in a more secluded place, so she crept toward him.

When she was a few feet away, he suddenly turned and lunged at her, grabbing her arms with a grip like tight lacings and holding her away from him. The lantern swung wildly, striking him in the arm, but he ignored it.

"I wouldn't try it, lad!" he warned, his voice low and stern.

"It's me," she gasped. "Diana."

He immediately released her. She opened the lantern shutters slightly and the candle flickered as she held it up so that he could see her face.

"Good God!" he whispered as he surveyed her in a way that made her feel half undressed. "What the devil are you wearing?"

She pulled the rough woolen jacket more tightly about her. "I thought it best to assume a disguise."

"*I* thought you were an urchin out to pick my pocket. Where did you get the clothes?"

"I borrowed them from my aunts' footman."

"Can you trust him not to tell them?"

"He doesn't know. I took them while he was sleeping." Diana turned to lead him toward the grotto. When they were inside, she set the lantern down and faced him. "They'll be returned before he misses them."

"They'll be wet."

"He won't need them till his half day anyway."

The viscount's lips turned up in a little smile. "You seem to have thought of every objection. Nevertheless, I feel duty-bound to note that if the watchman had come upon you, he probably would have thought as I did, that a lad dressed in such clothes in this part of Bath at night had a criminal purpose." He glanced at her chest. "On second thought, you wouldn't have fooled him as to your sex for long, my lady. Your disguise is most inadequate in some respects."

She felt herself blush and wished she wasn't. "A woman would attract more notice."

"I can't disagree with that, and if you had come in a gown and been discovered, the consequences might have been worse."

"Yes, if people found out I had come here alone at night, my reputation—"

"That isn't what I meant," he said, moving closer. "You might have been mistaken for something other than a pickpocket. As much as I want to be with you, this whole venture—" He stopped abruptly and put his finger to his lips.

Two voices drifted toward them, a man and a woman.

Fear gripped Diana. Despite the mist, they might have been spotted. The viscount might be right about people assuming she was a pickpocket or housebreaker, or they might recognize her.

She quickly closed the lantern shutter, grabbed the viscount's arm and all but dragged him further back into the grotto.

He said nothing as he stood close beside her. Very close. She held her breath as the couple drew nearer, her pulse loud in her ears.

Then she wanted to squirm, for the couple's conversation made the purpose of their visit to the gardens at this time of night, and in the dark, all too clear. Worse, they seemed about to complete their transaction under the nearby willow tree.

"I'm going to end this awkward situation before it goes any further," Lord Adderley said softly from his place beside her as he took hold of the lantern and pulled it from her grasp.

She opened her mouth to protest, but he had already left the grotto, ambling toward the couple beneath the willow. The woman had her back against the tree, and the man was close in front of her.

When the viscount was beside the tree, he halted and opened the lantern shutter wide, illuminating them.

Diana's first impulse was to look away, until she realized they had not yet gone far in their transactions.

"Well, bless my soul, is that you, Sissingsby?" the viscount inquired with his usual aplomb. "It's been an age."

The man drew back from the woman, who didn't seem to mind the interruption.

Diana stared. *This* was the man who'd stolen the heart of Lord Fallston's fiancée? His features had the bloated look of a habitual drunkard, and he obviously overindulged in food, too. His hat was on such a rakish angle, it was a wonder it hadn't tumbled to the ground, and his greatcoat was open, revealing rumpled evening dress.

"Who the devil are you?" Sissingsby demanded, clearly the worse for drink.

"Surely you remember your old school chum, Sissingsby. From Harrow."

"Adderley?"

"In the very flesh." The viscount eyed the woman. "I assume you've got your money already?"

She was slovenly dressed in a soiled gown that was too large for her thin figure. A threadbare shawl completed her wardrobe, and her wet hair coming down from its topknot indicated she had been out in the damp night air for some time.

Diana had never seen a whore before. According to Reverend Hamish MacTavish, she should be horrified that any woman would choose a life of sin. Yet as she studied the woman, she felt not revulsion or condemnation, but pity, and the compassionate certainty that no woman would freely seek out such a fate.

"I *ain't* got the brass," the harlot said. One

hand on her hip, she held out the other to Sissingsby. "Well?"

Glaring at the viscount, who made no move to leave, Sissingsby fumbled in his pockets. "Still playing everybody's mother hen, are you? I thought you were over that."

"Apparently not," Lord Adderley calmly replied.

After Sissingsby searched some more, without success, the viscount said, "What, all lost at the gaming tables again? Really, Sissingsby, I can't think what you're about. This young woman would have to come to your house to collect her fee, and how would you explain that to your wife?"

Sissingsby swore, and so did the woman, in terms that were most unflattering as to Sissingsby's physical development and potency.

"Shut up, you damned har—"

"That's no way to speak to a woman," the viscount said, his feet planted, his low voice filled not with the promise of passion, but with unmistakable menace.

Now he was indeed Count Korlovsky come to life—dark, powerful, frightening, the veneer of social polish completely stripped away to reveal the primitive warrior heritage beneath.

Yet there was one very important difference between Lord Adderley and her count: Adderley was using that power in defense of a woman, and a harlot at that.

"I won't," Sissingsby sneered. "She's nothing but a whore."

Lord Adderley's whole body radiated strength and the distinct possibility that he would employ it. "And you're a disgusting excuse for a man. Apologize, or so help me, I'll break your bloody arm."

He could and he would do it. Diana didn't doubt it for a moment.

Obviously neither did Sissingsby. "I-I'm sorry."

"Get the hell out of here."

Sissingsby obeyed, muttering curses at the viscount, the whore and women in general as he stumbled away.

Diana let out her breath, while the viscount retrieved the lantern.

Instead of fleeing the gardens as Diana expected, the woman moseyed up to the viscount, then ran her hands up his chest in a most suggestive manner. "Well now, sir, you've lost me some earnings. You're willin' to make it up to me, I hope."

The viscount removed her hands from his body. He reached into his jacket and held out some coins, which she snatched eagerly and shoved into the bodice of her gown. Diana was surprised they didn't fall right through to the ground, for she doubted the woman had on any undergarments.

"I suggest you retire for the evening," he said. "This weather can't be good for your health."

The woman laughed, a low, guttural sound that had no good humor in it. It seemed as hard as the life she must lead. "Is that all you're goin' to do? A fine gent like you, I don't mind earnin' it."

"I appreciate the offer, but I decline. Take yourself off, and I would steer clear of Sissingsby in the future."

"I will, and thanks." The harlot walked away, then paused and glanced back over her shoulder. "Callin' you a mother hen was a bit off the mark in some ways, but dead on, too," she said before she disappeared into the mist.

Diana silently agreed. The viscount's manner had been unmistakably kind and even gallant to the harlot, when he could have sent her on her way with a harsh word. He obviously played some sort of fatherly or brotherly role among his friends, too, as if he were years older than they were. Or perhaps it was only that he seemed older and wiser.

"I didn't think anybody would be here at this hour, for any reason," she said when he returned to her.

"Which demonstrates how little you know of life in Bath."

"If this were London—"

"Such things are certainly not exclusive to London." He set down the lantern again, crossed his arms over his broad chest and said, without any pretense of genial banter, "Now, my lady, why exactly have you asked me here?"

Lit from below by the feeble beam of lantern light, his angular face looked demonic. He was no supernatural being, though, but a man of flesh and blood. "I considered asking you to leave me alone."

After a long moment's silence that seemed to last an age, as her heartbeat thundered and her mouth dried, he raised one dark brow. "Am I bothering you?"

It was time to be honest—to a point. "You disturb me, yes. Our relationship—"

"We have a relationship?" He sidled a little closer.

She could discern nothing from his even tone, and his movement discomfited her. She could think better when there was more distance between them.

She stepped back. "Yes. No." She took a deep breath and silently berated herself. She sounded like a silly girl who didn't know her own mind.

She squared her shoulders and began again. "Although spinsterhood has certain advantages for a woman, I'd like to marry, to have a husband and children. My reputation will be tarnished if you persist in paying attention to me as you have recently, especially when I have my doubts that your intentions are honorable."

His eyes gleamed in the dark. "I must point out, my lady, that you started this relationship by studying me as if I were some kind of bug in a jar."

She flushed, but wasn't going to give up. "I don't know much about men and you seemed quite intriguing."

"*Seemed* quite intriguing? I'm not anymore?"

She didn't know what to make of the change in his voice, as if he was disappointed. "Well, yes, you're very interesting."

His devastating smile returned, and her heartbeat quickened in spite of her vow to remain composed.

"As a matter of fact, my lady," he said softly, "I find you intriguing, too."

Once before her heart had missed a beat or two, and it happened again, until her rational mind compared her to Adelina Foxborough. "I find that hard to believe."

His brow furrowed as he inched closer, so that his face was in shadow. "Why?"

She backed away. "Because I . . . I don't think I possess the necessary qualities and attributes to be attractive to a man like you."

"What qualities and attributes do you suppose I find attractive in a woman?"

She forced herself to think and ignore his proximity. The scent of tobacco. The whiteness of his shirt. The silhouette of his broad chest and shoulders. "Beauty, grace, accomplishments."

"I look for more than a pretty face and grace of movement, although you possess both. Playing the pianoforte or dabbling with watercolors and embroidering useless needlepoint items has never made a woman appealing to me."

He sounded completely sincere, and yet she was afraid to believe him. She was too different from the sort of women held up as paragons of what a woman should be. "Are these not the accepted criteria for a woman's personal worth?"

His voice dropped to a lower tone, one that made her knees feel like soft wool. "I learned long ago to distrust judgments made on appearance alone—at my father's knee, one could say. I admire intelligence. I tire quickly of a nitwit, and the ramblings that are the product of an uninformed mind." He reached out and touched the space between her brows. "You get a delightful little wrinkle here when you're deep in thought, which is more often than most young ladies of my acquaintance. You have a mind in here, Diana, and you aren't afraid to use it."

Good God, he sounded so serious, so sincere . . . as if he truly meant what he said.

"Shall I list my other reasons for enjoying your company?" He began to tick them off on his finger. "You speak your mind boldly and without fear, quite unlike most of the women I've met in my life. I also admire women who are capable of independence, and who occasionally exhibit a charming disregard for personal danger where the accomplishment of a goal is concerned. As for your looks, I've never seen eyes as bright and beautiful as yours. Or lips that make me want to kiss them as yours do."

Reaching out, he removed her cap, so that her hair fell loose about her shoulders. It was presumptuous and unexpected, and yet she said nothing. As she held her breath in anticipation, the words to chastise him slipped away from her mind like water through a sieve.

"I'm sure you could have contrived of a way to speak to me at a public gathering instead of all this subterfuge and disguise, if that was what you really wanted," he murmured, "but I'm glad you didn't. I like being alone with you very much."

She liked being alone with him, too. More than liked. She would gladly stay here, alone with him, all night.

So she didn't protest as he drew her to him, pulled her into his arms and kissed her passionately. Fervently. His mouth crushed down on hers with a heated yearning that she could scarcely fathom.

Indeed, she could scarcely think at all, except that she didn't want this moment to end.

The lantern fell to the ground, landing so that the opening was to the ground and they were plunged into complete, enveloping darkness.

It was as if she had left the everyday, familiar, constrained world of manners and polite, meaningless conversation, of fashions and gossip. As if she were completely free.

She clung to him tightly, reveling in the passion

of his kiss, the strength of his arms. The taste of his lips. She parted hers and when his tongue slipped between them, it was perfectly right, and wonderful. A low moan of ecstatic delight sounded in her ears and she realized it was hers.

His embrace tightened and slowly she moved her hands up his back, the jacket wrinkled taut beneath her fingers. His hand raked through her unbound hair, making her scalp tingle like the rest of her. Her limbs relaxed, nearly limp with need.

He guided her back until she felt the wall behind her, solid and cool. His hand slid up her shirt, along her ribs, until he reached the curve of her breast. He cupped her, and gently kneaded. Her breast firmed beneath his touch, while her body heated and her passion flamed.

With one hand, she pulled his head down more, as if she would devour him with her kisses. Her other eager hand circled his back and pulled him close, so that she could feel his whole body along hers.

His knee slipped between her legs. Instinctively she ground against the hard muscle of his leg. The rough fabric of her trousers and the finer fabric of her pantaloons rubbed the tender flesh of her inner thighs and her most intimate place.

As his tongue explored the warmth of her mouth, she pushed forward again. And again.

Her body tightened with tension. His hands caressed and stroked.

Then, suddenly, the tension snapped, catching

her unawares. Pleasure throbbed outward in waves of release. Panting, shocked, overwhelmed, she clung to him, holding his shoulders, not knowing exactly what had happened, but too sated to care.

She gradually became aware of his body, and felt the tension that still filled him.

No, he had not felt what she had. How could she make him relax? "What can I do?" she whispered, looking up into his strained face.

"For the moment, nothing," he said hoarsely. "Or I'll forget that I ever claimed to be a gentleman."

Then suddenly, like the sun bursting from behind a dark cloud, a beam of light caught her full in the face.

She gasped and blinked in the sudden illumination from the large lantern a grizzled watchman held up beside his face.

Edmond quickly shielded her.

" 'Ere now, what's goin' on?" the watchman demanded with obvious disgust. "Get away wi' ya, boy." The light swayed, as if he was waving his lantern to shoo her off. "We don't want none of that here."

Good heavens, what did he—?

Still hiding her with his body, Edmond reached down and picked up her lantern. "My lantern has gone out. May I use yours to relight it?"

The watchman's expression changed to one as

shocked as hers must have been. "Oh, beggin' your pardon, sir. O' course, o' course."

He held his lamp as steady as he could while Edmond lit theirs. When that task was accomplished, he gave Edmond a wary look. "Not here though, sir, eh?"

Then he hurried away as fast as his bow legs could take him, the light of his lamp bobbing like a large and erratic firefly.

Edmond let out his breath slowly.

Diana stared at him, aghast. "He thought that I—that you—that we—?"

"Very awkward," Edmond agreed. "I don't believe he realized you were a woman."

Despite what he said, he didn't sound the least bit worried. "But that . . . that's *worse*, isn't it?"

"As I said, very awkward. It could be that *my* reputation will be in jeopardy for our meeting here."

"How can you be so calm?"

"Because I don't think he knows who I am, or he would have called me 'my lord.' Likely he merely realized from my clothing that I'm rich and worthy of deference, no matter what lewd activities I engage in."

She clasped her hands together, thinking of the new stories that might be spread about him, and because of her. "Oh, this was a mistake!"

He reached out and pulled her close. "I don't agree."

He bent to kiss her again, but she wiggled out of his embrace. "I must go!" she said, grabbing the lantern.

"Diana, please." He took her shoulders in his hands and his dark eyes searched her face. "Tell me you aren't considering Fallston for a husband. Or is there another man I don't know about? Somebody in Lincolnshire, perhaps?"

He looked as if her response to his questions would either make him extremely happy or utterly miserable.

"I wouldn't marry Fallston if he were the last man in England and there's nobody in Lincolnshire I love."

He did care about her. His feelings were genuine and sincere. She'd never been happier in her life and she wanted to stay with him, yet she dare not linger any longer.

She lifted herself on her toes to buss him on the cheek. "Now I really must go. That watchman may return and I won't have more lies spread about you. Good night, Edmond."

With that, she turned to go.

He didn't want her to leave. He wanted to be with her, tonight, tomorrow and every day after that, for the rest of his life. He needed her. He loved her.

She started to run.

"Diana, wait!" he cried softly, chasing after her.

She didn't hear him, and although he ran as fast as he could, he couldn't catch her.

She dashed into the mews behind her aunts' house. Rounding the corner, he watched—both impressed and horrified—as she climbed up the garden fence, then the drainpipe and crept into an upstairs window.

He wouldn't be able to speak to her again tonight, but tomorrow he would. First thing in the morning, as soon as etiquette would allow, he would call on her and tell her how he felt. He would ensure that she never doubted him, or his feelings, or her own attractiveness, ever again.

Chapter 11

Trying to be as silent as they could be, Evangeline and Rodolpho hurried up the slick, damp steps of the tower toward the wall walk.

Rodolpho pushed open the ancient wooden door and, his back against the stone wall, headed outside. Evangeline followed, the cold rush of wind nearly knocking her off her feet. Dark clouds scudded across the moonlit sky and in the distance, closer to the sea, fog swirled near the shore, looking like a creature waiting to swallow them up.

But they would be safe if they could get to the cover of that fog and the boat Rodolpho had hidden on the shore.

The Castle of Count Korlovsky

The next morning, Reverend MacTavish's book lay open on Diana's lap, as she stared unseeing at the raindrops sliding down the drawing room windowpane. Lacking anything else new to read, she'd been making her way through this terrible book all day, thinking of Edmond with every word. What an unhappy, cheerless childhood he must have had, if his parents subscribed to Reverend MacTavish's notions of human weakness.

She hadn't been able to concentrate on her own book at all, especially as the hours passed and Edmond didn't come to call. Surely the miserable weather wouldn't deter a man like him from venturing forth. It might be his dread of encountering her aunts' obvious dislike that kept him away, but she couldn't quite believe that, either.

Today would be a perfect day for him to call, in spite of the weather. Aunt Calliope had retired to her bedchamber claiming a headache, and Aunt Euphenia was ensconced in her book room going over the household accounts. Talk of economical matters always sent Aunt Calliope to her bedchamber pleading an indisposition of one sort or another. It wouldn't be proper for Edmond to be alone with her, of course, but at least Aunt Calliope wouldn't be there, casting dark and condemning looks at him.

She contemplated writing him a note. Unfortunately, that would be as improper as his present of the book, until there was some official acknowledgment of the relationship between them—a relationship that made her heart sing, even though her doubt and dread that she was wrong to believe that a man like him could care about a woman like her were reviving with every passing hour.

"Diana?"

With a start, she turned to find Aunt Euphenia on the threshold. "Yes?"

"Lord Fallston has come to call."

Diana barely managed not to grimace. She'd hoped he'd realized that his suit was hopeless, but obviously he hadn't. It was easy to see how a younger, just as persistent, Fallston had annoyed Edmond and his friends.

Nevertheless, she would have to proceed with care and caution until she was able to prove to her aunts that Edmond wasn't the rogue rumor said he was.

Which she could do if he would come to visit!

If he wanted to visit.

If she wasn't wrong about him, after all.

Aunt Euphenia came into the room and sat on the sofa nearest the mantel. Obviously she intended to act as chaperon, something for which Diana was grateful.

"This might be a good time to tell Lord Fallston his suit is hopeless," Aunt Euphenia noted.

"Yes, you're right," Diana agreed, mentally girding her loins and preparing to be gentle, but firm.

His trouser legs a little worse for the weather, Lord Fallston appeared at the door.

"Good morning, Lady Harbage, Lady Diana," he said eagerly as he hurried forward to take her aunt's hand in greeting. He then took Diana's, holding it a bit longer than necessary. "It's too bad about the weather, but it's finally clearing."

His gaze was full of adoration; immediately, her jaw clenched. Was he really so blind to her feelings? Could he truly not see that she didn't reciprocate his? She rose and walked to the window farthest from them, getting as far away from him as physically possible.

"Yes, at last," Aunt Euphenia noted. Then she picked up that day's issue of *The Times*.

Diana surmised this was her signal that she was on her own. Lord Fallston interpreted it that way, too, for he practically trotted to her side and regarded her as if he was a desperate little boy.

"I'm sorry if my mother upset you when she visited the other morning," he said in a hushed voice before she could speak. "She spoke out of turn, and without my consent, and I would have stopped her if I had known her intent."

Diana felt a surge of relief. Perhaps he had realized courting her was a waste of his time and only wanted to apologize for his mother's visit. "She explained she was doing so only out of a mother's loving concern."

An unexpectedly hard look came to his face. "She forgets I am old enough that I don't need her assistance. I have been considering how to best apologize to you."

"You've done it very nicely," Diana replied, again keeping her tone polite, although inwardly she added, *So now you can go.*

"Then you forgive any offense she may have caused?"

"Of course." She smiled weakly. "She was only trying to be helpful, in her own way."

He smiled as if she'd just lifted the weight of the world from his shoulders. "Lady Diana, have you any idea how happy that makes me? That *you* make me?"

She sidled away from him and realized she was going to have to be blunt. "I'm sorry, Lord Fallston, but—"

"I don't pay any attention to what people say about you and Adderley. I'm quite certain your actions have been above reproach."

He sounded as if he were being very magnanimous, that she had seriously erred but he was willing to forgive her lapse.

She was immediately tempted to tell him about meeting Edmond in Sydney Gardens. *All* about it.

Suddenly, and regardless of Aunt Euphenia's presence, he grabbed her hands and clasped them between his sweaty palms. "Lady Diana," he whispered, "you know I love you. I adore you! I worship you! Please agree to be my wife, my angel! Otherwise my life shall be a desolate ruin—a graveyard!"

He said nothing about *her* feelings, she noticed as she tried to pull her hands free. She wondered why Aunt Euphenia didn't say something. Perhaps she was still immersed in the latest news from London; she couldn't tell, because her back was to her. "My lord, I really don't think—"

"If you accept me," he interrupted, his grip

tightening, "I promise I shall do all in my powers to make your life a paradise, my goddess."

She didn't doubt that would be utterly impossible, just as it was impossible to hear herself called an angel and a goddess and not want to laugh.

She was ready to be stern until she recalled his former fiancée's desertion of him. Out of pity, she softened her tone and quit struggling to get her hands out of his grasp. Surely Aunt Euphenia would soon notice and cough or indicate her disapproval some other way. "No, my lord, I cannot."

His eyes filled with a desperate longing. "But I've admitted I was wrong to be so critical of your opinions. I'm willing—no, anxious!—to be instructed."

As if she would want to be a teacher more than a wife! "My lord, I don't love you."

"But you will *come* to love me," he replied in a voice that was nearly a whine.

"No, my lord, I won't."

"I think you could," he said, a stubborn glint in his eyes, "unless you've fallen under Adderley's spell, like so many other foolish women."

That glint and his words removed her determination to be gentle.

She opened her mouth to tell him that she would never *ever* be his wife, in no uncertain terms, and prepared to yank her hands free with whatever force was required.

Before she could, Aunt Calliope came bursting

into the room, apparently completely recovered from her headache. Her sharp eyes fairly gleamed with query and delight as she looked at their clasped hands. Aunt Euphenia looked up from her paper and frowned.

"Lord Fallston, what a charming surprise!" Aunt Calliope cried as she swept toward them.

Diana gave a firm pull and finally succeeded in liberating her hands, which ached from his strong grip. "You misunderstand, Aunt Calliope," she began.

Before she could proceed further, however, Lord Fallston beat a hasty retreat to the door.

"If you'll excuse me, I have a previous engagement that calls me away. I hope to see you soon, ladies."

With that, he was gone.

Diana was glad to see the back of him, but she wished she'd been able to refuse him once and for all. She didn't want him going around Bath implying that she was eventually going to accept him.

"I thought I was going to have to speak to him about holding your hands," Aunt Euphenia noted.

Ignoring her sister's comment, Aunt Calliope rushed to Diana and drew her toward the sofa. "Well?" she demanded as she pulled her down beside her. "You accepted him, didn't you? Tell me that you did! Of course you must! Such a perfect match! Such a charming, genial young man!"

There was no point being vague. She wasn't going to marry Lord Fallston, and the sooner Aunt

Calliope realized that, the better. "Lord Fallston did propose, but I didn't accept."

"You *didn't?*"

"Since I don't love him, I wouldn't accept him."

Utterly flustered, Aunt Calliope reached for the smelling salts, which were usually somewhere in the sofa cushions. "Oh, my dear, what were you thinking!" she cried before taking an enormous whiff. "To put him off at all! Lord Fallston! Such a gentleman! So kind! So amiable! So suitable in every way!"

"But I don't *love* him, Aunt," Diana protested. "Surely you wouldn't want me to marry without being in love."

"Diana's perfectly right, of course," Aunt Euphenia said as she sat beside Aunt Calliope. "She has no need to marry for any reason other than love, and she shouldn't." She gently pried the smelling salts from her sister's hand. "Come, Calliope, we both know that she is wise to refuse if she isn't in love. We want her to be happy, don't we?"

Calliope's blue eyes welled with tears. "Well, of course I want her to be happy," she said, sniffling. "And that is why I want her to marry Lord Fallston. Such a fine young man."

"No, he's not," Diana answered. She was prepared to tell them what she had learned about Lord Fallston, and Lord Adderley, when the butler appeared on the threshold.

"I beg your pardon, my ladies," he said. "Another gentleman has arrived."

He presented a silver salver bearing a card to Aunt Euphenia. She stiffened slightly, then raised her eyes to the butler. "I told you before, Dalton. We are not at home to Lord Adderley today."

Diana stared at her aunt, then the butler, who hurriedly departed.

"Has Lord Adderley called here already today?" she asked, looking from one aunt to the other as she marched toward the door, forgetting this was not her house and fully intending to invite Edmond in.

"Diana, wait!"

Aunt Euphenia's commanding tone was so unexpected, Diana halted immediately and turned to face her. Before her aunt said anything more, Diana heard the muffled sound of the front door of Aunt Calliope's townhouse open and close.

Edmond was leaving! She ran to the window, prepared to throw up the sash and call him back, when Aunt Euphenia's stern words made her halt once more.

"Is there something you've been keeping from us?" Aunt Euphenia asked. "Something about the viscount?"

"Yes," Diana confessed.

Aunt Calliope bounded to her feet like a hound scenting a hare. "It can't be! Diana! The rumors—they're not *true*?"

"I haven't heard all the rumors and gossip, but I will say that if they imply Lord Adderley and I are intimately acquainted, they're right."

As Aunt Calliope moaned and collapsed onto the sofa, she faced her aunts squarely. "But there's nothing shameful about our relationship, or if there is, it's because I was the one who wanted secrecy."

"You made a promise, Diana," Aunt Euphenia said quietly.

"And I've kept it," she answered. "I haven't eloped with him, or let him seduce me. But he's not the scoundrel people think he is. Indeed, he's a finer, kinder gentleman than Lord Fallston, or any other man I've ever met except my dear father. If you would permit him to visit, you'd discover that, too."

"But Diana, the things I've heard!" Aunt Calliope protested.

"Lies, many of them started by this same Lord Fallston you think so highly of, in retaliation for a schoolboy prank that went a little awry."

"What of this other story I heard yesterday, Diana?" Aunt Euphenia asked with her usual quiet reserve. "A servant at the earl of Granshire's claims to have seen you on the terrace with Lord Adderley, in a very intimate embrace. If that is true, that is not the behavior of a gentleman."

"I was quite willing."

Aunt Calliope moaned and put her hand to her head. "You want to have your reputation destroyed?" she wailed. "To bring scandal to the family?"

"Of course not. And I didn't set out to harm

anyone, least of all you." She looked from Aunt Euphenia to Aunt Calliope, who was now wringing her hands. "I love you both dearly," she continued gently, "as if you were the mother I never knew. But I'm of age, and I must follow my heart. Disown me if you must and cast me out of your house, but I will not renounce my love for Edmond."

Aunt Calliope started to weep, while Aunt Euphenia regarded her niece steadily, dry-eyed and somber. "We will never cast you from our home, Diana, or disown you. Am I to assume from what you're saying that you're in love with him?"

"Yes."

"And he loves you in return?"

"I . . ." He hadn't actually said so, but she trusted her heart and the look in his eyes before he kissed her. "I believe so, yes."

"Has he asked you to be his wife?"

"No, not yet. He didn't . . . he hasn't had a chance."

"But you think he intends to."

For a moment, the last vestige of doubt tried to assert itself, but her love beat it back. "I believe his intentions are honorable, because he's an honorable man."

As Aunt Calliope sniffled, Aunt Euphenia's expression softened. "Then what more need be said, except that the viscount will be welcome to call in the future."

"Can't I send Dalton or one of the footmen to call him back?"

"It's late, my dear, and time to dress for dinner. If he loves you, I'm sure he'll call again tomorrow, and we shall be glad to visit with him then." She glanced at Aunt Calliope, whose nose was red and whose cheeks were tear-streaked as she dabbed at her brimming eyes with the edge of her scarf. "And I think some of us have had quite enough excitement for today."

Diana was too happy to argue or press the point. It was enough that Aunt Euphenia was willing to accept her relationship with Edmond. And she was sure Aunt Euphenia was right; Edmond would surely call again tomorrow. In the meantime, it might be wise to give Aunt Calliope time to get used to the situation.

Diana went to the door and paused on the threshold, turning back to smile at her aunts. "You'll discover what a wonderful man he is. And he loves books, too."

Smiling, Aunt Euphenia nodded as she left the room, while Aunt Calliope sniffled.

The moment she was gone, however, Calliope's mournful silence was replaced by her dismayed wail as she felt in the sofa cushions for her salts. "The viscount's ruined *everything!*"

Euphenia didn't reply.

"How can you be so calm?" Calliope demanded when she found the salts, glaring at her sister. "How could you say you'd let him come to call? Even if Diana's right about Lord Fallston—and I'm not saying she is—to accept *Lord Adderley* as her suitor. . . . Oh, this is terrible!"

Euphenia wasn't overly disturbed by her sister's protestations. "The viscount's not the sort of man we would have chosen for Diana, but he may not be the rogue we think he is. If nothing else, Diana's affection for him should tell us that. Even if he is, we shouldn't give her cause for grief, or secrecy. We want her to feel she always has a home with us, no matter what, don't we?"

"Yes, of course," Calliope agreed with a loud sniffle. "Should things turn out badly, we wouldn't want her to feel we would be angry with her, or that we wouldn't want to see her again."

"Exactly," Euphenia confirmed with a nod of her head. "Accepting the viscount may be difficult, but I don't want to lose Diana the way we did her father."

Scowling, Lord Fallston looked up to see his plump butler waiting by the door. "Well, what is it, Evans?" he demanded, turning his attention back to the glass of wine he held in his hand, wishing it was something stronger.

"I beg your pardon, sir, but there is a young lady who wishes to see you. Shall I say you aren't at home?"

Evans had the strictest notions of propriety and

he was obviously not at all pleased. The "young lady" must have come alone. There was only one woman of Fallston's acquaintance liable to flaunt society's conventions in that manner—Lady Diana Westover.

Joy and dread hit him in equal measure. Either she'd realized she was making a mistake by refusing him, or she'd come with quite another purpose.

Preparing himself for either eventuality, he said, "Show her in at once."

The butler didn't immediately move.

"And ask Mama to join us, please."

At that, Evans finally did as he was bid.

When he was the master in this house, Fallston sourly reflected, he'd fire the fellow, fifteen years of service notwithstanding.

While he continued to wait for Lady Diana, Fallston examined his appearance in the mirror and made a few adjustments to his cravat. He might not be quite as handsome as Adderley, but he was far from homely, as Lady Diana should appreciate.

He heard a sound and turned to the door, then stared in bewilderment at the extremely beautiful young woman hovering anxiously near the door. She was most certainly not Lady Diana. Her hair was dark, her complexion fair, her lips the color of red wine, her neck long and slender, and her attitude one of poise and grace. Dressed in a lovely gown of pink-flowered muslin, a soft cashmere shawl looped over her arms and wearing a bonnet decorated with delicate pink blossoms, she was the epitome of feminine perfection.

He suddenly wished he hadn't told Evans to fetch his mother.

"I do beg your pardon, my lord, for my outrageous presumption," she said in a very soft and sweet voice, "but I could think of no other way to speak to you, and in some privacy, too. I'm sure you'll understand why when I tell you the reason I've come."

He gestured toward a chair. She slid with graceful ease onto it and, clutching her silk reticule in her gloved hands, answered his unspoken question. "We *have* been introduced, my lord."

He thought he remembered meeting her, but where and when?

The Theatre Royal. He'd met her at the Theatre Royal.

"Good God, you're not an actress?" he gasped, as if actors were next door to leprous, which, in the eyes of his family, would actually be a step up for denizens of the stage.

"No!" the beauty cried, clearly outraged. "I'm Adelina Foxborough."

When he still couldn't make the connection, she fixed her exquisite eyes on him and said, very slowly, "I was with Lord Adderley at the theater. My father owns the Foxborough Distilleries."

"Oh, yes, of course," he replied flatly. She was a

woman of some education whose father had made a fortune in rum.

The fact that she had been with his enemy did not particularly elevate her in his estimation, either.

"What brings you here under these rather extraordinary circumstances, Miss Foxborough?" he inquired as he leaned against the mantel, affecting the sort of casual yet manly pose Adderley always managed to pull off with incredible ease.

"As you say, extraordinary circumstances," she replied. "I wouldn't be here if I didn't believe it was of the utmost importance, my lord."

He regally inclined his head. "Proceed."

"It is no secret in Bath that you are courting Lady Diana Westover."

His eyes narrowed, and Miss Foxborough hurried on. "It is also no secret that you and Lord Adderley are enemies of long standing. I also believe you must be aware that the viscount has noted your interest and seems to be determined to undermine your efforts."

If Fallston had noticed that, he wasn't about to admit it. "I don't think so."

"*I* do, my lord, and so do many other people. I understand there are even wagers being made as to when he'll succeed in thwarting your suit. . . ." She trailed off as if it was too painful to continue.

He came and sat beside her. "What sort of stories are being told?"

"She was alone on the terrace with him at Lord Bromwell's reception."

"With Lord Adderley?"

"Yes. One of the maids saw them."

"And this maid was sure it was the viscount?"

"Yes." Adelina cleared her throat delicately. "*My* maid ascertained that first you had been with Lady Diana, you were interrupted by the viscount, and then he, um, spoke to her, and . . . ahem . . . did a little *more* than speak to her, too, if you understand my meaning."

Fallston stared at her for a long moment, incredulous.

Adelina darted a look at Fallston that told him she was, indeed, the daughter of a canny businessman. "It's amazing what a little judicial use of money will accomplish when it comes to learning about people. My father says one must always know all one can about one's associates."

Fallston's hands clenched and his pride, already so battered and bruised by Adderley and his friends, felt wounded anew. "Mere rumors and unfounded speculation. I have already asked for the lady's hand and she has not declined."

"I haven't heard that she's accepted, either."

He frowned. "I don't see that my relationship with Lady Diana is any of your business."

"It isn't—but her relationship with the viscount is. To put it bluntly, my lord, I want to marry him, and I don't want her standing in the way."

He blinked.

"Until her arrival in Bath, our marriage seemed a distinct possibility."

"Yes, of course," he answered. "Your beauty alone . . ."

"And my money, too, I don't doubt."

"I hadn't heard Adderley needs money."

"Everybody needs money, or at least wants more than they have. That is another lesson I learned at my father's knee, and I haven't found anything to contradict it. Even you, my lord, would probably welcome an addition to your income, or an increase in your status."

"That is not why I want to marry Lady Diana."

She blushed. "Forgive me if I have insulted you."

He regarded her quizzically. "Why do *you* want *him*?"

"I'm wealthy and well educated, my lord, yet in the eyes of society, I'm still just a distiller's daughter. If I'm to make more of myself, I must marry above my station. I've spent years learning how to walk, talk, and dance like a lady. I can sing as well as any professional, and I play the pianoforte and harp. I've studied French, Italian, German, Latin and Greek until my eyes watered. I can paint in watercolors or oils, or sketch. All these lessons and hours of study have had but one goal—a titled husband. I won't have all that effort wasted, and the viscount seemed willing to consider me."

"Then you would be marrying Adderley only for that?"

"He is also a very handsome and charming man, my lord." A determination as strong as iron appeared in her visage. "And I won't be passed over for a homely little creature from the country just because she's a duke's daughter."

Adelina realized she'd raised her voice, and once again gave him a charming smile. "So you see, we have a mutual necessity, my lord, and that's to get Lord Adderley away from Lady Diana. I have a plan as to how that may be accomplished. However, I need your help to put it into action."

An unfamiliar sense of masculine protectiveness and power dawned upon Fallston. "I see. Provided I agree with you, and I'm not saying I do, what sort of assistance did you have in mind?"

"Realizing my interest in the viscount, my father set certain inquiries in motion, as is his habit when considering a new . . . partner. His man discovered a young French woman, a refugee from the Terror, living in London and whose history included an interlude with the viscount. She was working as a seamstress, and not a very good one, either. She was only too eager to reveal the details of her liaison with him, for a fee, of course."

"Of course."

"It was also an easy enough thing to persuade her to come to Bath. She is here now, and willing to be of assistance."

"For more money?"

"Yes. She's a very businesslike woman. I had no

trouble persuading her to wait until the most effective time to reveal herself and her child to Lord Adderley."

Fallston grinned like a gargoyle. "There's a *child*?"

Adelina's wine-red lips turned up in an answering smile. "The very image of him, too."

"Oh, this is too wonderful!"

As smug as a merchant who's sold his wares at twice the expected price, Adelina sat up a little straighter. "I thought you would be pleased. I also think meeting Madame Voisey and learning certain other facts should cause Lady Diana to reconsider her relationship with the viscount. Don't you?"

"Indeed, I do."

"However, I would rather not be involved in bringing the matter to her attention."

"You wouldn't want Adderley to know you were involved, either, in case that turns him against you," he guessed.

"Yes." She didn't look at all embarrassed by her machinations. "But if *you* were to introduce Lady Diana to Madame Voisey, you would be perceived as saving her from a disastrous liaison."

Adelina smoothed her sleeve from her elbow to her slender, graceful wrist. "Afterward, I daresay Lady Diana would need a shoulder to cry on, and someone to listen to her remorseful sobs. And to be generously forgiven for a silly flight of fancy . . . well, gratitude may be a powerful inducement to affection, or even marriage, my lord."

He saw the merit in her plan at once. Yes, he would be looked upon as doing this for Diana's own good, and if he were to welcome her back into his affections, she would have to be grateful. Her aunts would thank him, too.

His only regret was that he hadn't thought of a similar scheme himself. He must remember this tactic involving an enemy's past and using his history against him. "What a clever woman you are!"

Smiling, she brushed her fingertips across the neckline of her bodice. Suddenly very aware of her luscious breasts, Fallston swallowed hard and tried not to stare.

A bustle in the upstairs corridor heralded his mother's impending descent. No matter what he thought of Adelina Foxborough—and his opinion was improving by the minute—he could all too easily imagine what his mother would say if she found a distiller's daughter, who had arrived alone, sitting in her drawing room. "It would be better if you would leave now, Miss Foxborough," he said as he hurried to the drawing room door.

She rose and produced a piece of paper from her reticule as she came toward him. "This is Madeline Voisey's address in Bath."

Their hands touched as he pocketed it, the contact thrilling him. Impulsively, he grabbed her gloved fingers and pressed a fervent kiss upon them. "If things work out as we hope, I shall be in your debt, Miss Foxborough,"

"And I shall be in yours," Adelina replied softly as she glided from the room, a smile of satisfaction on her very beautiful face.

Chapter 12

Evangeline gazed at the count in disbelief as his men surrounded them. "Love?" she repeated. "It isn't love that tries to force a woman to stay against her will. Love is generous and unselfish, and it cannot be compelled into being. Love is given, not taken."

"Have I not been generous?" the count demanded as his men held Rodolpho despite his struggles. "Have I not given you everything you wanted, everything you needed? What more can I do? You have but to ask, and it will be yours."

"Then give us our freedom," she replied defiantly. "If you truly love me, you will let us go."

He scowled. "No."

"Then what you offer is merely lust. If you want me, it is only for my body, not my heart, which you will never ever have. I will love Rodolpho until the day I die."

The count drew his blade. "Or until he does."

The Castle of Count Korlovsky

As dusk fell, Edmond paced the floor in his library like a restless animal, as he tried to figure out some way to see Diana again.

Despite a heavy rain that had kept most of the residents in Bath indoors, he'd gone to her aunt's townhouse as soon as he possibly could, only to be informed that neither Lady Diana or her aunts were at home.

He didn't believe that for a second. However, he could believe that Diana was still abed, after her late night, so this order might come solely from her aunts. With that hope, he'd gone away and returned later, only to be given the same cold answer.

And again. And again.

After the kisses he had shared with Diana—soul-searing, wonderful kisses—he was sure this wasn't Diana's doing. Her feelings for him would be like the woman herself, strong and sure. But her aunts had heard all the rumors and the lies about him. They believed him to be a rake and a gambler, and probably worse.

This was the price for not stopping Fallston from spreading his malicious lies and rumors, and making false accusations. If he had, surely her aunts wouldn't be so set against him and they would at least let Diana see him. But they didn't approve of him, and as she was a guest in her aunt's home, Diana was subject to their rule.

His bold, resolute beloved was surely chafing at their restrictions. He could believe she was likely planning to sneak out of the house as soon as it was dark to see him. Her footman, should he awaken later, might find his clothing missing, and

Ruttles might be startled to find an urchin on their doorstep.

As anxious as Edmond was to see her, he hated to think of her taking the risk of climbing down from her window again. Even if she'd done it successfully before, it was too easy to imagine her slipping and plummeting to the ground below. And then there was the whole host of dangers that awaited a lone woman on the streets at night.

He wished he could send her a note, telling her to be patient and he would see her somehow, but he was sure her aunts would intercept it. He could try bribing a servant to deliver it to her, but that couldn't be done tonight.

He would have to try to get to her first. He could get into Lady FitzBurton's townhouse the same way she'd gotten out. He'd had some experience in that regard at Harrow.

It would mean running the risk of being caught sneaking into the townhouse like a criminal. He was sure Diana would defend him, but he was equally certain her aunts would charge him with housebreaking.

Yet up against that risk was the one of Diana falling and breaking her neck, or being seized on the street by thieves, or worse, so in the end, there was only one thing to do. As soon as it was dark, he would make his way to Lady FitzBurton's townhouse and when he thought it safe, he would climb up the drainpipe and into Diana's window. Until then, he would watch, in case she started to climb out. He would show himself and make sure she stayed inside, and then he would go to her.

It wasn't the way he wanted to court her, but he wasn't willing to take the chance of her risking her own safety, and he so desperately wanted to be with her—

His aged butler appeared in the door. Before he could speak, Brix strode past him.

"Close the door, Ruttles," the Honorable Smythe-Medway commanded, shocking the elderly man in a whole new way. Nobody who'd met Brixton in the past ten years would ever have suspected he possessed such a tone of voice, let alone would use it.

Ruttles did as he was told, while Brix regarded his friend as if he'd never been so disgusted in his life. "Is it true?" he demanded, his hands balled into fists at his sides.

"Is what true?" Edmond answered, wondering what exactly Brix had heard to make him act this way.

"That you've been intimate with Lady Diana. You were seen together on the terrace at Buggy's reception, kissing."

As he got to his feet and faced his friend, Edmond wished he'd been more open and honest about his feelings for Diana with his best friend. He would be now. "Yes, that's true, but—"

"Good God!" Brix cried, his face reddening. His whole body quaked with a volcanic rage that shocked Edmond. He hadn't ever seen Brix so angry—hadn't known he could even *get* so angry. "It was just supposed to be a bit of a *joke*. You weren't going to seduce her. You weren't going to ruin her reputation. That's what you said. It was to be a little recompense because she made you uncomfortable, and because she didn't seem to find you attractive. I warned you this was danger-ous, but I trusted you—and you gave me your *word*!"

"I've kept my word, Brix. I—"

"You have *not*," Brix snarled, "You've *ruined* her reputation. Wagers are being made on whether you've already succeeded in seducing her. There's another bookmaker who believes you haven't yet and he's taking bets on the day you do. Another one is taking wagers on who'll win the duel, you or Fallston."

Painful as it was, Edmond ignored Brix's de-nunciation of him. "What are they saying about Diana?"

"What do you care?" Brix cried, waving his hand as if he'd like to sweep Edmond out of the room. "It's all over Bath that some maid saw the two of you together on the terrace at Buggy's re-ception and Sissingsby's claiming you were with her in one of the grottos in Sydney Gardens in the middle of the night."

"That's all true. I was with Diana in one of the grottos. If you'll give me the chance to explain—"

"What other lies have you told me?" Brix demanded. "Did you mean to seduce her all along, despite your sworn oath?"

"I meant what I said when I made my promise to you," Edmond replied, his patience fraying. "I didn't set out to do anything but pay her back for making me feel like an odd sort of bug in a jar."

"Oh, that makes me feel better," Brix retorted sarcastically. "What made you change your mind and break your oath? Have you come up with some new scheme to pay her back? Are you trying to make her fall in love with you and then you'll break her heart? Or is this aimed at Fallston after all? You want to take her away from him, and *then* you'll break her heart?"

"No! I've tried to keep my word to you. I meant to. I didn't know she was going to be on the terrace. She asked me to meet her in the grotto. As for the way I feel about her—"

"Oh, so this is all *her* fault? You agree with the people who're saying that for all her book reading, she's an ignorant country miss who should have stayed in Lincolnshire rather than risk running afoul of you? Even those most willing to take her part will be watching her and counting the days before they can expect to see a little living token of your affection."

Edmond could easily imagine the things people would say, the way they'd look at her. Her searching gaze would have nothing on them. "I assure you, Brix, I haven't seduced her."

"Not yet, eh?" his friend countered, striding around the room as if his anger required motion. "And damn it, if you haven't, it isn't for lack of trying, is it? I should have known you weren't going to be satisfied with just following her around. I should have guessed there was more to it than that. You set out to ruin Fallston's chances with her. Gad, and I thought Fallston was a vindictive little rat!" He halted and glared at Edmond again. "I'm disgusted with you, Edmond, really disgusted to think that after all these years you could play such a rotten trick after giving me your word!"

"I never set out to ruin the match but by God, if I have, I won't be sorry," Edmond answered, his feet planted, anger and frustration bursting forth. "I don't want her to marry him. I want her to marry *me*."

Brix stared as if he'd been turned into a sculpture entitled Man, Dumbfounded.

"I love her, Brix," Edmond declared. "I'd marry her tomorrow if I could."

"But you . . . but she . . . *what?*"

A little calmer now, Edmond spoke very slowly, as if Brix was in a stupor, which in a way, he was. "I love Lady Diana Westover and I want to marry her."

Brix felt for a chair, lowered himself, missed the seat and had to try again. "You . . . *love* . . . her? Lady Diana? The one who stares?"

"I love Lady Diana Westover, the one who stares," Edmond repeated.

"Good God! You're absolutely serious!"

Edmond relaxed against his desk. "I've never been more serious."

"And you really want to marry her?"

"I do, if she'll have me. I haven't asked her yet."

"Well, my friend," Brix said after the longest moment of silence they'd ever shared, "I think if she's kissing you on terraces and dancing with you at balls and meeting you in grottos, I expect she will."

"I'm afraid it's not that simple. Her aunts don't approve of me, and maybe never will. That means I can't court Diana properly, as a gentleman should, and that will only confirm her aunts' poor opinion. Still, if I must, I must, because I don't want to lose Diana."

"Faint heart never won fair lady," Brix muttered, still stunned. "I begin to see that being the notorious Lord Adderley might actually have some drawbacks."

"It certainly does and never more so than now." Edmond ran a hand across his forehead. "Gad, Brix, I've been an idiot! I think I've loved her from the first moment I caught her staring at me with those marvelous eyes of hers, and I still haven't had a chance to tell her how I feel, not even last night in Sydney Gardens."

"Last night . . . *where*?"

"Sydney Gardens, after the ball. While we were dancing, she asked me to meet her there, and I did. She and I . . . well, I discovered how she felt about me, and finally realized how I felt about her. But we were interrupted by a watchman who assumed we were having an illegal assignation and ordered us to move along. She did—she ran home and climbed back up the drainpipe."

Brix continued to regard him with baffled amazement. "She climbed up a drainpipe? In a *dress*?"

"She was in disguise, in a man's clothes."

"She was climbing drainpipes, running about Bath dressed in men's clothing and having secret rendezvous with you? Good God, I'm beginning to think you're both half mad."

"Maybe I am, but she's not. She was just using the determination and the intelligence God gave her."

The glimmer of a smile appeared on Brix's face. "Perhaps she's not half mad, as you say."

"And when we kiss—"

Brix held up his hand. "Spare me the details and raptures, my friend. The point is—and as incredible as it seems—you seem to have fallen in love with this woman and want to marry her, but her aunts are like Gorgons at the gate and you can't get by them."

"That's basically the situation," Edmond agreed.

"Well, I suppose if anybody can change women's minds, it's the charming Lord Adderley."

"I don't want to use charm, as you put it. I'd rather use the truth, and sincerity. I really do love her, Brix, with all my heart."

Brix grinned, although his eyes were full of sympathy. "Then all my righteous indignation turned out to be for nothing. Pity, really. I've never been so worked up in my life."

Edmond gave him a wry smile. "I didn't expect your tirade, either."

"Shocking, was I? I must remember that. But I must say, Lady Diana's not at all the sort of woman I thought you'd marry. I mean, I could see Buggy falling in love with her—they'd probably spend their honeymoon in the library—but you?"

"Can't you envision me spending my honeymoon in a library?"

Brix reflected a moment. "Even if I can, that's not quite the point."

"Yes, it is. I think we'll suit admirably. To be sure, I didn't appreciate her merits myself at first. I do now."

Brix's mouth lost its merry twist. "The rumors are going to run rampant. Fallston will have an apoplectic fit."

"I hope his reaction won't be quite that drastic, but I don't expect him to be pleased. I suppose he'll say I stole her from him, although I don't think he ever had her affection to begin with."

Brix chewed his lip. "It may be worse than that. We both know he doesn't hesitate to start false rumors, and there's already plenty enough going around. He'll probably claim she has to marry you because you seduced her. It couldn't be because she preferred you to him."

"I never should have kept quiet about his false accusations and the other rumors he spread," Edmond said, "but I kept hoping he'd weary of playing the helpless victim and stop."

Brix regarded Edmond gravely. "If you love her, Edmond, and it certainly sounds as if you do, I wish you both the best. If there's anything I can do, just ask."

Edmond clapped his friend on the shoulder. "Thank you, Brix, I will."

His friend grinned. "Do you need a plan to get past the Gorgons at the gate?"

Edmond smiled. "As a matter of fact, I've already got one."

Diana woke instantly, listening intently. The sound coming from the vicinity of her window sounded exactly like a rat scratching at the wall.

She sat up slowly, watching for it in the moonlight that spilled in through the narrow gap of her drapes.

Her breath caught as the drapes moved, and it wasn't from a breeze. She reached for the candlestick on her bedside table, her fingers wrapping around the cool metal. Moving slowly, so as not to make a sound, she slipped out of the bed and, arm upraised, crept toward the window and drapery. If the rat stayed behind the curtain, she could clout it without having to look at it.

The drapes moved more. She raised her weapon higher.

Something . . . someone . . . grunted.

That was no rat! It was a housebreaker!

She was about to make a dash for the door when a deep, familiar voice stopped her in her tracks. "Diana!"

She wheeled around. "Edmond?"

"Yes! I need your help."

She put down the candlestick and rushed to the window. "What are you doing?"

"Trying—rather unsuccessfully—to climb in your window," he said as she reached down to grab him by the shoulders.

"Put your feet there, on that ledge," she commanded, nodding to his left. "That's right. You should have some purchase there."

"Ah!" He did as she told him, and soon scrambled over the sill. Panting, he brushed off his rough woolen jacket. His gaze flicked over her and she was instantly reminded she was clad only in a thin nightgown, her hair in a thick braid down her back. Instinctively she grabbed her dressing gown from the end of the bed and hurriedly put it on.

He crossed the room to her. "I realize I've taken a risk and it could be a disaster if your aunts find me here, but I had to see you. I tried all day, and the butler kept saying you weren't at home. Then I thought you might try to come to me, and that would be even more dangerous, so I decided to follow your example. I do have some experience with climbing, from my days at Harrow." He winced as he rotated his shoulder. "Although it seems the intervening years have taken their toll."

"Oh, Edmond, I should have sent you a note," she said with a rueful smile. "They've changed their minds. You can visit."

His delighted smile dazzled her. "I can? They won't object? How did this happen?"

"I explained to my aunts exactly why I wouldn't marry Lord Fallston and told them I was in love with you."

His eyes betrayed his vulnerability, the unmasked yearning of a man who fears his hope will be denied. "You love me?"

She rested her hands on his shoulders and gazed into his face. "With all my heart, Edmond."

His eyes shone with joy. "I love you, Diana, with all my heart and from the bottom of my soul."

"Even though I'm not like other women? I'm not pretty or—"

He put his finger to her lips to silence her, and looked deep into her eyes. "Diana, for the first years of my life, I thought I must be the most homely, misshapen creature on earth because of the way my parents treated me. Then, when I was eight years old, I discovered that people stared not because I was ugly or disfigured, but because I was the opposite." He touched his chest. "Yet I knew that inside, I was still the same boy, no matter how

I looked. In here, I was neither homely or handsome, I was simply Edmond. I've never paid much heed to what the world considers beauty since."

He took hold of her hands, his clasp firm but gentle. "Even that first day in the Pump Room, I looked at your shining eyes, and saw the blue of sky in springtime. Your smile gives a joy that I feel in the depths of my soul. Most of all, when you look at me with admiration and respect, for the first time in my life, Diana, I feel that I am worthy of those things, no matter what my parents or the world might say about me. Here, in my heart, you make me feel a way nobody's ever made me feel, and that is why I love you."

He placed their hands over his heart. "You're the most beautiful, wonderful, bold, brazen, exciting," he smiled "—delightfully exasperating woman in the world, and I can't imagine going through the rest of my life without you."

All her doubts and worries dropped away. Her insecurities disappeared, and her love for him—unbounded, liberated—burst forth, as strong and determined and vital as she had ever been. Her smile beamed. "I've tried not to love you and told myself I mustn't, but it seems I'm not good at obeying my own orders."

His dark gaze locked onto hers. "Diana, will you marry me?"

She gave him a pert look, comfortable and sure enough in their love to joke. "Considering that you have had the effrontery to accost me in my own bedchamber, of course we must marry, my lord." Her gaze softened as she raised herself on her toes to kiss him. "Besides, I'll be miserable if I don't."

In the next moment, his lips captured hers in a kiss that robbed her of breath, but gave her a hint of a new life, with him.

A vibrant, exciting, passionate life. A life as a woman beloved. A life she had always dreamed about, but thought forever beyond her reach.

A life better than anything she had read about or imagined and it began here, in his arms.

She encircled his neck and leaned into him, giving herself over to the passion that swirled through and in her. Released from all constraint, confident in his love, she dared to kiss him completely. Her mouth moved over his with sure certainty, tasting and touching, as desire unfurled.

His tongue slid between her parted lips and eagerly, she accepted. With slow deliberation, hers danced with his.

His hands glided down her back, holding her closer still, his touch tingling and heating her skin. The barrier of her nightgown was nothing; she might as well be naked.

Oh, yes, she wanted to be naked. The image of him nude burst into her mind, fueling her burning desire. With anxious fingers she shoved the jacket from his shoulders, or tried to.

Breathing heavily, his dark gaze still on her face, he drew back and sloughed it off, letting it drop softly to the floor. She undid his shirt buttons, her fingers working swiftly to get them open. She peeled back his shirt and discovered that his naked chest was every bit as magnificent as she had suspected. A smattering of hair as dark as that on his head stretched between the dark circles of his nipples, and then again from his navel to disappear below the waist of his trousers.

"Do you like what you see, Diana?" he asked, eyes gleaming like a jungle cat, all trace of vulnerability gone, replaced with that virile power he possessed that had nothing of cool sophistication about it.

"Oh, yes," she sighed. A knight of the round table—Lancelot, Gawain—would have a chest like this, shoulders like this, arms like this.

His lips curved up slowly. "High praise indeed."

He reached out and slid his finger between the knot of the tie at the neck of her nightgown and her skin. Did he want to see her naked?

The thought didn't frighten her, or shock her. It seemed only natural, to be expected, exciting and arousing.

He tugged gently, so that she stepped forward at the same time the knot came undone. She held her breath as he slowly, slowly, loosened the opening and slid her gown off one shoulder. Gently holding her arms, he brushed feather-light kisses along the curving slope toward her neck.

Then he stopped. With a ragged sigh, he pushed the gown back into place and with another ragged sigh, stepped back. "I think, Diana, that I had better go. Now."

He was right, of course. What they were doing was wrong, in the eyes of society and certainly her aunts', if they discovered Edmond there. Even though he had asked her to be his wife and she had gladly accepted, they were not yet wed.

So she gave him a wistful smile and fought to master the passionate yearning coursing through her body. "You really are a gentleman."

"At the moment, I wish I weren't."

"At the moment, I wish I weren't a lady."

His gaze searched her face. "You're serious."

"I assure you, I'm perfectly serious. Unfortunately, I also think you're right, and you shouldn't stay. If you do, I'll never be able to let you out of my bed."

"Good God, Diana, are you trying to torture me?"

"No, my lord. I'm merely being honest."

"You make me feel like a feudal lord when you address me that way. My name is Edmond."

She stretched like a cat after a long nap, or as if she herself had only just awakened. "Edmond . . . I like it."

"I'm glad you like it." His voice lowered to that deep purr that seemed to make her very soul tremble, and he tugged her back into his arms. "If I were to be completely honest, I would tell you that I'm extremely tempted to carry you to that bed and stay there until we're both too sated to move."

Her breathing quickened. "Too sated to move?" she managed to whisper.

"Too sated to move," he confirmed, his voice a low, husky growl.

They gazed at each other, silent, the tension stretching, building.

Until his mouth crushed hers in a kiss that robbed her of all coherent thought and caused the simmering passion within her to explode into a conflagration.

In the next instant, he had lifted her in his powerful arms. In two strides, he was at her bed, laying her upon it. His breathing ragged, her magnificent Hades stared down at her, until she crooked her finger through the waist of his trousers and tugged him down on top of her.

Her hands moved over his chest, her lips following. He was hers, to love and desire. She was his. Did anything else matter?

He rolled, so that his hips were between her legs. Bracing himself with one hand, he nuzzled her gown lower, kissing her breasts, as his other hand slid slowly up her naked leg, pushing her nightgown upward. Then she gasped as he sucked her nipple into his mouth, and her whole body stiffened. She hadn't known . . . hadn't suspected . . . hadn't even guessed . . .

Gently, he flicked his tongue across the hardened peak and a different tension took hold, one that combined with the desire already coursing through her.

Glorious tension. Wondrous desire. She arched, silently begging him to continue.

His hand cupped her between her thighs. She moaned softly as he shifted his hand and pressed his body where it had been, his erection rubbing against her although he was still half dressed.

Anxious need consuming her, she raised herself and captured his nipple with her mouth, imitating what he had done, swirling her tongue around the dark nub as he groaned softly.

Then he moved back, kneeling. "I don't think this is wise."

She raised herself up on her elbows. "I don't think love is supposed to be wise."

He shifted around until he was sitting on the edge of the bed. "No, but we should be. I want you so much, it's like torture to stop, but what if I got you with child? People can count days and months back from a child's birth, and they will."

She knelt behind him, wrapping her arms about him, her breasts against his back. "People will accuse you of seducing me, and your reputation has already suffered enough."

"It's yours I'm thinking of, as well as your aunts' opinion of you."

"And their opinion of you would be worse, too." She caressed his cheek. "You're right. I should look beyond what I'm feeling, so I suppose you should go."

"I must."

"And I must let you." She ran a finger along his glorious lips. "You do realize there is going to be one very serious consequence of your visit this evening?"

"We're going to be married."

"And I'm going to have very great expectations for our wedding night."

That brought a smile to his face as he got off the bed and went to pick up his shirt. "I promise to do my best to live up to them."

Diana raised herself on her elbow and studied him as he dressed. He caught her looking, and frowned. "Your stares really are disconcerting."

"I'm admiring you."

"Oh, in that case, carry on."

As he had said to her on a certain memorable evening, she asked, "What the devil are you wearing?"

His eyes twinkled with merriment, and a deeper joy beneath. "A disguise. My footman's clothes fit better than I anticipated. I'll have to have a word with my tailor about his claim that I am difficult to fit."

The clothes did hang rather remarkably well on his broad, muscular frame.

She climbed off her bed and went to him as he pulled on the jacket. "There's something very attractive about you wearing a footman's clothing. It makes you seem less intimidating."

"You never found me intimidating."

"I certainly did."

"You hid it very well."

"I don't anymore, of course." She ran her hand under the lapels of his jacket.

"Diana, I appreciate that you're a bold and brazen woman, but this isn't helping my gentlemanly resolve."

She withdrew her hands and clasped them behind her back. With her brown hair braided, white nightgown and that innocent expression, she might have looked like an angelic and virtuous being, except for the mischievously seductive gleam in her eyes.

"Diana, Diana, what am I going to do with you?" he moaned with dismay.

"Marry me, my lord."

"That's likely the only way I'll ever know a moment's peace," he noted as he reluctantly went to the window and put one leg over the sill. "Although with you as my wife, I'm not sure that'll be any guarantee." He grinned, his expression the embodiment of merry devilment. "And I wouldn't have it any other way. Now kiss me quick, my darling, and send me on my way, until tomorrow."

She did, and after she watched him climb down the pipe and hurry away, she did a little jig of pure, unbridled joy.

Chapter 13

"No!" Evangeline screamed as the count's rapier pierced Rodolpho's side.

Blanching, her beloved looked at her with anguish in his eyes, then slipped to the ground, unconscious.

Silhouetted against the full moon, his black cloak whipped about him by the wind, the count stood over Rodolpho's prone form like a malevolent spirit. "He lives, my love," the count said, raising his shadowed eyes to look at her. "What are you willing to do to ensure that he continues to do so?"

She stared at the count, too worried about Rodolpho and horrified by her enemy's words to speak.

"Do you think I will ever let you go, Evangeline?" the count demanded, his voice low and as harsh as the ravens that lived in the ruins. "A life for a life, my lovely Evangeline. Stay with me, and I will let Rodolpho live. Refuse, and his body will be dashed on the rocks below."

"How will killing the man I love make me want you?" Evangeline cried above the howling wind of the rising storm. "I will hate you even more if you kill him."

"You hate me now, but surely knowing your
sacrifice has saved his life will give you comfort as
you share my bed. And you will share my bed,
whether he lives or dies."

The Castle of Count Korlovsky

A soft knock interrupted Diana's reading of the latest draft of this important scene. She'd been too excited to sleep after Edmond's visit last night, and had happily, feverishly worked on the confrontation between Evangeline, Rodolpho and their enemy, the count, the first writing she'd done in days.

Fearing it was Aunt Calliope, she hastily thrust the pages into her writing desk and closed the lid. "Yes?"

"My lady?" Sally called beyond the closed door. "Your aunts want you to come to the drawing room. You have visitors."

Diana eagerly got to her feet. This early, it must be Edmond. "Do you know who it is?" she asked as she opened the door.

Sally dropped a little curtsey. "I believe it's Lord Fallston and some acquaintances."

"Oh. Thank you," she replied, subduing her disappointment that it wasn't Edmond.

"Do you need me, my lady?" Sally asked, obviously surprised to find Diana not just awake, but dressed.

"No, thank you. I'll go straight down."

As she did, she reflected that it was probably just as well it was Lord Fallston. She could tell him that she wouldn't marry him before her relationship with Edmond was confirmed to be more than rumor and speculation. That would be better than letting him hear it from somebody else.

She wondered if his mother was with him. She winced, but at least she'd get all the unpleasantness over at once.

Then she was going to marry Edmond, her heart fairly sang.

She entered the drawing room and came to an abrupt halt. Lord Fallston stood with his back to the hearth, arms behind his back like a soldier at ease. His expression was anything but easy, however; his eyes fairly shone with delight and something darker. It took her but a moment to realize what it was—malicious triumph.

His expression changed almost immediately, to his usual genial amiability, but she didn't doubt what she had seen, and her mind screamed caution.

Her gaze darted to her aunts, seated stiffly on chairs near the hearth. They looked distinctly uncomfortable, although the other guests were a harmless-looking, well-attired, young and pretty woman and a little girl, seated side by side on the sofa. The woman's coloring was fair, her chin delicate, her cheeks plump and pink, and her posture graceful. Her ensemble was extremely fashionable, as was the little girl's. The child's coloring, however, was dark.

"Lady Diana," Fallston said, stepping forward, "allow me to present Madeline Voisey and her daughter, Amelie."

After Diana murmured a salutation, Madame Voisey said, with a Parisian accent, "How is Lord Adderley these days, my lady? Still breaking hearts, *non*? Of course, he is, a man like that—so handsome, so passionate, as I have cause to know."

Her back straight, Diana lowered herself to a chair opposite the sofa. The meaning of the woman's words and her manner was all too obvious. She'd never expected Edmond to be a virgin, yet to meet this woman, to hear her speak of him that way, and in front of her aunts . . . ! They might never form a good opinion of him now.

But betray any distress in front of Lord Fallston or this woman she would not. "Lord Adderley is well."

"You are probably wondering how I am familiar with the dear viscount."

The tension in the room grew as thick as smoke from a fire of green branches as Diana struggled to maintain her self-control. "I think it's safe to assume that you were intimate acquaintances."

Lord Fallston cleared his throat. "Then I have no doubt, Lady Diana, that you can also guess who fathered this little by-blow."

Diana's breath caught, for she'd done nothing

of the kind. She'd been thinking more of her aunts' reaction to Madame Voisey and her innuendoes.

She ran a swift, studious gaze over the little girl. Edmond had never mentioned a child, but the likeness was certainly there, in her coloring and her eyes, the slope of her chin, even the carriage of her head.

Had she been wrong to believe that he was different from other wealthy noblemen who kept mistresses and fathered illegitimate children?

"I thought it only right that you should know the sort of man he truly is," Fallston said with chastising condescension. "Sometimes, it seems, words alone are not enough."

Diana glanced again at the little girl, who looked as confused and uncertain as Diana felt. Whatever motives Fallston and Madame Voisey had for this visit, she was but an innocent child.

"Amelie," she said in French, ignoring Lord Fallston for the moment to address the child, "would you like to look at some books I have in the other room?"

The little girl's eyes brightened, and she resembled Edmond even more. "Oh, yes, mademoiselle!" she said, also in French. "I adore books."

Diana held out her hand and the little girl eagerly accepted it.

"I'll return in a few minutes," Diana said to the others as she escorted Amelie to the book room and got down a volume about birds and another of fairy stories with many illustrations, both of which elicited cries of delight. "You won't be afraid to be left alone for a little while?"

"*Non, non*, I am often alone. Oh, look at this dragon!"

Satisfied, Diana was about to leave when she hesitated. "Have you ever met your papa?" she asked Amelie, who was happily studying the pictures.

"*Non*," Amelie replied, glancing at her and shaking her head. "Maman says he is a great man. A handsome man, and I look just like him."

She shouldn't have asked, Diana thought as she hurried back to the drawing room.

But given the look in Lord Fallston's eyes, it was also obvious what he was up to. In spite of what he said, he wasn't doing this for her benefit.

Galvanized by her certainty that this was far more about Fallston's hatred for Edmond than any concern for her or the child, or Madame Voisey, she strode briskly into the drawing room. "Aunt Calliope, Aunt Euphenia, will you excuse us, please?"

Aunt Calliope didn't move, but Aunt Euphenia rose at once. "Of course." She took her sister's hand and pulled her to her feet, then propelled her resistant sister from the room via a hand on the small of her back. "Come along, Calliope."

Once they were gone, Diana ignored Madame Voisey and addressed Lord Fallston. "So, my lord, you have kindly asked Madame Voisey here to tell me about her liaison with the viscount and show me her child, who appears to be his as well, is that it?" She glanced sharply at the pretty French-woman. "Well, madame, is that not so?"

Madame Voisey didn't look at all upset. "*Oui.* Edmond was my lover. A very fine lover." She smiled as if she were sharing a secret. "But I think you already know that, my lady."

Diana wasn't about to answer her. "I wonder, madame, how the viscount came to be traveling in France, given that we were at war with that country for so many years."

Madame Voisey merely smiled more. "We did not enjoy our liaison in France, much as that is to be pitied. We met in London, where I have been living since my family was forced to flee during the Revolution. He was so young then, so passionate, so enthusiastic, so virile!"

"I'm sure," Diana said evenly.

It wasn't difficult to imagine a younger Edmond freed for the first time of the constraints of his parents' strict house or the discipline of school, indulging his desires.

She could understand if he'd had lovers, and gambled and drank to excess. She could also see how an enemy would make use of that past and turn it into evidence of continuing debauchery, exaggerating if necessary and speaking as if Edmond had never changed.

But whatever he'd been like in his youth, Edmond had changed. He wasn't a decadent scoundrel, or an example of the selfish aristocrats of the *ton*. He was a decent, honorable man who happened to be a viscount.

"He swore his eternal devotion to me, and even promised to marry me," Madame Voisey continued, her eyes shining with the same venomous pleasure as Lord Fallston's, "but when I told him I was with child, he abandoned me. One morning he just went out and never came back. He left me without so much as a penny—and I carrying his child!"

While Diana could believe this woman had been Edmond's lover and Amelie their child, she couldn't—she wouldn't—believe that Edmond could be as hard-hearted as Madame Voisey was implying. That he would callously walk away from his responsibilities, even if the affair was over. . . . "What proof have you of all this?"

"I have the child, and for the rest, ask him."

If Madame Voisey's story was a complete fabrication, would she suggest that?

"If he is an honorable gentleman, he will confess, will he not?" Madame Voisey went on. "He will surely beg your forgiveness even as he swears his eternal devotion. Edmond is very convincing. I was not fresh from the countryside, and he fooled me. He would have made a fortune on the stage. Or perhaps he seeks a fortune in another way."

"He doesn't require a fortune," she said.

Madame Voisey shrugged. "If you say so."

"He hasn't told you about his debts, either, has he?" Lord Fallston asked. "His estates are all heavily mortgaged."

Diana slowly swiveled on her heel to look at him. His voice sounded sorry, but his eyes glowed with malicious delight. "You see, my darling? He's a scheming cad, just as everyone says."

She stood as still as one of the vases on the mantelpiece. "Madame Voisey," she said without looking at her, "would you please join your daughter in the other room?"

The woman gracefully shrugged, and obeyed.

"You are very keen to make the viscount out to be a villain," she said to Lord Fallston the instant they were alone.

He had the wisdom to look a little penitent. "I'm only trying to protect you."

It was too late. She'd already seen his pleasure in her pain. "Are you, indeed? How kind," she said without trying to hide her cynicism. "However, what I feel for anybody except yourself really isn't any of your concern. As for protecting me, I neither seek nor require your protection."

His gaze hardened. "My lady, I have lost a woman to a charming cad before."

"A foolish, flighty creature, so my aunt described her. Do I strike you as a foolish, flighty creature, my lord?"

"No, but Adderley has twice the charm of Sissingsby. I'm acting in your best interests, my lady."

"You're acting in *your* best interests, my lord. You haven't done this out of love for me, or the urge to protect me. Vengeance for past hurts can be a powerful motivation, and Edmond hurt you very much. While I can understand the cause, I cannot excuse your behavior. Your tactics are unworthy of a gentleman."

"And his behavior toward this unfortunate woman and her child *is*?" Fallston demanded.

"I didn't say that."

"My lady, if you will champion that man—"

"I love him."

Fallston's jaw dropped. "*What*?"

"I love him."

Fallston's face flooded with rage. His hands balled into fists as he glared at her, his expression murderous as he came toward her. "You, too? You women are all the same! A handsome face, a pleasing manner, a few kisses in the moonlight—!"

He raised his hand to strike.

Diana's hand shot out, straight, her fingers making a wedge that she jabbed as hard as she could into the soft flesh of his armpit.

With a cry, he fell back.

"Try to touch me again—in *any* way—and I'll have you flat on your back begging for mercy," she said through clenched teeth. "Just because I've lived in the country, my lord, doesn't mean I haven't learned something of human nature." She grinned devilishly. "Books are a great help there, as well, as you might have discovered if you'd ever troubled to read one."

Clutching his armpit, he stared at her. "You're . . . you're unnatural!"

"Yet only moments ago you were condemning me for being like the rest of my sex. You can't have it both ways, my lord." She went to the door of the drawing room and held it open. "And now, my lord, I give you good day. Please take Madame Voisey and her child with you. Oh, and pay the woman whatever you agreed to, even if this hasn't been quite the success you'd hoped. That's not her fault. It's *yours.*"

Still pressing his hand where she had hurt him, Fallston stumbled out the door. As she walked back to the sofa, breathing hard, Diana heard Lord Fallston, Madame Voisey and Amelie leave the house.

In the next moment, Aunt Calliope and Aunt Euphenia rushed into the room. Not unexpectedly, Aunt Calliope was wringing her hands. Aunt Euphenia's eyes were full of concern.

"I shall most certainly *not* be marrying Lord Fallston," Diana announced.

With that, she swept from the room and strode out the front door without bonnet, wrap or gloves, leaving her stunned aunts staring after her as if she'd lost her mind.

* * *

Her hair disheveled, perspiration staining her gown, Diana barged into Edmond's bedroom.

"Diana!" Edmond cried, turning, his shirt unbuttoned. "What the devil's happened? Are you hurt?"

His valet, his face red as his scarlet vest, scurried back into the dressing room, holding the viscount's morning coat by the shoulders and carrying it in front of him as if it were a shield. Ruttles arrived behind her, breathless and distressed by not being able to prevent this unknown harridan from barging into the house.

As Edmond walked toward her, Diana stuck her arm straight out to hold him off and regarded him steadily. "Who is Madame Voisey?"

Edmond started as if she'd shot him, then answered immediately, without prevarication. "She was my mistress." He glanced at the butler. "You may leave, Ruttles."

His expression stony, Ruttles immediately turned on his heel and left the room, closing the door softly behind him.

"How did that relationship end?" Diana demanded, staring at Edmond, the man she loved. The man she wanted to believe could be trustworthy and faithful.

His cheeks flushed, yet again, he didn't hesitate. "Badly."

"So I understand. I have had her version of events. I want to hear yours."

"Madeline's here in Bath?"

"Lord Fallston brought her to my aunt's house."

He stared at her incredulously as they faced each other. "Fallston—I might have known! But how did he—?"

"Madame Voisey also brought your daughter."

Edmond paled. "My . . . *what*?"

"Your daughter, Amelie."

His eyes narrowed and vitality again emanated from him as he firmly answered. "I don't have a daughter. Madeline and I never had a child."

"She looks very much like you, my lord."

"She *can't* be mine. Madeline would have told me if she was carrying my child. Good God, she would have used it to squeeze more money out of me before I realized what she was and . . ."

"And?"

He rubbed his hand over his forehead. "I'm ashamed to admit the way I left her. I just walked out one day and didn't go back."

"You abandoned her without a penny?"

He frowned. "There was plenty of food and wine in the apartment, my clothing and toilet articles to sell. She also had several men anxious to take my place as her 'protector.' I doubt she was without funds for more than a week."

"But you don't know that for certain."

"No, I don't."

"And given your abrupt departure, how can

you be so sure she wasn't carrying your child? It's possible she wasn't certain, so she hadn't told you yet."

"You don't know Madeline. If there'd been the slightest chance, she would have told me. That would have meant more money for her, you see. Even if she'd discovered it later, she would have come to me and demanded more."

"You seem very certain of what another person might do, Edmond, although you've never been in those particular shoes. If things had got to the point where you would leave her in that heartless way, perhaps she wouldn't have come to you. She might have her pride, or maybe she didn't think there was any use."

"I left her after I realized I was nothing to her but a bank for withdrawing funds. She never loved me. I don't think she even particularly liked me. Oh, she liked my looks, but that was all. It was my money she adored, and the moment I realized that, I saw no point in lingering. So I left." He planted his feet and faced Diana squarely. "But if I'd known there was a child, I swear to you, Diana, on my honor, that I would have made certain it was well taken care of."

"Even though you harbor such an ill opinion of her mother?"

His hands balled into fists. "Gad, *especially* then. I would have made it worth Madeline's while to do so."

"How could you afford it?"

His brow wrinkled. "What?"

"I have been told your estates are heavily mortgaged."

His eyes flashed fire. "That's an outright lie. Two of my estates are mortgaged, I grant you. One paid for Buggy's expedition, and the other for Charlie's legal defense over . . . a private matter. I don't regret doing that for an instant. But heavily mortgaged? No. Absolutely not."

Believing him in this, and everything he said, Diana let her breath out slowly and ran her hand over the back of the nearest chair, the damask smooth beneath her fingers.

"Diana, you do believe me, don't you?"

She looked at him. "Yes, Edmond, I do."

"Thank God!" He crossed the distance between them in a stride and gathered her into his arms.

She stood stiff and still, willing herself not to be swayed by the desire his embraces always engendered. "How many other lovers have you had, Edmond?"

"It's you I love with all my heart, you I care about. I've never loved any woman as I do you."

"Did you say that to them, too?"

He drew back, his eyes full of anguish. "No!"

She regarded him steadily. "You're certain the love you feel for me is different from the passion you felt for them? You're sure you will love me for the rest of our lives?"

He answered without hesitation. "Yes, Diana, I am."

"Do you know the history of my Aunt Euphenia and her unfortunate marriage?"

He nodded.

"Then I hope you can appreciate why I'm going to make this request of you, and I hope you'll agree to it." She took a deep breath, and as she did, firm resolve strengthened her. "I want you to stay away from me."

He gasped, then listened dumbfounded as she relayed the plan she had devised as she had hurried through the streets of Bath, ignoring the people pointing and staring and whispering.

"Leave me alone for a year, Edmond. Don't try to see me, or talk to me, or come anywhere near me. In a few weeks I'll be going home to Lincolnshire and if you still love me in a year, come to me there. I have to know if your love will stand the test of time and distance. I believe mine will, but I must be certain of yours. Absolutely certain."

Her own heart ached to think of that long separation and the look in his eyes nearly stripped her of her determination. But she meant what she said: she had to be sure of his devotion.

He straightened his shoulders. "I'll love you until I die, Diana, and if that's what it takes to prove it, painful though it will be, I'll do what you ask."

She held out her hand and willed away tears. "Then farewell, Edmond, until a year from today, in Lincolnshire."

He lightly kissed the back of her hand. "Not

farewell. Adieu," he whispered as he lifted his dark eyes to look at her, just as he had that first day in the Pump Room.

She caressed his cheek. "Adieu, my love. I hope to see you a year from today."

"You will, Diana, you will," he quietly vowed as she ran out of the room.

Chapter 14

It was a single word, softly spoken. "Mercy!"

As the count's hand clutched hers and his feet tried to find purchase on the crumbling wall, Evangeline wanted to ignore his plea, to leave him there, to abandon him to his fate, because of all that he had done.

But she could not. He was still a human being and she couldn't leave him to fall to his death. To do so would be to let herself become what he was.

She grabbed hold of his arm and pulled with all her might. But he was heavy, dragged down by the weight of his rain-soaked cloak, and she was weak from hunger after being kept in his dungeon.

His fingers started to slip, even as it felt as if her arm was being pulled from its socket. "Pull harder!" the count commanded, fear full on his face.

She braced herself against what was left of the wall and pulled again.

A blinding flash of light split the night sky as a bolt of lightning struck the nearest tower. The count gave a startled cry and loosed his hold. At that same moment, the stones at Evangeline's feet shifted and crumbled.

With a horrible scream, the count fell backwards into the dark abyss.

The Castle of Count Korlovsky

Lord Fallston's butler raised a brow as he regarded the well-dressed man on the doorstep. "Yes?" Evans inquired, his tone as frosty as the top of a mountain in the dead of winter.

"I wish to see Lord Fallston," the man declared with outrageous arrogance.

"I'm not sure he's at home, sir. Whom shall I say is calling? Have you a card?"

"I'm Lord Adderley, and if he's not at home, you'd better tell me where he is."

Although the nobleman made no overly threatening moves, there was something in his voice, his very attitude, that gave Evans serious pause and made him think his life was not worth sacrificing in the service of his employer.

"I do believe he has returned," he said, bowing his way out of the door to let Lord Adderley enter.

Edmond strode past him, then paused. "Where will I find him?"

"I regret I'm not precisely sure, my lord."

Edmond looked sharply at the footman hovering nearby, who stammered, "I-I think he's in the study." He gestured vaguely up the stairs.

"Where exactly is the study?" Edmond demanded.

"Third door on your left."

Edmond dashed up the stairs two at a time until he reached the main floor. Ignoring a middle-aged maid who scuttled out of his way, he continued toward the third door.

He entered without so much as a knock, to find Fallston seated by the hearth, a wine glass in his hand. The man started, then a damnably smug smile bloomed on his face. "Good afternoon, Adderley," he said as he set the wine down. "Trust you to make a rude entrance, but I assumed you'd arrive eventually."

Edmond marched to him, hauled him up by his jacket lapels, then let go of him as if touching him disgusted him, which it did. "Where are Madeline and the child?"

Fallston smiled. The damn prig smiled, his eyes full of gloating jubilation. "I see somebody's told you your secret isn't a secret anymore. Who was it, I wonder?" He pretended to think a moment, clearly enjoying himself immensely. "Ah, could it have been Lady Diana? Yet somehow, I don't think that's what you were discussing on the terrace after I left you. Or when you were dancing at the ball."

"It doesn't matter how I found out. All that you need concern yourself with is that I have, and I know who's responsible, you loathsome little—"

"I'm not the one who callously abandoned the mother of my child."

Edmond tried to batten down his rage. He

didn't owe this piece of dung any explanation for his past mistakes, and how Fallston had found Madeline and Amelie wasn't the most important thing now. "Where are they?"

"Gone, as soon as we left Lady Diana. With the money I gave her, your lovely former paramour promised they would disappear completely."

Edmond could well believe that. Madeline was not a stupid woman. Greedy, devious and, he'd thought, so lacking in maternal instinct she wouldn't hesitate to rid herself of a child if she got pregnant, but not stupid.

Fallston laughed, his delight at Edmond's distress fairly emanating from him. "What's this? Is Hades upset? Is he at a loss at last?"

"I didn't know about Amelie."

"How unfortunate," Fallston sneered. "But such things happen when a man who thinks he's Adonis and Apollo combined traipses through London seducing women. If he's an intelligent Adonis and Apollo combined, he would expect such things and plan for them. He would ensure the woman he abandoned was not with child at the time. He might even take some pains to find out her fate, so that she isn't eager to see him get his comeuppance for leaving her. Sadly, you are not nearly as intelligent as you think you are."

Finally, Fallston had his vengeance.

Because Edmond knew that he was right. He shouldn't have abandoned Madeline so abruptly.

He should have tried to find out what had happened to her.

"Poor man, you didn't cover your tracks as well as you thought you did, did you? Apparently even gods sometimes make mistakes. Very big ones." His eyes gleamed with malice. "Not as bad as frightening a boy nearly to death, but bad enough to give him a taste of misery."

The Adderley's pride roused. "That was an accident, Fallston! How many times do I have to tell you?"

"The result was the same, you fool!" Fallston snarled, walking around his chair so that it was between them. "You humiliated me, you and your cohorts. Always so splendid, always so bold!" He leaned forward, hands gripping the back of the chair until his knuckles turned white, and he was nearly nose to nose with Edmond. "How does it feel to lose, Adderley?"

Edmond's fists clenched, but he dominated the urge to strike his enemy down. "Is that what this is about, *revenge*?"

"It's about teaching you a lesson!"

"What about Diana? Where is she in this *lesson*? You don't care about her at all, do you? She's just a means to an end."

Relaxing his grip, Fallston gave Edmond a twisted, bitter smile. "You really don't understand me at all, Adderley. Of course I care about her. I'm going to marry her. She's a duke's daughter, after

all. But I'm not fool enough to love her. After Lucinda, I swore I'd never allow myself to love another woman, for that gives them the upper hand,
the power to hurt me even worse than you and
your friends did. You can appreciate that now,
can't you, Adderley? What did Diana say to you?
Did she tell you she never wanted to see you
again? And her aunts—oh, they'll make sure all of
Bath—London—England!—knows of your shameful abandonment of your child."

Edmond's lip curled with scorn. "You disgust
me, Fallston. You always were a spoiled little prig,
crying and whining and running to the masters
any chance you got. Even before your dunking
you nearly got Charlie sent down just because you
thought he had a better bed. Oh, you didn't think
we knew that? Apparently, I'm not the only one
who's not as clever as he thinks."

Fallston smiled, but it was strained, tense. "Say
what you like. I've got what I wanted—or almost.
On the day I marry Lady Diana, I'll be satisfied,
and I'll finally have shown you I'm better than you
and your friends."

Edmond's fist clenched and he batted the chair
away, sending it clattering across the floor as Fallston stumbled backward. "Do you honestly think
that Diana would *ever* marry you?"

"Why not?" Fallston cried as he regained his
balance. "I am such a very *nice* young gentleman,
after all. Her aunts certainly think so."

He tried to stand up straight and speak defiantly, but his voice shook and his body trembled although Edmond hadn't laid a hand on him.

Edmond laughed, and it was a sound to chill the marrow of bones, or make a coward quake even more. "You don't know her at all. If you did, you'd know she's too smart not to see you for what you are."

Fallston edged toward the hearth and wrapped his hand around the poker. "Perhaps not. But at least you won't have her. For once in your privileged life, you'll have lost something you really care about."

"No, I haven't," Edmond said as he watched, hoping the weasel would try to hit him. Then he could hit him back. "She loves me, despite your attempts to discredit me. Instead you've shown your true colors, and for nothing, Fallston."

"You're lying!" Fallston cried like a petulant child denied his favorite toy as he raised the poker. "She can't love you anymore! She can't!"

"My lord, is everything all right?" the worried butler inquired from the doorway.

Fallston dropped the poker as if it was red hot. "We are quite finished," he said limply. "Show the gentleman out."

Edmond started for the door, then turned back, and his lips curved up in that devilish smile Fallston loathed. "You're wrong if you think we're finished. I'm only getting started. I'm going to put a stop to you, Fusty, like I should have years ago. That was a mistake, I grant you, but you've made a worse one. You've underestimated Diana."

"Here she comes!" Calliope cried from her vantage point at the window.

"Sit down," Euphenia softly commanded. "And don't trouble her with a lot of questions. I think we both know where she went."

"But Euphenia—!"

"Let her tell us in her own time, Calliope. Interrogating her may drive her away."

Calliope nodded, albeit reluctantly, as Diana appeared in the doorway.

"Oh, my dear," Euphenia said as she led an obviously exhausted Diana to the sofa.

"I'm all right," Diana whispered as she sat.

Aunt Calliope anxiously began searching for her smelling salts under every available cushion.

Diana had already regained her breath and her self-possession by the time Aunt Calliope finally found them.

"I'm fine, really," she said as she smiled at her solicitous aunts, now seated on either side of her. "I want to explain."

"There's no need to do that now," Aunt Euphenia said. "First a bath and a clean gown and some tea."

"I asked Sally to draw a bath the moment I came in the door," Diana replied, "but before I do anything more, I need to tell you what's happened between the viscount and me."

"Only if you want to, my dear. We can wait for explanations."

"No, I'd rather do it now. At once." Wanting to get this over with, she didn't pause for any further encouragement. "I went to see Edmond. I had to hear his version of what had happened with Madame Voisey. He didn't try to deny what she said. He did abandon his mistress—but he didn't know about the child. I believe that. I also believe he was being honest and sincere when he said he regrets how he ended the liaison."

She looked wearily at Aunt Euphenia as exhaustion stole over her. "And although I still love him, I remembered what you said about a feeling that seems like love, but is actually false and fleeting. I want to be sure that what I feel, and what he claims is love, truly *is* genuine and lasting. So I've asked him to stay away from me for a year. If his love for me is true and constant, he'll come to me then. If not . . ." She drew in a ragged breath. "If not, it is better to lose a year waiting than be miserably married."

Aunt Euphenia struggled silently for a moment with her thoughts, then spoke. "Because I love you like a daughter, Diana, I must ask you this. How can you be certain he'll be honest about how he's spent that year if he returns to you? He might claim to have been constant, and not be."

Diana gave her aunt a wry, sardonic little smile. "Gossip, Aunt Euphenia, gossip. For once, I'm very glad Aunt Calliope has so many loquacious friends, and I'm counting on her to tell me if she hears a whisper of anything. But I honestly don't think she will. I have faith in Edmond."

"Then I hope you're right, my dear."

Aunt Calliope burst into tears. "Oh, Diana! Euphenia was right! You *are* a sensible girl!"

Obviously trying to conceal her extreme curiosity, Sally arrived and announced that she had drawn Lady Diana's bath.

Diana rose and glanced down at her gown. "I look a wreck, and I've probably disgraced myself entirely and completely ruined my reputation. I'm so sorry, Aunt Calliope."

"Oh, who cares what the people in this provincial little town think!" Calliope cried, jumping to her feet and hugging Diana fiercely. "It's your happiness that's important. Let them gossip!"

"And they will," Diana said softly as she laid her head on Aunt Calliope's soft shoulder. "When they hear everything that's happened, they will."

That evening, Brix stared at Edmond seated at his desk in his study, furiously writing. "What do you mean, you're going to France? When?"

"I leave tomorrow, at dawn."

"What for?" An answer apparently came to him, and he winced. "Oh, good God. You're not giving up on Lady Diana? I thought you loved her and I must say—"

"No, I haven't given up on Diana," Edmond interrupted, realizing that was the only way he was going to get a word in. "I love her and she loves me."

"Then you managed to see her?"

Edmond gave him a brief smile. "I did and she consented to be my wife."

"Then why are you leaving?" Brix asked. "Shouldn't you be planning a wedding or at least interfering while she plans a wedding?"

Edmond put down his pen and sighed. "It's gotten complicated."

"It was damned complicated already."

"Sit down, and I'll explain."

"This should be fascinating," Brix muttered as he obeyed, sprawling in a plain oak chair opposite the desk.

"You remember my affair with Madeline Voisey?" Edmond began.

"I remember you were very upset about it. You went on quite a rant about mercenary women in the club one night. Made a real impression on Charlie, I recall."

"She's in Bath, or at least she was this morning."

"Ah! How much does she want? I hope you don't intend to pay her, after the way she cheated on you with that actor fellow."

"She didn't ask me for a penny. In fact, I never actually saw her at all, and that's why I'm leaving. I've got to find her."

Brix sat up straight. "Good God, man, what for? Is this some bizarre notion of chivalry? Or is it guilt for the way you left her?"

"It's a little girl named Amelie that Madeline claims is mine."

Brix's mouth opened, but nothing came out for the first several seconds until he stammered, "A-a child? She claims she had your child?"

"Our *friend* Fallston was good enough to introduce them to Diana."

Brix shot to his feet. "I knew it! I knew I should have challenged that sanctimonious little rodent to a duel!"

"Sit down, Brix. It's done, and besides, you're a terrible shot. I wouldn't want you killed by that sanctimonious little rodent."

Brix muttered something about ridding the world of prigs, which Edmond ignored. "The thing is, although I'm not sure that the girl is mine, I have to see her for myself, and try to find out the truth. If she is mine, I must make sure she's well provided for. That means going to France. I found out that much by bribing Fallston's butler." He gave Brix a bit of a smile. "Madeline always wanted to go back to Paris, but only if she could set herself up in style. It seems now she's got the money to do it."

"It won't be easy," Brix said doubtfully. "It's a big city with lots of places to hide if one doesn't want to be found. Let me go with you, Edmond. I can help search."

Edmond smiled. "I'm grateful for the offer, Brix, but your French is appalling."

"What about Drury? He speaks French like a native and he might know some people in the government to ask."

"Considering the sort of thing he did in the war, I rather doubt he's on friendly terms with the French government. I think I'll have better luck on my own, and I've got plenty of time."

Brix gave him a puzzled look. "What about Diana? Does she know you're leaving?"

Edmond shook his head. "No, and it doesn't matter. She doesn't want to see me."

Brix shot to his feet again. "That poisonous little weasel! He's convinced her—!"

"Of nothing."

Brix blinked.

"She realized he was trying to discredit me, and came to me at once. She wanted to hear my explanation. I told her that I did abandon Madeline, that I regretted it, and that if there was a child, I hadn't known or I would have ensured it was well taken care of. She believed me, Brix."

His friend lowered himself back into his chair. "Then why doesn't she want to see you?"

"It's not forever, although it will certainly seem an eternity. She's asked me to keep my distance for a year. She has to know my love is genuine. Long-lasting. Forever."

"Gad, it's a test!"

"Exactly."

"And you're going to put up—?"

"I'm going to pass it with flying colors," Edmond said firmly. "And before you say anything, no, I don't blame her. How can I, after she met Madeline and heard what she had to say? How can I fault her for wanting to have some proof that I can be constant?"

"You're a better man than I am, I must say, to take this so well."

Edmond looked at his friend, and shook his head. "I'm *not* taking it well. It's tearing me up inside, but I've got to respect her wishes. And I've got to find out if Amelie is my child."

Brix sighed, and after a moment said, "Tell me you at least gave Fallston a black eye."

Edmond picked up his pen. "I would have liked to, I'll admit, but his butler interfered."

"So you're just going to let him get away with this? Good God, you know what he's going to do, don't you? He'll play the martyr again and the devil only knows what kind of rumors he'll spread this time."

Edmond looked up from his letter and smiled. "I'm not letting him get away with anything anymore. For years he's been lying about me and saying we were trying to kill him to anybody who'd listen, so it's more than past time I sued him for slander and defamation of character, don't you think?"

Brix stared incredulously. "You're going to take him to *court*?"

"Yes. It should finally make him stop saying such things, and think twice before he spreads any more lies about me, or anybody else."

Brix frowned. "He'll fight the charges tooth and nail."

"I sincerely hope so," Edmond replied, his devilish smile growing. "I want everyone to be talking about the case."

"It'll be a terrible scandal," Brix said, obviously wondering what had got into his friend.

Edmond laughed softly. "Exactly. But thanks to all Fallston's lies, what's a little more scandal to *me*? Fallston, on the other hand, has a horror of it, and his mother even more." He brushed his chin with the tip of his pen. "It's rather too bad he never wrote to *The Times* about me, because then I could add libel. Maybe he accused me in letters to his friends and acquaintances. I'll have to get my solicitor onto it."

Brix grinned, then sobered. "A case like this could cost you a pretty penny and drag on for years."

"I don't care. It's about time somebody called him to account, and I intend to do it."

"Then there's only one thing to do, Edmond," Brix replied solemnly. "I insist you let me join you in the suit. I won't be surprised if Charlie and Drury want to, as well."

"Are you sure?"

Brix's smile became positively beatific. "I almost feel sorry for the sanctimonious little rodent."

Several weeks later, Aunt Euphenia watched Diana finish packing away her writing desk. "You're adamant, then? You won't stay for Christmas?" she asked.

"I do appreciate your invitation, but I'd rather spend it at home," Diana replied gently, but with resolve. As far as she was concerned, it was past time she went back to Lincolnshire. "I need the quiet and the calm. Bath is too hectic for me."

That brought a smile to her aunt's face. "I think you're the only person under fifty who's ever thought so."

"Well, I do. I'll be glad to get back to the peace of the countryside."

Peace, and plenty to do, among people she'd known all her life, and with whom she felt comfortable. People who had no interest in the gossip and scandals that seemed the very lifeblood of Bath—and none had stirred the resort town quite like the news of the lawsuit Edmond and his friends had brought against Fallston. Coupled with the ending of the relationship between Diana and Fallston, and the suspicion that Lord Adderley was responsible for it, excited speculation had spread through Bath like a fire through dry straw. The gossips had many theories, and many questions, which they didn't dare to ask Diana, although she didn't hide at home. To be sure, going out and catching the surreptitious glances, sly looks, the whispers and enduring the few bold questions about Edmond's departure had been unpleasant, but she was adamant that she not appear to be ashamed of anything that had happened, because she wasn't.

Going out and about had another, more serious drawback, though. Everywhere she went in Bath, and no matter how she tried not to, she half-expected—and more than half-hoped—to see Edmond, even after she'd learned he'd left Bath. Once, she'd nearly waved and shouted a greeting at a complete stranger in Bath Abbey just before services were to begin. She'd had to cover her mistake by pretending to be reaching up to adjust her bonnet.

It was ridiculous to expect to see him since she was the one responsible for his leaving, but she simply couldn't help it. She thought the best remedy for what was fast becoming an obsession was to go home to Lincolnshire and wait out the year there.

She faced her aunt. "You and Aunt Calliope will come to Lincolnshire next spring, won't you?"

Aunt Euphenia regarded her intently. "Are you sure?"

Nodding, Diana fussed with the latch of her writing desk. "If Edmond doesn't come, I don't want to be alone." She raised her eyes and smiled wistfully. "If he does, I'll want to share my happiness with the two other people I love most in all the world."

Aunt Euphenia's eyes filled with tears, which she immediately wiped away. "We'll be there, of course. And in the meantime, we'll do our best to stem the tide of rumor and gossip."

"Thank you," Diana said, truly grateful, because that wasn't going to be an easy task. "If you receive any letters for me, you'll forward them on?"

"Of course."

She'd heard nothing from Edmond since that last meeting, although she hadn't asked him not to write. And they *were* engaged.

On the other hand, she'd been so firm that they not have any contact, she had herself to blame if he didn't. She was the one who had forced them on this course, and if they were to truly be certain of their mutual devotion, perhaps silence would be best.

As anxious as she was for news of Edmond, however, he wasn't the only person she was hoping to hear from. She was also wondering if she'd receive a letter from Jamieson and Son, Publishers, in London.

In the first few weeks after Edmond's departure, she'd finished her manuscript, revised it until she'd almost had the whole book memorized, then decided it was now or never if she was going to try to get it published. She'd mentally girded her loins, bundled it up and sent it off to London.

Once it was actually out of her hands, however, the overwhelming sensation had not been joy or relief or even hope. It was rather akin to nausea.

Now she worried about it all the time, although with a different sort of anxiety than she felt for Edmond, wondering where he was, what he was doing and if he was all right. So far, Aunt Calliope had heard from various friends that he'd gone to Paris, then returned to London. Her friends reported that he was living very quietly. Alone.

She could guess why he'd gone to France, and she imagined his meeting with his daughter a hundred times. As for what would happen next, she couldn't be sure, but she was certain that he would ensure Amelie was well taken care of.

Aunt Calliope burst into the room in a whirl of feathers and silk, brandishing that morning's post. "There's a letter for you, Diana."

Diana's heart thundered as she rushed to take it and eagerly tore it open.

It wasn't from Edmond.

"I don't know what sort of friends you left behind in Lincolnshire, Diana," Aunt Calliope complained, "but they've addressed it very poorly. They left off your title."

Now that the first rush of disappointment had passed, Diana noticed the company crest on the top: Jamieson and Son, Publishers. She could scarcely breathe as she began to read.

Dear Miss Westover:

That was the name she had used so they wouldn't know she was titled in case that gave her an unfair advantage over other writers. She'd wanted her book judged on its own merits, not the author's lineage.

We are very pleased to inform you that we would very much like to publish your novel, The Castle of Count Korlovsky.

She stared at the glorious words as if they might disintegrate.

But they didn't and there they were in black ink on white vellum. Jamieson and Son wanted to publish her book!

It was almost as wonderful as the first time Edmond kissed her.

"What is it?" Aunt Euphenia asked worriedly. "Not bad news I hope?"

"No, no, it's wonderful news! Marvelous news!" Diana felt for the chair near her dressing table and sat, devouring the rest of the letter from Jamieson and Son. It went on to discuss contracts and payments and would it be possible for her to visit London in the next few months?

"Is this something to do with the lawsuit? Is all

that nasty legal business concluded?" Aunt Calliope asked hopefully. "For your sake, I hope Lord Adderley has won."

Diana's happy gaze took in both her aunts, although beneath her joy, there was a pang of sorrow, too, for the one person she most wanted to share this news with was not there. "It's not about the lawsuit. I've written a book and a company in London is going to publish it."

"You've done *what?*" Aunt Calliope cried, as horrified as if Diana had announced she'd just assassinated the Prince Regent.

"I've written a book. A novel. And it's going to be published," she repeated, giddy with triumph.

"A novel? What sort of a novel?" Aunt Euphenia asked, only slightly less shocked than Aunt Calliope.

"It's called *The Castle of Count Korlovsky* and it's a romance about a young woman named Evangeline and her true love, Rodolpho, and an evil count who abducts her—"

With a cry like a wounded bird, Aunt Calliope sat heavily on the foot of the bed and covered her face with her plump hands. "Just when I thought it couldn't get any worse! A *writer* in the family," she wailed.

Diana hadn't really expected any other reaction from Aunt Calliope, yet it certainly took the bloom off the moment.

"Aren't you happy for me? Aren't you proud of me?" she asked Aunt Euphenia. She'd hoped

Aunt Euphenia would understand, and was hurt by her less-than-enthusiastic reception of her niece's success.

"Happy? Proud? It's a *terrible* thing to have a writer in the family," Aunt Calliope cried before Aunt Euphenia could speak. "Look at *Byron*. And Shelley, cavorting about in Greece. And there's Caroline Lamb and her horrible book, portraying everybody in such a terrible light. I'm surprised nobody's sued her for libel. Fiction, indeed! Don't you believe it!"

"There are good books, too," Diana protested.

"Not by anybody in *our* family!" Aunt Calliope charged.

She wasn't making a critical remark about Diana's talent, yet her comment rankled nonetheless. "What about Lord Bromwell and *The Spider's Web*?"

"He's a *man*!" Aunt Calliope retorted. "And it's not a novel."

"This *is* slightly different," Aunt Euphenia said when she could get a word in. "And Calliope is right. We've had more than enough scandal touch our family lately."

"I'm not going to withdraw my book," Diana said firmly. "I worked very hard on it, and I'm glad it's considered good enough to be published. More than glad! Delighted. Pleased and *proud*. If Papa were alive, he would be, too."

Aunt Euphenia's expression altered. "You're right, Diana," she said. "I'm ashamed of myself for thinking of anything but this reward for your efforts. Congratulations."

Aunt Calliope looked from one to the other, then made a decision. Rising from the bed, she hurried to her niece and threw her arms about her. "My dear, you're right, and I'm an old fool."

Diana held her close, and a solution dawned. "I do understand your worry that there may be more scandal." She drew back and regarded her aunt steadily. "So I'm willing to make a compromise. I'll use a pseudonym."

"A what?" Aunt Calliope asked, as if she feared it was a disease.

"A false name." She mused a moment, and the perfect one came to her. "I'll use Diana Cyril, for Papa. He loved books so much and passed that love on to me, so it's only fitting that his name be on one, don't you think?"

"Oh, my dear Diana!" Aunt Calliope cried as she pulled out the edge of her scarf and started to dab her eyes.

"What a wonderful idea, Diana," Aunt Euphenia seconded. "Your papa would be so happy."

And then she burst into tears.

Chapter 15

Holding him gently in her arms, his head cradled in her lap, Evangeline looked down into Rodolpho's pale face. A trickle of blood ran from his mouth and he scarcely seemed to breathe.

"Rodolpho," she whispered, holding back her tears as she willed her strength into him. "Rodolpho, my beloved, come back to me. I love you so much, Rodolpho. My life will be a desert without you. Please come back to me, my love. Please . . . come back. . . ."

The Castle of Count Korlovsky

In the drawing room of Diana's manor in Lincolnshire, the candles had burned low. Seated on a camel-back sofa near the hearth, Aunt Euphenia pretended to continue reading *The Times*'s account of the successful conclusion of Edmond's lawsuit. Several people, including the famous author Lord Bromwell, and other men who had been at Harrow with him and the other co-plaintiffs, made it very clear that Lord Fallston's version of the prank and other tales of Edmond's activities were not just gross exaggerations, but

345

malicious enough to be slanderous. When Fallston had realized he was going to lose, Edmond and his friends had agreed to drop the suit if Fallston would leave England.

Fallston had departed and the gossip in Bath was that a certain distiller's beautiful and accomplished daughter had sailed on the same ship. It was rumored Lady Ellis had gone to Baden-Baden to recover from the double shock.

While Aunt Euphenia read, Aunt Calliope attempted to concentrate on her embroidery. She'd had to redo a particular section six times after dinner, and was no closer to finishing than when she'd started.

Her shawl wrapped about her, Diana stood at a set of French doors that overlooked the curving drive, where she had been all day except when it was time to eat. She made no pretext of doing anything else but watching the drive. It would have been pointless and impossible to do otherwise. Her aunts knew as well as she what day it was.

Since arriving in Lincolnshire eight months ago, she'd filled her days with activities—helping prepare *The Castle of Count Korlovsky* for publication, visiting, charity work—but always she was thinking of Edmond and longing for this day.

This morning, she had awakened with a sense of giddy anticipation, any doubts that he would come quite subverted. Her love still burned as strong as the last day she'd seen him and she was full of hope that his did, too.

When he had not arrived by midmorning, doubts had begun to taint her hope, but she was still optimistic. He'd probably stopped for the night in a village, and it might take some time for him to get from there to her house.

By noon, her anticipation was losing ground to anxiety. Surely, unless he'd stopped for the night in Lincoln or Stamford, he would be here by now.

As the hours ticked by after that, and her aunts grew progressively more reserved and silent, fear replaced hope.

Maybe he was sick, or hurt, she told herself, a new set of worries developing.

Yet if that were so, surely he would have sent a message. He must realize that under such circumstances, her command for him to keep his distance wouldn't apply.

Maybe she'd been wrong to dismiss his complete lack of communication during the past year as his determination to obey her stricture. She might be a fool for carrying her belief in him to this extreme.

By the time dinner was served, after a delay of over an hour in case he arrived, she began to seriously consider that he might not be coming because he didn't want to.

Now it was getting toward midnight and her nerves were stretched as tight as a bowstring before the arrow's loosed.

Aunt Euphenia, glancing at the remains of the nearest candle, caught her niece's eye. "Diana, dear, don't you think it's time to go to bed?"

"Not just yet, Aunt Euphenia," she replied, barely able to speak for the lump in her throat. "You may retire if you like. It's . . . it's been a very long day."

Aunt Calliope and Aunt Euphenia exchanged sorrowful looks. "Very well, my dear," Aunt Euphenia said. "We'll see you in the morning, then."

"Good night," Aunt Calliope said gently after she put away her embroidery. "I'm so sorry, my dear. I was hoping he'd come, for your sake, and that I'd been wrong to be so critical of him before."

Diana fought to keep her voice steady. "If he doesn't love me, it's better that he doesn't."

"But knowing that doesn't make the pain any less," Aunt Euphenia said as she slipped out the door, followed by a teary-eyed Aunt Calliope, whose only benediction was a sniffle.

Alone, Diana turned back to look at the drive visible in the light of a full moon. A great wave of sorrow and loneliness washed over her, as it had after her father's death. In those first miserable days, before she'd decided what she would do next, she thought she'd never be happy again.

She felt the same now.

A sob broke from her throat, but she willed herself not to cry. As before, her pain would lessen over time, just as she'd recovered from her father's death. She had her aunts for company, and her friends. She might even meet another man . . . another man who wouldn't be Edmond. Who was not nearly so exciting and passionate. Who didn't make her heart race and her blood pound and her whole body tingle as if shocked by lightning.

She fell on her knees, her face in her hands. She loved Edmond so much, and he hadn't come.

She'd waited and longed for this day, and he hadn't come.

She'd been a fool to ask him to wait so long, and was a bigger fool for loving him still.

"Dear God," she whispered, "what will I do?"

Write another book.

The answer came to her strong and vibrant, rising like a phoenix out of the ashes of her broken heart.

Write another book, and go on.

She lowered her hands from her tear-streaked face. Yes, that's what she'd do. She'd write another book.

As she drew in a deep, shuddering breath, sure of another path than the one she'd been envisioning for so many months, the draperies further down the room shifted. A latch clicked.

Hardly daring to breathe, she struggled to her feet.

The French doors flew open and Edmond stumbled into the room. Panting hoarsely, nearly doubled over as he tried to draw breath, his hair disheveled, his boots caked in mud, his riding jacket torn and filthy, his cravat nonexistent and his grimy shirt open at the neck, he leaned on the latch for support.

"Diana, thank God!" he gasped. "Forgive me for coming so late. This morning my coach lost a wheel and I had to get a horse but it took me forever to find one that wasn't decrepit and then the damn beast threw me and bolted about ten miles back—"

His explanation was cut short as Diana ran down the room, threw herself in his arms and kissed him passionately, her whole body behind it.

"Oh, you're here. You're really here!" she cried as she pressed more kisses onto his cheeks, his chin and any other part of his face she could reach regardless of the sweat and grime.

"Late. I'm sorry—"

"Shhh. Just kiss me."

He willingly obeyed, holding her close as his lips captured hers with all the fiery passion she remembered.

But the memories were like the faintest echoes now that he was here, in the flesh, warm and solid, his hands caressing her.

He broke the kiss and held her tightly. "I gather from this reception that you still love me and want to marry me?"

"Of course I do. Now kiss me again, Edmond, or I'm going to scream."

He frowned with patently false dismay. "What, and wake the house?"

"Edmond!"

He held her away from him and looked down at his soiled jacket and muddy boots. "I'm filthy."

"Lord Adderley, at this particular moment, I wouldn't care if you were covered in dung."

He grinned, his eyes lighting in that devilish way that went straight to her heart and sent it strumming like the strings of a harp. Again his lips covered hers, but this time leisurely, as if he wanted to reacquaint himself with her slowly. Although his kiss seemed indolent, her whole body tightened with anxious desire, and her nipples pebbled beneath her gown.

Sensing the change in her, he shifted and deepened the kiss. She ran her hands beneath his jacket and up his back. How strong, how wonderful he was.

Their lips parted, and their tongues entwined, each touch within the warm interior sending new waves of pleasure through her.

Still kissing her, he bent forward and slid his arm beneath her knees. She wrapped her arms around his neck as he lifted her in his arms and carried her to the sofa, stepping over her shawl, which had fallen to the floor when she'd run to him. He turned, sat and settled her on his lap.

Of course, his legs must be aching if he'd come all that way on foot. "You must be exhausted," she whispered, lips against his cheek as her hand meandered down the edge of his gaping shirt.

"I was. I'm strangely revived. I wonder why?"

She tilted her head and pretended to reflect. "Perhaps because you're sitting down."

"With the woman I love on my lap," he confirmed, just as apparently serious, "and a very fine place it is for her to be. It makes it so much easier for me to kiss that little spot on her throat just where it meets her jaw."

He demonstrated, and delightful sensations reached all the way to Diana's toes.

"This was worth the wait," he murmured.

"If I'd known how difficult waiting was going to be, I would have made it a month."

"Then I wouldn't have been able to return in time. I needed two months to find Madeline and Amelie." He grew serious. "I also found out the truth. Amelie isn't my daughter."

Diana gasped with surprise. "She's not? Whose is she, then?"

"I don't know, and neither did Madeline. She's not Madeline's child, either."

Diana could scarcely absorb that last bit of information. "But Amelie called her Maman."

"Madeline spotted her among a group of orphans on an outing. She noted the likeness to me and the little girl's accent, not expecting to hear a French child in London. When a man came to Madeline asking questions about me, she remembered the child and thought she could use the poor girl to her gain, by claiming she was ours. She even told Amelie she was adopting her, but once she didn't need her anymore, she sent her straight back to the orphanage."

"Oh, no! The poor little thing!" Diana frowned.

"That means Amelie is in London. We can't leave her in an orphanage."

Edmond kissed her gently. "I haven't, and I suspected you would feel that way, too—which is another reason I love you. I only regret it took as long to find Amelie as it did. First I had to go to Paris to find Madeline, which took some time. She's not a stupid woman, and she knew I'd be looking for her. Once I found her, it took more money for me to persuade her to tell me about Amelie, and what she'd done with the child. From there, I went to the orphanage." He made a wry little smile. "It wasn't difficult to convince the matron that I wanted to take Amelie from there and put her in a school. You should have seen the way she looked at me, and then Amelie. She obviously believed Amelie was my natural daughter, too. Her scrutiny wasn't quite so disconcerting as another young lady's gaze across the Pump Room, but nearly."

"If the likeness made it easier for you to help Amelie, I'm glad. She seemed such a sweet child."

"I thought so, too. She's in an excellent school in Kent, and is quite happy. The food was a great help in that regard, not so much the quality but the quantity. We can visit her, if you'd like."

"I would. In the meantime, I must send her some books. She was very fond of them, which is another reason I thought she might be yours."

"As pleased as I am to hear you thought a child

of mine would enjoy books, I hope you're not intending to do that right this moment."

"No," Diana said, nestling against him. "Not right this moment."

Edmond sighed as he held her gently. "I fear Amelie may be harboring the hope that I'm really her papa, but I'm keeping it a secret for some mysterious reason of my own."

The seed of a plot suddenly sprouted in Diana's mind, about an orphan who goes seeking her real father and winds up nearly being captured by pirates before being saved by a handsome naval officer, but she shut it away for the moment. "Who was this man asking questions? Was he sent by Fallston?"

"No. Adelina Foxborough's father wanted to find out about the man he thought was seriously interested in his daughter."

He smiled ruefully. "I wanted to write to you a thousand times during the year, about that, and Amelie and everything else, but I wasn't sure if I'd be violating our agreement."

Diana rested her head on his broad shoulder. "There were many, many times I'd wished I'd drawn up a list outlining exactly what our separation entailed, but at the time, I hadn't thought things through. I did have rather a lot on my mind."

"I should say so—and not just our situation. Buggy told me about your book, Diana Cyril. Apparently the literary world is as small as Bath, and just as prone to gossip. There are very few secrets among writers and publishers."

He didn't sound annoyed. He sounded happy for her.

She flushed with pleasure to think he knew and approved of her accomplishment, and then wondered if he'd yet to realize he was the model for the count. "Have you read it?"

He grinned. "I have, and I thought it was marvelous." He laughed softly. "You really are the most astonishing woman."

He must not have made the connection yet. She wasn't sure whether to be relieved or not. "And you, my lord, are a very exciting man."

"Naturally. I look and sound exactly like the dastardly Count Korlovsky, do I not? Lately several people have been so kind as to note the likeness."

"You're not angry?"

"Actually, I was quite flattered—until he tried to murder poor Evangeline. Why didn't she jab him in the neck?" Edmond touched his finger to a spot below her throat, sending a delicious tremor through her. "I seem to recall a simple blow here is extremely effective."

"Because Evangeline was delicately reared in a convent, of course," Diana pertly replied.

Edmond sighed melodramatically. "I may have to retire to the country because of your book. Women keep staring at me. None of them as outrageously as you, but half of them look like they think I'm going to gobble them up for dinner."

"Poor Edmond," she said without a jot of sympathy, since he seemed amused and not angry in the least.

"I must say, Lincolnshire seems quite nice. Rather welcoming, too."

She took a deep breath and voiced a worry that had been troubling her since she'd received the news that her book was to be published. "I intend to continue writing, Edmond, after we're married."

"I should hope so. Only a selfish fool would try to keep you from doing something you're so good at, especially if you enjoy it. But perhaps next time, the dark, mysterious, exciting stranger could be the hero."

She hugged him with delight, and some relief, even as another plot seedling began to sprout. "I'm so glad you're not going to object to my writing!"

He bent down and brushed his lips over her forehead. "I have a confession to make. After I had Amelie settled, I got out the journals I wrote when I traveled through the Alps. I'd enjoyed writing them, and reading them gave me some hours of entertainment."

Her eyes lit up. "I'd love to read them, if I may. The Alps would make a wonderful setting for a book."

He reached into a pocket of his jacket and

pulled out a small, slim leather-bound volume, which he handed to her.

It was titled *A Journal of a Journey through the Alps*, by E. Haddes.

"What's this?" she asked as she slowly turned the pages. Then she reached the simple dedication: *To Diana, the goddess of my heart.*

She gasped and looked at him, to see a delighted grin spread across his moonlit face. "I'm E. Haddes," he said, as irrepressible as a mischievous schoolboy. "I didn't just reread my journals. I decided to polish them up and send them off to Buggy's publisher. He agreed they had some merit. Not enough to warrant a large run, unlike a certain young lady I could name, because he says it has limited appeal—unless I wanted to add a woman fleeing an evil uncle or stepfather or some such thing. I told him I had no talents in that line. Still, he thought my descriptions delightful and almost poetical."

"Oh, Edmond, this is wonderful." She read a bit near the start and then stared at him, aghast. "Was there really an avalanche? You could have been killed!"

"Obviously I escaped, my love, and fortunately so did all of my party."

"Oh, yes, of course." She continued to read, until his lips brushed the top of her ear. "As pleased as I am that you seem to find my writing fascinating, I didn't mean for you to read it all right now." He wrapped his arms about her. "And it's rather disconcerting to be overlooked for a book, even if it's mine."

She closed it, then turned so that they were face to face. "It's your fault for writing such an exciting opening."

He grinned. "Wait till you get to the banditti."

"Banditti!" She was about to open the book again, but he gently took it from her and set it on the side table. "That can wait until tomorrow. We have more important things to do right now."

She gave him a fraudulently innocent smile, as she had the first day they met. "Such as?"

"Getting reacquainted." He ran his hands down her arms to her fingertips. "Let me see. Where do I begin?" He brought her hand to his lips. "Ah, yes," he murmured. "I think . . . here."

Just as the first time he kissed her hand, warmth and what she now knew to be desire thrilled through her at his touch.

She splayed the fingers of her other hand on his chest. "Your breathing still seems a bit erratic, my lord."

He closed his eyes and bit his lip as she continued her exploration. "It's likely to stay erratic if you keep doing that."

"I am merely reacquainting myself with you. Do you want me to stop?"

He slowly shook his head. "No."

He gasped when she leaned forward and pressed her lips to his heated skin. "You're a bold and wanton woman, Diana. I saw that from the start."

"Because you make me want to be bold and wanton."

"You make me want to take advantage of that."

"Please do."

Regarding her steadily, he began to caress her. "We might wake the household."

"I don't care."

"And here I've spent a year trying to establish that Lord Adderley is not a scoundrel."

"I know you're not."

"And that I'm a gentleman."

"This is no time to be coy, Edmond."

"No? You would rather I do . . . this?"

"Yes . . ."

"And this?"

"Yes, *please*. . . ."

"And not that I should leave and come back tomorrow, properly attired and on my very best behavior?"

"No!"

"You would not have me on my best behavior?"

"If that means as docile as a dog brought to heel, certainly not."

His eyes gleamed in the moonlight, as if her words had unleashed all the primitive power she had ever sensed in him. "Careful, Diana," he warned. "I have only so much patience."

"The time for patience is at an end. For both of us."

He studied her face, and when he saw that she meant what she said, the last of his restraint fell away. For a year he'd waited, trying to be patient, and do nothing that would jeopardize her good opinion of him. The latter wasn't nearly as difficult as the former, because Diana would be the reward.

And now he was with her again, holding her in his arms where she felt perfect and so right.

With eager, inflamed need, he pulled her to him. His mouth captured hers, igniting what passion was left unkindled in her.

Encouraging him, she pushed his jacket from his shoulders. He broke the kiss long enough to tear it off and throw it to the floor. Then he leaned back and pulled her down, so that her body lay atop him.

Their kiss deepened while his fingers untied the lacing at the back of her bodice. When it was loose, he pushed the gown lower, and her chemise with it.

The air was cool on Diana's shoulders, chilling her hot skin for a brief moment before he slipped his hand inside her slack garments. How warm his palm was on her back! She inched backward, sitting up slightly as she trailed kisses down the column of his neck, the evidence of his arousal hard beneath her.

His eyes dark with desire and hunger, he put his hands on her shoulders and gently eased her garments lower, the movement of the fabric a delicate pressure that foreshadowed his plans.

He took her breast in his hand and his thumb lightly brushed against the pebbled nub. Exquisite sensations throbbed through her and she arched back. He cupped her other breast, then both, until his ministrations made her bite her lip to keep from crying out.

He raised himself on his elbows and with one hand to steady her, brought his mouth to her nipple. He sucked it in, making her gasp, then used his tongue, swirling it over and around the tender tip before he pleasured the other.

"You're so beautiful," he murmured as he lay back and looked at her. "I've dreamed of seeing you naked in the moonlight."

"And I, you," she whispered as she lowered her head to kiss him.

As she did, she unbuttoned the rest of his shirt. She pushed it back, then explored his exposed chest with her lips and tongue, seeking to arouse him as he had her.

His eyes closed, a groan broke from his throat, and then he sat up, startling her. "What's the matter?"

"Are you sure, Diana? Absolutely sure?" he demanded in a hoarse whisper.

"Yes, I am."

"Then this sofa will not do. The mud from my boots will ruin it. Stand up."

Clutching her gown to her breasts, she scrambled off him. "I'm not worried about the mud."

"Well, neither am I. That's an excuse to get out

of my boots," he said, tugging them off and letting them fall where they may. "Besides, it's too short for what I have in mind."

She swallowed hard.

He tore off his shirt, then tossed the sofa cushions onto the floor.

They landed in a pool of moonlight. "The better to see you with, my dear," he said, a wolfish grin on his face that made her limbs turn to water. The wolfish grin disappeared, to something gentler. "May I see you?"

Nodding, she let go of her gown. It fell to the floor, puddling around her feet. Her chemise and petticoat followed, until she stood before him naked, and unashamed, because the way he looked at her made her feel she was wondrous and special.

He watched as she walked to the cushions and lay upon them, raising herself on her elbow. "Now let me see you."

His gaze never left her face as he stripped off his clothing, revealing a body just like a statue of a Greek god, as she had always expected.

"Come to me, my love," she whispered, holding out her hand.

He did, and she lay back as he knelt between her legs.

"I love you, Diana," he whispered.

"I love you, Edmond."

He put his hands beside her and lowered himself, his weight gloriously welcome. "You want me?" he asked softly.

"Yes!"

"You won't be sorry we didn't wait until we're married?"

"No. We've waited long enough."

He leaned forward and his lips brushed over hers, tantalizing her. She, meanwhile, skimmed his skin with her fingertips, lingering on his hardened nipples.

She felt him against her and parted her thighs in silent invitation.

He hesitated and she opened her eyes, to see him looming above her, still uncertain. She reached down and guided him to her. "I have no qualms, Edmond. None at all."

"I'll be gentle."

"I know."

They looked into each other's eyes as he slowly slid inside her, only a little at first. He kept watching her as he withdrew, then entered again, a little further. He did it again and each time, she was more prepared, her body more moist and accommodating. But tight. Sweet heaven, tight.

Then came the moment when he thought she was ready. He thrust deep inside her and felt her maidenhead give way. He stopped at once and held her to him, waiting, yet barely able to control himself as he nestled inside her. He murmured endearments, soothing her, promising the worst moment was over, and all the while fighting the guilt, wondering if he had made a mistake, gone too far, expected too much, been too impatient. He'd waited a year; what was a few more days . . . weeks . . . until they could be married?

He felt her smile, her lips against his chest. And then she . . . squirmed. "That feels so good," she sighed.

He nearly choked. The shock lasted only a second, though, as the realization that she wasn't in pain crashed into him.

She began to move, undulating, and that was enough to shatter his control. He thrust inside her again and she gasped not with pain or dismay, but pleasure.

Again, and she grabbed his shoulders, pulling him closer. She wrapped her long, slender legs around him, arousing him as he'd never been before, her excitement contagious and liberating. He loved her with fierce passion, and all the nights he'd imagined this moment seemed but pale watercolor images of the glorious reality.

How wonderful she was, and perfect. Intelligent. Creative. Passionate. Desirable.

Special beyond special.

She cried out and her muscles tightened about him, the sensation sending him over the edge, into that abyss where nothing existed but the release of impassioned tension.

Panting and sated, he lay his head on her sweat-slicked breasts.

"I could never imagine anything like that," she murmured as she stroked his hair. "Aunt Euphenia didn't make it at all clear."

He levered himself up on his elbows. "I beg your pardon?"

"She tried to tell me that there were parts of married life I would miss if I remained a spinster. I had no idea."

He withdrew and snuggled against her, her head upon his arm, then leaned over and reached across her body for her shawl, which he tucked around her.

"Do you think you can endure the quiet life, Edmond?"

He kissed her gently and looked down at her with love and commitment shining in his dark eyes. "Of course I can, as long as you're my wife."

A shocked little shriek broke the tender moment. Clutching the shawl to her naked breasts, Diana sat up abruptly to see Aunt Calliope and Aunt Euphenia on the threshold, clad in their nightclothes and illuminated by the single candle Aunt Calliope held in her hand. They looked like two middle-aged gothic heroines encountering a scene of unbelievable horror.

Blushing furiously, Diana hastily rearranged the shawl to cover as much of both of them as possible.

"Diana, what is the meaning of this?" Aunt Calliope demanded when she found her voice. "Have you fallen? Are you ill?" She spotted Edmond. "Oh! That is . . . that is the viscount, I trust?"

Edmond gave Diana a look of mock dismay. "Were they expecting somebody else?"

"No! It's all right, Aunt Calliope. Please go back to bed."

"Bed? How can I go to *bed?* My poor nerves! Where are my salts? And right in the drawing room, too!"

Recovering her customary equanimity, Aunt Euphenia grabbed her sister by the arm and started pulling her out of the room before Calliope could start searching in the sofa cushions for her smelling salts. "This is not the time, Calliope. We can . . . discuss . . . all . . . this . . . in the morning."

"But Euphenia—!"

"*In the morning, Calliope!*"

After they had gone, Aunt Calliope exclaiming and Aunt Euphenia trying to calm her—and both probably rousing the entire household in the process—Diana sighed and ran a slow, measuring gaze over Edmond. "Oh, dear. We've just been discovered naked together."

"Then there's no help for it," he replied gravely. "We *have* to marry."

"I seem to recall you saying you wouldn't marry me even under these exact scandalous circumstances."

"Yes, I did." He lay down and pulled her into his embrace. "But that was before I fell in love with you. I assure you, I feel quite differently now. In fact, I can think of no finer fate than marriage to you."

She bussed him on the cheek. "Fortunately, my

lord, I feel exactly the same way about you. Nonetheless, I think we'd best get dressed. I expect the servants heard my aunts and we'll soon be discovered by the rest of the household. I wish to keep the sight of your naked body all to myself."

"I'd say you were a selfish creature, but I don't want anybody else seeing you naked, either. That is a treat I intend to reserve solely for your husband. In other words, *me*."

"You'll get no disagreement there," she said with a smile. "But in the meantime, I think we must observe some of the proprieties. Otherwise, we might scandalize the entire neighborhood."

"Yes, I daresay evincing love and passion for one's intended wife is likely to cause a stir. We'll probably be snubbed by the *ton* completely."

She grew serious. "I don't really give a hang about what anybody says, as long as I've got you."

He smiled and tucked a strand of errant hair behind her ear. "You do, Diana. You most certainly do."

Forgetting everyone but the man she loved, Diana looked at him with joy and tenderness. "And you have me, Edmond. Forever."

He murmured a heartfelt "Thank God," as he gathered her close and kissed her.

As Rodolpho leaned upon her for support, Evangeline and her beloved watched the sun set behind the smoking ruins of the count's castle. So much pain, so much fear—yet now it was all over. He was dead, and they were free to begin their lives together.

"Come," Rodolpho said as he turned away. "Let us not look on that horrid place another moment. Let us forget what happened here."

"I doubt I ever can," Evangeline said as she gazed into the eyes of the man she loved. "It was where I learned how strong our love is, Rodolpho. Stronger than any man and his minions, stronger than hatred and evil, no matter how determined."

Rodolpho smiled down at her, his love shining in his blue eyes. They kissed tenderly, then slowly walked toward the road, their heads high, their bold spirits ready to face whatever other troubles might come their way.

Together.

The Castle of Count Korlovsky

Epilogue

〜◦ΘΘ◦〜

His long legs stretched straight out in front of him and crossed at the ankles, his fingers steepled, the Honorable Brixton Smythe-Medway sighed and regarded his friends seated around the enormous library of the late duke of Dilby. Buggy sat in the corner by the wide windows, absorbed in a book he had found. Hands behind his back, properly at ease, Charlie examined a model of a ship in a bottle on the mantel. Drury's attention was on one of the maids passing by the door with a load of linen.

The remains of the wedding supper had been cleared away and the happy couple departed for their honeymoon in Europe. Tomorrow, the remaining wedding guests would go their separate ways, although there would be meetings in London and Brighton and possibly Bath as circumstances permitted.

"Well, that's it, then," Brix said philosophically. "The end of an epoch. Trust Adderley to lead the way in this, too."

"Aren't you going to be next?" Drury asked as he took a sip of his wine.

"Heaven forbid," Brix cried. "I've always said I'm not going to wed till I'm fifty and I'm damn well going to stick to that."

Buggy turned his studious—and dubious—gaze onto him.

"I have *some* self-discipline, you know," Brix retorted in response to his silent query.

Drury snorted skeptically.

"I have!"

"Haven't got the gun ports right," Charlie muttered as he ceased his contemplation of the vessel and turned toward his friends. He crossed his arms. "Care to make a wager on that, Brix? Say, a hundred pounds?"

"What, only a hundred?" Brix demanded as if Charlie had insulted his financial status.

Charlie's grin was as devilish as Edmond's had ever been. "All right, then. A thousand. I'm willing to wager a thousand pounds you'll be married before you're fifty."

Brix's chin jutted slightly. "Very well. A thousand."

"What if he dies before he's fifty?" Drury demanded.

"He looks like a fairly healthy specimen to me," Buggy said solemnly. "On the other hand, a sudden ague or apoplectic fit, possibly a prolonged head cold—"

"I never get sick."

"What about Fanny Epping? I don't think she'll wait till he's fifty," Drury remarked.

"I wouldn't marry Fanny Epping if she were the last woman on earth!"

"An extra five hundred says it'll be Fanny who finally brings him to heel," Charlie said.

"I say! I'm sitting right here, you know!" Brix jumped to his feet. "And how many times do I have to tell you? I will not marry mousy little Fanny Epping! I'd just as soon marry my scullery maid!"

"I'm in," Drury said, still ignoring Brix. "I'll keep the book."

"*I'll* keep the book," Charlie said, patting his uniform jacket for something to write on, and with. "I *always* keep the book."

"All right," Drury agreed. "There's probably some paper in the top drawer of that secretary." He gestured at the large piece of furniture on the other side of the room. "That's where my father always kept his. Are you in for the five hundred on Fanny, Buggy?"

"Of course."

"I'm not going to marry Fanny Epping!"

Charlie and Drury exchanged amused, patronizing smiles.

"Then we'll all be out five hundred pounds," Buggy calmly noted.

"*Fifteen* hundred," Brix retorted. "Because I'm not going to marry till I'm fifty and I'm not going to marry Fanny, so you're all going to lose!"

"Twenty-two years is a long time to keep track of a wager," Charlie mused aloud. "I could be lost at sea, or marooned on some desert island. Or dead of wounds received."

"There are several specimens of spider that are quite poisonous," Buggy gravely reflected. "I might encounter one."

"And I might die of boredom on the bench," Drury noted.

"Either way, I'm winning. And this is very charming talk at a wedding, I must say!" Brix said sarcastically. "I'm glad you at least waited until the wedding supper was concluded."

"Wouldn't want to spoil the bridal couple's day, would we?" Drury said without a hint of a smile. "Say, is it true that Diana's book's selling out all over the country?"

"Yes, it is," Buggy confirmed. "Her publisher's delighted and mine is having kittens."

"Your book's still doing well," Charlie said.

"Nevertheless, my publisher actually asked me if I didn't know some noblewoman I could use as a model for a romantic interest." He pulled a face.

"Can you honestly believe any woman would be willing to travel through the jungle looking for spiders?"

"Why not?" Charlie replied. "If you can do it—"

"I'm a man!"

"I don't think Edmond's bride would shirk from something like that if she took her mind to it," Brix said. "Maybe there are more women like her—"

"I doubt it."

"All right, Buggy, have it your own way," Charlie said, his tone placating. "Edmond got the only woman in England bold enough to go hunting spiders in the jungle."

"Say," Brix said, brightening. "You could take Fanny. Maybe lose her there."

Buggy gave him a disgusted look. "She wouldn't do. As my publisher so poetically put it, the unknown romantic character should have *a whiff of scandal about her*. Fanny's as virtuous as they come."

"What if you fell in love, Brix, the way Edmond did?" Charlie asked. "You wouldn't want to wait until you're fifty then."

"*If* I did fall in love—with somebody who is *not* Fanny Epping—then I suppose I'd lose a wager. And Edmond is in love, isn't he? I've never seen him so happy." Brix surveyed the vast room and collection of books. "I daresay he'll think he's in heaven here, eh?"

There was more than a hint of envy in Drury's expression. "Happy he certainly is, but I don't think this room has anything to do with it." He lifted his glass. "Here's hoping we're all so lucky in love, eh?" He darted a glance at Brix. "Whether it's before we're fifty, or after."

The irrepressible Brix grinned, then added his "Here, here!"

COMING NEXT MONTH

LOVE WITH A SCANDALOUS LORD by Lorraine Heath
An Avon Romantic Treasure

With a well-worn copy of *Blunders in Behavior Corrected*, Miss Lydia Westland has dreams of marrying a proper British lord. But while the first titled man she meets is dashing and oh-so-tempting, the Marquess of Blackhurst is anything if not scandalous . . . and he's about to teach Lydia that all rules are made to be broken.

&

OPPOSITES ATTRACT by Hailey North
An Avon Contemporary Romance

The last thing Jonni DeVries needs is the notorious Hollywood womanizer Cameron Scott around her recently broken heart. Lucky for him he was in costume when they first met or Jonni would have surely kicked him off her property. Now all this sexy hunk has to do is prove he's not the cad the tabloids made him out to be.

&

THE CRIMSON LADY by Mary Reed McCall
An Avon Romance

Fiona Byrne wants no part of her former notorious life and instead adopts the disguise of a simple seamstress. Then she is discovered by Braedan de Cantor, a dashing stranger who threatens to expose her. Braedan has no choice but to seek out the legendary lady outlaw to save his sister, though he never imagined the peril to his own heart and soul.

&

TO MARRY THE DUKE by Julianne MacLean
An Avon Romance

While her matchmaking mama is picking out suitably titled gentlemen, heiress Sophia Wilson is dreaming of her Prince Charming. She thinks she's found him in James Langdon, the Duke of Wentworth. But soon after the wedding the groom announces that this will be a marriage in name only!

REL 0503